These Lingering Shadows

A Last Waltz Publishing Anthology

hugs & bloody kisses
♡ Deana Olney

Last Waltz Publishing

Copyright © 2022 Last Waltz Publishing

Last Waltz Publishing

5 Midland Avenue

Pompton Plains, NJ 07444

Owner: R. R. Chiossi

This is a work of fiction. Names, characters, places, and incidents either are the products of the author's imagination or are used fictitiously. Any resemblance to actual persons, living or dead, events, or locales is entirely coincidental.

Cover design by Christy Aldridge

Edited by 360 Editing Services (a division of Uncomfortably Dark Horror).

Foreword by Candace Nola

All rights reserved. No part of this book may be reproduced or used in any manner without written permission of the copyright owner except for the use of quotations in a book review. For more information, address:

lastwaltzpublishing@gmail.com

https://www.lastwaltzpublishing.com/

Contents

Praise for These Lingering Shadows	V
Foreword	VII
	IX
1. The Far Field By Heather Miller	1
2. Hallow House By Jo Kaplan	17
3. Nory's By Michael J. Moore	41
4. Behold, Death Arrives, A Duet of Ash and Fang By Jae Mazer	47
5. Hell Hath No Fury By Diana Olney	69
6. A Halloween Ghost Story By Christy Aldridge	97
7. Mine By Matt Scott	119
8. The Dare By Tony Evans	129
9. Cries of the Night By Guy Quintero	143

10. The Feeding By D. E. Grant	161
11. Belladonna's Curse By Danielle Manx	173
12. Devlin's Manse By Daemon Manx	197
13. Flesh and Chocolate By James G. Carlson	225
14. Riding the Ghost Train By Jack Wells	249
15. A Dream of Dead Leaves By Jeremy Megargee	267

Praise for These Lingering Shadows

"Anthologies are a chocolate box to suit all tastes, and when it comes to These Lingering Shadows horror lovers will want to devour every gruesome bite. With fifteen macabre offerings featuring woods and witches, rituals and revenants, and cottages and crematoriums, this casket of chilling gothic tales will make your spine tingle and your toes curl. These Lingering Shadows is essential Halloween reading." —Lee Murray, four-time Bram Stoker Award®-winner and author of Grotesque: Monster Stories

"These Lingering Shadows is filled with wonderfully spooky stories that have twisted endings. It delivers all the shivers, including Halloween themes, ghosts, haunted houses and other hauntings; yet all the stories seem fresh and original. I highly recommend this book." –Jeani Rector, Editor of The Horror Zine

"Rarely does a story follow me for days like Jae Mazer's contribution to this anthology. Behold, Death Arrives, a Duet of Ash and Fang is beautifully atmospheric and layered with haunting imagery. These Lingering Shadows is the perfect blend of scary stories for the Halloween season, offering a variety of styles to satisfy every horror appetite." – Kate DeJong, reviewer and interviewer for Grimoire of Horror, author of Soup and Nightmares.

"A smoky Halloween treat of an anthology offering such creepy delights from hungry specters to devilish witchery, from vast, labyrinthine houses to ghostly mansions holding ghastly family secrets. Mix in haunted lovers, zombified fathers, Halloween dares, werewolf-inspired vengeance, trick-or-treater legends, and a host of wandering spirits and ghouls, and you have a recipe for an entertaining autumn night in." – Kenzie Jennings, author of the Splatterpunk nominated Reception and Red Station

Foreword

BY CANDACE NOLA

Autumn is a time of reflection for many as the leaves change to a dizzying array of gold, amber, bronze, red, and copper and drift slowly down to cover the ground. The air grows crisp with the cool scent of snow just beyond the horizon. Fairs and carnivals and pumpkin patches crop up everywhere you turn along with hayrides and haunted houses. It's a reminder that the year is drawing to a close and that things are constantly changing and evolving.

It also becomes a nostalgic time as we remember those cool fall nights of our childhood spent carrying pillowcases and plastic bags across neighborhood streets yelling "Trick or Treat" or crowding around campfires toasting marshmallows and listening to scary stories. We remember the haunted house on our street or in our town with fond smiles and maybe a shake of our heads as we remember how scared we were of its big wrought iron gate, and imposing front porch. We recall the many stories that we heard about it, or one just like it, and we chuckle as we sit on the front step with a mug of steaming cider and lose ourselves in the memories of past autumn nights.

The Far Field by Heather Miller will leave you breathless with emotion and lush images of days gone by, while A

Dream of Dead Leaves by Jeremy Megargee will leave your soul enraptured and longing for more. Riding the Ghost Train by Jack Wells and Mine by Matt Scott sing with prose worthy of Poe and gloomy Victorian nights. Hallow House by Jo Kaplan, Hell Hath No Fury by Diana Olney, and The Dare by Tony Evans will summon you back to those campfire nights from childhood.

These Lingering Shadows lovingly presents all of those memories of childhood, wrapped up in one delicious tome of old lore and lost love, of haunted houses, hayrides and scary stories by the fire. This is your cider on the front porch moment. Grab a blanket, settle in, and linger in our shadows a while.

-Candace Nola
Author of Bishop & Hank Flynn

"What would your good do if evil didn't exist, and what would the earth look like if all the shadows disappeared?"
— *Mikhail Bulgakov*

Chapter One

The Far Field

BY HEATHER MILLER

There's a heaviness to the air today. We've reached the late end of summer, and closer to the house, the first harvesters are hard at work beneath the blazing sun. There's nothing to reap here in my little meadow, however; no crops grow here with which to feed the bellies of the gentry or fill the storehouses and coffers of the important man who oversees these lands. All that grows here is the bounty which Nature herself has sown. Tall grasses wave, pale in the sunlight, and in between, a hundred different flowers flash their colors. I walk slowly through the verdant abundance, trailing my fingers along the stems and blossoms of the ironweed and goldenrod, the foxglove and indigo, the asters and the harebell. The wild mints release their fragrance each time the wind passes through, and the milkweeds are bent heavy with their burden of striped caterpillars. All around flit the fluttering wings of butterflies, bees, dragonflies, beetles.

I'm not bothered by such things, by the insects which fly and creep and sometimes seem to hover in miniature clouds directly in my path. Nor do I mind the lizards or the toads or the small sleek snakes which slither and hop and run among the grasses at my feet. I might have been wary of them at first, when this place was fresh and new to my eyes, but that was over a year ago now, and I have grown accustomed to the things which live out their busy little lives among the stalks.

The sun is tilting toward the west now; the workers will soon wipe their sweat-soaked brows and turn toward home. It's almost time. I'm waiting for someone, and they cannot come until the fields are cleared of laborers, the paths deserted. Our meetings are secret, our words meant for no ears but our own, our plans the stuff of hushed twilights and midnight bargains.

The heat lays oppressive over everything, making the landscape shimmer. I shimmer along with it.

It was not so stiflingly hot, the first time I came here, the first time he showed this place to me. Meet me at the far field, he'd whispered as we passed, he in his fine silk shirt and I in my rough woolen work dress. I'd dipped my head and blushed as I hurried past, a thrill of anticipation and fear running like lightning through my veins.

I'd spent the whole afternoon repeating those three words over and over to myself as I went about my work: the far field, the far field, the far field. When I was finally dismissed from my duties, I did not turn homeward as I normally would. I stopped for a moment at the small mirror which hung near the servant's entrance and tucked a few stray golden hairs back into my braids. I licked my fingertips and rubbed at a smudge of dirt which marred my cheek. Then I smoothed my dress and splashed a bit of Cook's rose water across my collarbone.

I walked the long and winding paths toward the edge of my employer's property. It was spring then, and the cool dampness which filled the air, seeping into the trees and the dirt, felt pleasant against my flushed face. My heart raced within my chest as I drew nearer to that secluded bit of land known as the far field.

The meadow was oddly shaped, a remnant of acreage where my master's land butted up in crooked angles to that of another, surrounded on three sides by a forest of ancient trees and hidden almost entirely from view as the trees had begun to encroach along the fourth side as well. Because of its peculiar shape and location, the field had never been cultivated, and only wild things grew there.

We were wild things, Nathaniel and I, when we spent time together in that hidden haven. I can remember the intensity with which he looked into my eyes as he slid the fabric of my shift over my shoulders and let the garment fall to the ground. I will never forget the smile that quirked about the corners of his mouth as his gaze lingered, roaming over the whole of me, my pale skin glowing in the twilight. And his hands – I shall never, ever forget the feel of his hands, firm, insistent, pressing and caressing every part of me.

Our love was impassioned. Our love was pure. Our love was a secret, a thrilling knowledge that I carried with me throughout the day, a feeling both giddy and heavy, like a white-hot stone that I kept hidden in my pocket which would, were I not careful, burn a hole right through my skirts and reveal the shocking knowledge of our indiscretions.

Spring turned to summer. We lay together in the hidden moments between dusk and dawn, the moon and stars and nighttime creatures the only witnesses to our secluded rendezvous. One evening in August, as we lay, tired and panting, letting the sweat on our bodies cool in the stifling air, my eye was caught by a shape which I had not seen before in the woods which surrounded our field, our secret place. The grin on Nathaniel's face told me that this was some wily project of his and I convinced him without much effort to reveal his plans.

It is a special place, just for us. A place for you to live, a place where I can keep you secret and safe forever.

The words seemed romantic to me when he spoke them.

They hold a different meaning, now.

As summer turned to autumn, the small house reached its completion. Nathaniel showed it to me, giddy as a schoolboy, excited to present me this most special gift. Although the structure was not large, it was to be mine – all mine. For a girl who had grown up in a home with five siblings and never an inch of space to call my own, it was like a mansion. The house sat back just far enough into the surrounding woodland that it blended in and disappeared among the trees. Even I, who knew it was there, often had to scan the area two or three times to spot it.

Nathaniel swore me to secrecy. The house was for me to live in, but I was not to tell a soul. He would bring me all the food and supplies I needed, and I would dwell there in happy solitude, awaiting his arrival whenever he could spare an hour or two to spend with me.

For two months I lived in that little house. For two happy months, I rose each morning, swept the floor, dusted the shelves, and made sure that everything was just so. Once a week, I would take my clothes and the bedlinens to the quiet creek that flowed through the woods just a few hundred feet from the back of the house and scrub them clean, then hang them on the bare tree branches to dry in the late autumn sun.

Soon the weather grew colder. Nathaniel would build up the fire in the stone fireplace and we would lie together on the fur rug in front of it, our own body heat helping the flames to warm the little cottage. He brought me candles and books and candies that melted on my tongue. It was a blissful life.

While it lasted.

As Christmas approached, I was busy with plans, racking my brain for a way to purchase or make some kind of gift for Nathaniel.

But all my plans and schemes were for nothing. Nathaniel came to me a week before Christmas. The sound of his horse's hooves thundering toward the meadow was startling to me. He had never ridden to the far field before. As he approached, I could see why he did so this time. Attached to his horse was a small cart, loaded with firewood and packages wrapped in brown paper. Nathaniel carried all these things quickly into the house, his cheeks red with the cold. I invited him to sit and warm himself for a while, but he brushed me off.

Something about him troubled me that day, a shiftiness of the eyes, a tightness to his lips. He held me at arm's length, stared wordlessly at me for a moment, then paced in circles around the front room while he spoke. He told me that his family was going away for the holidays, that they would be gone until after the start of the new year. This was why he had brought such abundant provisions. I would be alone for nearly three weeks, there in the house by the far field.

Before he left, he showed me a small package wrapped in green paper. This, he said, was my Christmas gift, but I must not open it before that day. In fact, he said, I must leave the box exactly where he put it until Christmas morning. He placed it carefully atop the mantel.

He held me then, crushed against him so hard that I could feel the pounding of his heart in a discordant rhythm with my own. He kissed me then, too, kissed me with a passion as strong as the first day we'd met here in the far field, kissed me firmly, almost violently. He rested his cheek for a moment against the crown of my head and went wordlessly out the door.

And then he was gone. The stack of firewood along the outer wall was taller than it had ever been. The packages when unwrapped revealed a feast of food.

The house seemed suddenly like a lonely prison instead of a home.

I saw no one for the next week. Nathaniel was gone, his family gone with him. The many servants who made up the household staff were sent to their own homes for the holiday, with only a scant crew left to deal with any situations that might arise at the manor house. No one walked the paths just beyond the trees. No farmers worked the fields. The grasshoppers and the beetles, the frogs, and the bees, all had disappeared. Even the birds had gone away, except for a trio of crows that soared in endless circles above the field, stopping occasionally to perch in the treetops and shout their condescending caw-caw-caws down at me.

When Christmas morning came, I rose and braided my hair. I washed my face in icy water and put on my nicest dress. I built up the fire and tidied the two rooms. I waited.

Although Nathaniel had said his family would be gone until the new year, I had half-convinced myself that he would show up on Christmas Day, unable to stand being apart from me for so long.

The day passed slowly.

Finally, when the pale winter sun began to sink below the trees in the west and a cold twilight rose to meet it, I resigned myself to the fact that he was not coming after all. I took the green-wrapped gift from the mantel and sat alone at the small table by the window. Night spread across the forest and the field beyond. I lit a candle and simply sat for a while, mesmerized by its hypnotic dance. Then I sighed, shook my body as if to shake the loneliness and melancholy out of my heart, and pulled the package toward me. I opened it carefully, trying not to tear the thick, expensive paper. Inside was a beautiful ivory box, its lid carved with flowers. I smiled as a tear ran down my cheek. It was beautiful, but it was no replacement for the warmth of Nathaniel's arms around me. I picked up the lid to inspect it more closely under the light of the candle. Now, here was something unexpected. Nestled into a wrapping of kitchen paper inside the box were half a dozen small shortbreads, pressed into the shape of hearts, thin and delicate.

I ate the first one with love, the second with longing. The third and fourth I swallowed without thinking, choking back the bitterness that rose within me at being abandoned on this special day. The final two I devoured in rage.

Perhaps if I had not been so greedy, the poison would not have taken effect so quickly. Perhaps if I had been more ladylike and stopped at one, the symptoms would have spread slowly enough that I could have run to the village, to my father's house, to my mothers and sisters for help.

But no, within minutes I was on the floor, my body curling in on itself, my vision blurring, my mouth gasping for air that could not enter my lungs. Within a quarter of an hour, I was dead.

But I was not gone.

I was there still, a spirit heartbroken and enraged, lingering in the corner of the room when Nathaniel returned a fortnight later. He covered his mouth and nose as the stench of my corpse assaulted his senses. The weather had been cool enough that my body had not decayed excessively, but still the odor filled the small room. He pushed at my stiffened body with his boot, as if the smell wasn't enough to assure him that I was dead. Then, satisfied, he went out behind the house and dug a grave.

"I'm truly sorry, darling," he said, once he had wrestled my unyielding body into the hole in the ground. "But things are going to change around here, and I can't have you messing them up."

He covered my body with dirt while I stood in the shadow of an old pine tree and watched. He left the shovel leaning against the wall of the cottage and walked away without a backward glance. The sound of his whistling lingered long after he had traveled beyond my sight.

And then time passed.

I discovered that I could, when I stretched my senses a little, hear bits of conversation from the manor house. Mostly, I heard the silly gossip of the kitchen maids and the harsh tones of the men in the stables as they boasted of their conquests. Sometimes, I heard the refined tones of Nathaniel's mother as she gave out orders to her staff. And then, I heard the thing which I had both anticipated and dreaded.

I heard the news on a particularly dreary January day, while snow fell like gray ash from the sky, dirty before it ever touched the ground. I heard her name on the lips of a dozen servants. I heard of her dowry in the voice of Nathaniel's father.

I heard the carriage approach the day before the wedding, and the nervous fluttering of her heart as her new husband laid her down in their marriage bed that first night. I heard the gasp and the moan, and I felt it within me as if I had a body of my own still to feel it with.

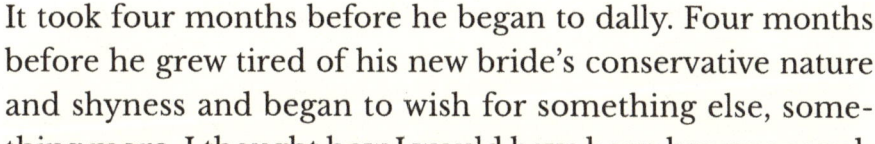

It took four months before he began to dally. Four months before he grew tired of his new bride's conservative nature and shyness and began to wish for something else, something more. I thought how I would have been happy enough to stay hidden in the house beyond the far field and live as his mistress, had he not seen fit to murder me. The thought filled me with shame. And then, once more, with anger.

It took me no time at all to plan my revenge. For the first time in nearly a year, I ventured beyond the far field. I followed a light which shone like a beacon in the night, a light which only I could see, a light that called to me. I sought out those who could help me, and I made my plans.

And then I waited.

It seems that old habits die hard. He brings her to the far field. His new mistress's appearance shows that he has a type, for she looks so like me that we might be sisters. He lays her down in a spot so familiar the grass seems to still hold the shape of my own body. He whispers words to her that sound like echoes to my ears, words he spoke to me just a year ago.

They do not visit the field as often as he and I did. He has appearances to keep up now, a wife back at the manor who expects his attentions. But they come often enough. She has hair like sunshine and eyes like a winter sky, and her laugh sounds like the tinkling of crystals. She rakes bloody furrows down his back, and I laugh from where I watch in the shadows, wondering how he'll explain that to the good lady back home.

Sometimes, she comes alone. Sometimes, she sits inside the little house, near enough that I could touch her if I wanted, near enough that I can hear the things she thinks but does not say aloud. Today she brought something, a small item that glinted with a dull shine as she hid it away within the house. "Be patient," she whispers to the empty room, "Wait until the time is right."

Autumn turns the field to a sepia monochrome. The flowers fade away and the dried grasses rustle in the wind. The trees flash brilliant colors for a brief time and then they, too, fade to brown. Along the creek, the cattails bend and sway, the sound like the clattering of old bones.

For a few nights, the Hunter's Moon rides high in a sky the color of loneliness, and I know the time is near.

It's a dark night when they come, the moon now nothing more than a waning crescent behind a drift of scudding clouds. The rain fell heavily earlier in the day, and everything drips in the storm's aftermath. I hear them before I see them, hear their hurried footsteps and furtive whispers.

She resists him when he tries to lower her to the ground. It's cold and it's wet, and she wants to know why they can't go inside the cottage where it's dry. He refuses at first, but she's walking away from him, backward toward the house where it hides in the trees. She's undoing buttons and laces as she goes, calling him onward with her laugh and the look in her eyes.

His reluctance amuses me. He has not been inside the house since the day he buried me. Is he haunted by memory, by guilt, or simply by fear? Finally, he gives in, and they fall through the door in each other's arms, half-undressed already. The fur rug still lies before the cold fireplace, a little dusty perhaps, but otherwise still soft and warm.

I watch from the doorway. Their bodies twist and tangle, hands and mouths, hair and teeth all moving wildly in a frantic display of passion. Within the shifting form that is my consciousness, I feel something very much like desire for the most fleeting of moments. I remember his hands on my skin, his mouth against mine. For half a second, I forgive and forget and slip back in a blissful memory, but I'm brought back to the present by a cry of pleasure mixed with pain.

She's flipped him over onto his back and is mounting him now, coupling in a way that the more pious people in town would call debased and unnatural. Nathaniel has his head thrown back, eyes closed, mouth open and moaning.

He does not see her hand slip beneath the rug.

He does not see the knife she pulls out, the flat metal blade with a handle of carved bone. He does not see it, but he feels it as it slides in.

His eyes open wide in surprise.

She pushes harder against the hilt, burying the blade deep between two ribs, puncturing the lung beneath.

Nathaniel's mouth opens and closes like a fish. No words come out, only a faint gurgling sound as his lung fills with blood.

She pulls the knife out and Nathaniel's body contracts around the wound. She's naked in the darkness, crimson blood covering her pale hands as she holds them up in the moonlight. She's loving every minute of this, I can tell.

She buries the knife into the opposite side, with a moan that sounds more ecstatic than any sound she's ever uttered while lovemaking.

He won't have long now.

Perhaps it's because his own spirit is wavering between worlds now, but suddenly his eyes shift toward me, and I know that he can see me as I watch in the shadows. I step forward and kneel beside them on the rug. My nearness makes her skin break out in a rash of goosebumps. She turns toward me and smiles. In those final moments he realizes it. His eyes flick back and forth between us, and he takes in the striking resemblance. He's gasping for air, but he still manages to raise a hand and point, from me to her and back again.

Of course, he'd never bothered to ask me – or her – about our families. He never bothered to learn that I was the oldest of six girls, or that my next oldest sister, Samantha, and I looked uncannily alike. He certainly never bothered to learn that our father was an old soldier who taught his daughters to defend themselves, or that our mother came from a long line of wise women.

Without this knowledge, then, how could he ever have known that the females of our line can commune with the dead, can cast a glamour over ourselves to disguise our true appearance, can seduce even the purest of men with the help of a few unwholesome ingredients and well-timed words?

He couldn't. He couldn't have known, and woe to him for his ignorance.

Samantha digs the grave herself, dressed only in her shift, the work keeping her warm despite the cold October night. She digs in the exact spot he buried me nearly ten months ago, and when she pauses and presses the back of her hand to her mouth, I know she's found what's left of me. I don't look. I don't want to see it. She wraps him in the rug, then grunts and heaves, pushes and pulls, and finally rolls Nathaniel's bloody body on top of my decayed one.

She snatches up the bag she dropped earlier and pulls from it a handful of dried leaves and petals, which she scatters into the grave before filling it in, murmuring under her breath as she goes. I recognize some of the herbs from their fragrance:

sage and basil, lilac and yarrow. She's banishing his spirit and his memory from this place. I stand back and let her do her work.

The faintest hint of pink is in the sky as she tamps down the small mound of dirt that now serves as a double grave. She skips away through the woods and washes herself in the freezing water of the creek, then pulls her dark dress on over her dirty shift.

"Well," she says, and she looks into my eyes. "That's that, then, dear sister."

I nod my head and stretch my hand out toward her in thanks. It was she who shone the beacon of homecoming for all those nights after I stopped returning to our house in the village. It was she who saw me in my spirit form and listened as I told her the true circumstances of my disappearance. I looked at her now and felt overwhelmed with a sense of love and pride. She would take my place as the eldest sister, and help our mother teach the younger girl the secrets of the wise.

"You coming home now, then? Or ... going on?" she asks, gathering her hair up into a bun and pinning it into place.

I look around. I let my eyes roam over the softly swaying grasses; I listen to the song of the crows as they circle above us. A breeze blows through the surrounding forest, dislodging a few dry leaves from their branches.

"I'm going to stay here," I say, and my voice sounds like an echo half-lost on the wind. She looks at me for a moment and then nods. "I'll come and visit you then, when I can."

I smile at her. She smiles back and then turns decisively toward the path, heading away from the far field, away from the manor, toward her home.

There's a lightness to the air today. A cold wind sweeps through and cleanses the stink of hurt and despair from the air around me. Half-frozen dewdrops sparkle on a thousand curling blades of grass. The far field is quiet and peaceful, and finally, I feel quiet and at peace along with it.

Chapter Two

Hallow House

BY JO KAPLAN

Jordan Robertson's youth existed now in the golden hues of nostalgia and blurred Kodachrome photographs. He thought of his childhood as a simpler time when the world was not so angry and crowded and addicted to the constant availability of tragic news. He'd never married, but if he'd had grandchildren, he imagined they would be, as he saw most children these days, depressed, anemic, and terminally bound to the internet. The mystery was all gone from their lives, it seemed.

He lived alone in his retirement, in a modest two-bedroom house purchased on the comfortably middle-class pension of a small-town college biology professor. When the Girl Scouts came selling their cookies, he always bought a few boxes, though they never seemed to come around anymore these days; and when the kids came trick-or-treating each Halloween, he made sure to have a big bowl of candy ready—the good stuff, too, with chocolate and caramel and nougat—but fewer and fewer seemed to come around anymore these days. Jordan didn't know if it was because they had their parents drive them to the nice part of town, where the rich folks gave away those full-size candy bars, or whether they'd been warned too many times against knocking on strangers' doors. He usually ended the night with a nearly-full bowl of candy that would go uneaten, and he would feel sorry about it, wondering what had happened.

Time had a habit of moving faster the older you got, he'd found. The longer you lived, the quicker it went.

When he was a kid, Jordan had spent most days—and most nights, matter of fact—carousing with his friends, getting up to mischief: throwing toilet paper over the school librarian's yard, stealing a beer from his father's stash to share between them, or daring each other to go up to the local haunted house and knock on the door. Simple joys. But life went on, unraveling into ever-greater complexity even as it seemed ever more of the same: buying toilet paper, drinking beer with his buddies, walking up to his house and wondering if it was really his or if he'd find a strange family there, himself only an echo, a haunting.

Sometimes he thought he'd lived past his prime, or rather that he'd lived a life that wasn't meant for him—a life on extra time he shouldn't have had. He wouldn't say this, of course, to his drinking buddies or his doctor. And it wasn't because he thought he had nothing to live for. It wasn't anything that could have been solved with children or grandchildren. It was something he'd felt since he was twelve.

That was how old he was when all his friends disappeared.

Natural selection tends to maximize two biological elements: metabolic capacity (through increased surface area exchange), and internal efficiency (through minimizing transport distance). Such design principles result in branching networks, such as capillaries and the dendrites of a neuron. As a result of these fractal networks, though living beings occupy three dimensions of space, one might consider their internal physiology as having an additional fourth dimension.

—Jordan Robertson, PhD, from "Natural Selection, Allometric Scaling, and the Fourth Dimension of Life"

※

"You ever heard of the Hallow House?" he asked his drinking buddies during their five o'clock happy hour at the local bar now decorated with fake spiderwebs. It was Halloween again, and the house was on his mind. Jordan had moved back to his hometown when he retired; sometimes it felt like he'd never left at all.

"What?" shouted Mike, who refused to use a hearing aid even though he needed one. "The Holler House?"

"Hallow House, you deaf old fuck," said Carl as the others chuckled. He turned to Jordan. "Oh, yeah. We were all scared of that place, back in the day. My sister used to tell me stories that scared the piss outta me." He frowned. "Weren't there some kids that disappeared in that house?"

"Peter, Jermaine, and Vincent," Jordan said. "Vin." He almost added Jordy as if he had disappeared that night too, and all this life was one long dream he simply hadn't woken from yet.

"Now that was a story." Carl grinned.

"What was?" Mike yelled.

"They used to say if you went in that house after dark on Halloween, you weren't coming back out again. So naturally, all the neighborhood kids would test their mettle by seeing who would dare get closest."

"Whatever happened to that place?" asked John Jacobs as he fished out his evening medication. "It still around?"

"Not for much longer. They're planning to demolish it, put up some fancy new apartments," said Jordan. "I just heard."

"Damn shame." Carl shook his head. "A piece of history is what it is."

"That whole area's a blight though," said John, rattling pills. "Good riddance."

Jordan finished his beer with slow sips, tried to make it last even though it had gone warm. A contingent of twenty-somethings burst in the door with a flurry of wind and leaves, each of them dressed for the holiday, loud and happy, and he felt that old tingle of autumn—a whisper-chill, at once redolent of his boyhood friends' laughter echoing in the cool night and filled with the knowledge that all those friends were dead, had been some sixty-odd years. Their graves, long grown over, and with a scant twelve years between birth and death, remained empty. He rolled the bottle between his palms, wondered if this was his last chance at least to fill those empty graves, to remind everyone those friends had existed, once.

"It'll be gone soon enough," he murmured, set down the bottle, tried to imagine hip youngsters moving into new apartments, walking in the same spaces Donna Martin once walked. Taking pictures of their lattes to post on social media, a bright new digital footprint erasing history, erasing all the people who'd already been erased by that black hole of a house.

He fished out a few bills, tossed them on the bar, and was on the move before the others could object. He knew the house would be gone by next Halloween, and by then it would be too late to find them again. Peter, Jermaine, and Vin.

Peter, Jermaine, Vin, and Jordy.

---◆○◆---

Electrical signaling in animal nervous systems is a fractal process. The second law of thermodynamics states that entropy must always increase in a closed system; for this reason, fractal systems can only pass information in one direction. Because backward extrapolation is impossible, it is likewise impossible to determine the rule governing the fractal.

—Jordan Robertson, PhD, from "Natural Selection, Allometric Scaling, and the Fourth Dimension of Life"

---◆○◆---

These days, the house wore its neglect in scabs and scars, a shabby exterior of missing shingles and rotting wood. Jordan had never understood why the looming three-story Victorian was called Hallow House, but its regal position set back from the road and flanked by trees did give it an air of mystery. Now it was a trap house. Broken windows stood like black daggers against the attic, while the ground floor was all boarded up.

He remembered what it looked like when he was a kid: painted pink, its edges sharp and clean, its gables triumphant. Back then, the house had only been empty for a few years, ever since Donna Martin had disappeared, a pregnant new bride who'd called it her dream home when she had moved in with her husband. They picked out furniture, decorated the nursery, welcomed their new baby. They didn't ask about the house's history. Why would they? Who even knew its story? Where had it come from?

Three guesses what day it was when Donna vanished.

Her husband searched up and down for her, but she was nowhere to be found. Eventually, he and his son moved away.

Kids in the neighborhood said that on Halloween, if you looked up at the second-floor bedroom window, you might see Donna Martin's face in the moonlight. This is what Jordy and his friends had heard, and it was why they'd all decided to go to Hallow House that night. He could still hear their voices as they'd laughed their way across town, dusk turning the trees black.

"I hear she was a real knockout," said Jermaine, holding his hands in front of his chest to simulate the size of Donna Martin's breasts. He wore a black cloak, jaw stuffed with plastic vampire teeth that muffled his voice and made him suck in spit loud as pulling a drink through a straw.

Peter guffawed, but he looked excited. He was always trying to catch a glimpse of the Playboys at the magazine stand. That night, Peter was wearing a clown costume with a red wig, his face painted white, black rings around his eyes.

Vin, who towered over the others following a recent growth spurt that made his arms and legs too long for his clothes, was dressed as a scarecrow. His pants and sleeves hung a few inches too short, making him look even ganglier. "You're not supposed to talk about the dead that way, Germy," he said. Jermaine wrinkled his nose.

"Who says she's dead?" asked Jordy. He'd been dressed as a ghost that night, a simple sheet with eyeholes cut out.

"The folks who see her ghost in the window, that's who."

"Aw, I don't believe in that stuff," said Jermaine. But as soon as he said it, they were there; Hallow House loomed as the sun left the horizon, its pink paint, in the twilight, now the color of a bruise. They looked up, searching for Donna

Martin's face (Peter perhaps searching for a different part of her body), but they didn't see anything. "Told you," said Jermaine. "No ghosts."

"Dare you to go knock on the door," said Peter.

Vin's eyebrows skyrocketed. "You crazy?"

"Why?" asked Jermaine. "Not like anyone would answer. Nobody lives there."

But Peter wouldn't let up. "I'll give you half my candy if you do."

"I wouldn't do it for all the candy in the world," said Vin.

"I'll do it."

It was Jordy who accepted the dare. Sometimes he wondered what might have happened if he'd begged off like the others, if they would have simply turned around and gone trick-or-treating, come home later that night with sacks full of candy. He wondered what they might be like now if they hadn't gone in. If they'd had the chance to grow up.

Jordy had been small for his age, and maybe that was why he felt he had to prove himself. His parents didn't pay him a whole lot of attention—partly the reason for the shoddy costume. So, he took a breath and approached the house, trying to remind himself there was nothing to be afraid of. He stepped onto the porch, raised his fist, and rapped three times on the door.

Nothing happened.

Vin let out a whoop, and the others came rushing up, grabbing his shoulders, commending his bravery. Jordy was on top of the world. He felt like more than just a ghost in a cheap old sheet.

But then he heard a click and saw the front door creak slowly open. His heart lurched up his throat.

"What the heck?" said Vin. If Jermaine's face hadn't already been painted white, they would have seen him go pale.

"Hello?" Peter shouted. His voice echoed in the dark foyer. "Anybody home? Mrs. Martin? We've come to fix your pipes!"

Jermaine laughed while Vin shot Peter a look of horror and hissed at him to be quiet. Peter didn't listen. He stepped across the threshold, pushed the door the rest of the way open, then reached over and flipped the light switch. Jordy didn't know why he was surprised when the lights flickered on.

They looked inside, where a stately oak staircase went up and turned and went up again. A tufted armchair stood beside the stairs, a teddy bear seated upon it.

"Come on," said Peter. "Let's check it out."

Vin exchanged a look with Jermaine. "I don't know. Maybe we should just go trick-or-treating."

Peter rolled his eyes, peered up the staircase, grabbed the stuffed bear. "Sure, if you all admit you're scaredy-cats."

"Not me," said Jermaine, joining him in the foyer.

"Dracula's in," said Peter. "Who else?"

Vin took one reluctant step, then another. "But only because I want to see if it's true."

"If what's true?"

He held his hands in front of his chest, mimicking what Jermaine had done earlier, and Peter let out a peal of laughter. Then he looked at Jordy, the only one still on the dark porch rather than the lighted foyer. "You coming, Casper?" Peter held the bear by its foot, and it dangled at his side, black button eyes gleaming.

He wondered, sometimes, what might have happened had he gone inside with them, and he couldn't really say now, all these years later, what held him back. He could pretend it was some kind of premonition, as if he'd known what was going to happen, but this was likely just him projecting his current knowledge onto his past self. More probably, at twelve, Jordy had simply found the prospect of stepping into that house more frightening than the act of defying his friends, so he shook his head and stepped away. This moment had become surreal for him over the years. He didn't remember if they shut the door, or if they left it open; he didn't remember if they walked off right then, or if they stood there looking out at him with disappointment. He saw himself as he backed away—saw himself drift, ghost-like, down the porch steps, far enough now to look up again at the second-floor windows, and to see, or imagine he saw, a woman's face peering out at him, with black button eyes.

The next day, Jordy found out his friends hadn't made it home that night. He talked to the police, said they'd gone to Hallow House. The police searched it top to bottom but found no trace of them. They asked him where his friends had gone after that, but Jordy had no answer.

Why are there no Victor Frankenstein's among us? Simply this: his creation is a fiction. If we do not know the governing rule of life, we cannot hope to replicate its complexity. We can only extrapolate forward, not backward.
 —Jordan Robertson, PhD, from "Natural Selection, Allometric Scaling, and the Fourth Dimension of Life"

It was Halloween, but you couldn't tell, not on this side of town. Trash littered the front lawns of decrepit buildings, and there weren't any decorations in sight—certainly no trick-or-treaters. The sun had become a sliver of gold on the horizon as Jordan stood staring up at the old Victorian, trying to catch a glimpse of a face in one of the second-story windows. Over the years, he'd come to think what he'd seen that night was just his imagination. But sometimes, when the air felt just like it did back then—crisp, thin, expectant—he could almost convince himself he had, in fact, seen a ghost.

Now, he could see nothing beyond the boarded-up ground-floor windows as he stepped onto the porch, where the front door hung askew on rusted hinges. He gave the knob a turn. Inside, bulbs flickered dimly on faded wallpaper peeling like dead skin and empty cans strewing the floor.

He hesitated at the threshold, the certainty that had propelled him to this point abruptly doused. All his life he'd lived never knowing what had happened to them. All his life he'd been afraid of this place, building walls around it in his mind until it became something monstrous, hungry, impenetrable. No matter how much he studied the rules of life, how many degrees he acquired, there was still one thing in this world he had never understood. His body's adrenal mechanisms urged him to walk away now, to let it go—let them demolish it, let this wretched place finally be gone from this world. Let it stop haunting him.

But he was haunted, too, by those three empty coffins.

He stepped inside.

To the right of the foyer, he found a sitting room with a battered settee. A man and woman—mid-twenties, perhaps, but aged beyond their years, skin sallow, eyes sunken, hair matted—lay slumped against the wall beside a few discarded needles. As he stepped past them, a hand grabbed his ankle, and he looked down to find the woman staring with wild eyes.

"Don't go back there," she mumbled. "You can't go... in the void... like Sharon..." Her voice trailed off as her eyes glazed over, head lolling, and Jordan gently shook his leg until she loosened her grip.

"You ought to get yourself right," he said, unsure if she was listening. "You should stay right there, and once you've sobered up, go out that front door and never come back here again. This place is a trap."

"It's a trap," she said with an odd, giggling cadence. "It's a trap!"

Jordan sighed. He couldn't do anything for them. Either they would clean themselves up, or they wouldn't. You couldn't force someone to do something they didn't want to do.

Ahead, he found a dining room and a kitchen. Broken glass littered the floor, another fellow passed out in the corner. Graffiti spray-painted the walls.

What were they searching for? These people who had become so in love with the feeling of being high they could no longer stand to be sober. Maybe they were searching for that lost feeling of childish joy, trying so hard to extrapolate backward to its source, to know happiness again, but finding only this poor facsimile.

Jordan returned to the foyer. He supposed he could leave now. He'd seen the inside, after all these years, and it was nothing he was looking for. He sighed, hesitated, then peered up the staircase. Was that where they'd headed, after he'd walked away? They must have gone upstairs, looking for Donna Martin.

He turned away from the front door.

The stairs groaned under his weight like they might collapse at any moment, and he arrived at the second-floor hallway better kept than the first, its wainscoting intact and its doors retaining their brass handles. Jordan tried one, found a linen closet, tried another, found a bedroom. He stepped inside where a bed still sat, mattress impressed with the shape of its owner. He went to the window and looked out but could see little in the darkness, and he wondered if this was Donna's window. A cold finger went down his spine. He turned and stepped back into the hallway.

But it was not the same hallway he'd come from.

Sure, it looked the same—just the same. But now he looked left, right, saw no stairway. Just a long hall with doors and more doors, and no way to get back down.

Impossible, he thought, his heart wheeling.

But was it less impossible than his friends vanishing into thin air?

He traversed the hallway, then from room to room, from room to new hall, from new hall to new room, each a near-identical replication of the last, each turning in directions which the geometry of the house should not have allowed, each orthogonal, somehow, to the previous, and to the previous, and to the previous. After one turn through yet another bedroom, he heard a sound, muffled by many walls, like a baby crying, and it raised goosebumps on his arms.

He called out, "Hello?"

He was surprised when another voice echoed his greeting. He entered the room where he'd heard the voice, dark but for the hall light slanting in.

"Oh, thank god," he laughed, the anxiety which had crept up on him dissipating in the presence of another person. "Do you know how to get downstairs from here?"

The figure nodded, resolving, in the thin light, into a woman with wild hair, wearing baggy sweats. "Sure you want to go down?" she said. "There's also up. And across. Left, right. Sideways and slantways and longways and backways..."

"Just the stairs down, I think."

The woman turned, said, "Suit yourself," and opened a closet door that revealed another hall, waved him forward. They went through a bathroom next, at the back of which what had seemed a cabinet opened into a long stone corridor.

"What is this place?" he asked. She glanced at him, the hall light turning her eyes to wet stones. A grin quirked over her mouth.

"You're in the Hallow, baby," she purred. "Where you think you was?"

Here, the baby's crying had returned, seemed louder now, echoing against the stone walls even as he saw no child. Again, something in the sound drew a shiver of dread down his spine. Something about it didn't seem right—though, having little experience with children, he couldn't quite say why—and he wished to be rid of it.

"Keep up, baby!"

He looked up, saw the woman ahead of him, far down the corridor.

Hurrying to catch up with her—she was much younger than him, and his joints creaked—Jordan followed her through a peaked wooden doorway at the end of the corridor. The layout of the room beyond reminded him of the dining room on the first floor, except much older, rough-hewn, its stove a fireplace burnt to cinders, its walls more of the same old stone as the corridor.

"How long have you been here?" he asked. "Wherever here is?"

The woman shrugged. "Time ain't time here, baby." She looked around with a frown, searching. "Sometimes, it changes, you know? You gotta pay attention." She started moving along the wall, tapping experimentally.

"How do you know where to go?"

"Been exploring, ever since I got lost. I know all kinds of ways, now. But you can't draw a map. Maps don't work." She discovered an egress, beckoned him forward, and Jordan hurried to follow, not wanting to lose her. He remembered being twelve years old, suddenly friendless—how he had spent the following years feeling like he lived on the edge of the world, about to fall off at any moment. Eating lunch alone, sitting on his front porch summer evenings watching other kids chase each other down the block, while he had no one. He'd ridden his bike back and forth to Hallow House so many times, but he was always afraid to go as far as the porch, always afraid—and that old fear crept up on him now, lighting up his nerve-endings. He shouldn't have come here. He should have left before he stepped inside.

"I think of it like a mind," said his guide. "Intuitive, like. This place doesn't make logical sense. Doesn't make geographical sense. But it makes mind-sense, you know? And mind-sense is like dream-sense, which is to say it don't make much sense unless you're asleep."

"But we're not asleep."

"Ain't we?" The woman flashed a grin, missing a few teeth. They passed along another hall, where Jordan spotted something on the floor—something she stepped around but that he paused, puzzled over.

A stuffed brown bear with button eyes.

His guts lurched into his throat as he bent to pick it up. "You were here," he murmured, the bear's face staring up at him, inscrutable. "You came through here."

Peter's voice echoed in his ears, *you coming, Casper?*

It took him a few minutes to stand up again, aided, thankfully, by the woman. He clutched the bear as he followed her, and he thought he could hear again, somewhere in the distance, the baby crying. "Does sound travel the normal way, here?"

The woman frowned, shrugged. "Let me tell you something, baby. Ain't nothing travels here in a straight line. Things might seem far away, but they're close, because of how the halls have folded over each other. Now, I used to be on some shit. Heroin, mostly, but other stuff, too. And when I first ended up here?" She shook her head, eyes bulbous in her gaunt face.

"I thought I was trippin.' But there ain't no trip like the Hallow, you can believe that. Some folks come through here, they say it goes on forever. Far as I can tell, it does. Most folks come through here, they keep going. One thing they don't ever do?" She nodded to a doorway that lay ahead in darkness. "Come back."

They stepped through and found a room where long weedy grass, half-dead, burst from the broken floor and vines crept up the walls. Jordan was stopped short by the sight of a figure in the buzzing light that flickered like the moon passing behind clouds, arms out at his sides as if held up by wooden poles. Like a scarecrow.

"Vin?" Jordan gasped.

The scarecrow looked up—and, yes, yes, it was. And yet—he remembered Vin being so tall, towering over the others, but now he seemed so small, so scrawny, so impossibly young.

"Vin," he said again. Slowly, like coming out of sleep, the scarecrow looked up. "Hey, Vin. It's me. Jordy."

Vin said nothing, kept his pose.

"Come on," said his guide. "We're not far now, you want the stairs down."

"But—" He couldn't leave without him. "Come with us," Jordan begged. "We're going back down." Nothing. He tried again: "What about Jermaine and Peter? Where are they?"

"You're a ghost." Vin's voice was dry whisper, like dead grass.

Jordan reeled away from him. "Vin, buddy, listen. It's me. It's Jordy."

Vin blinked slowly. "You're not Jordy," he said. "You're old."

"You can't reach him," said his guide. "He's been here a long, long time. Way longer than me. His mind's gone, now. Thinks he's a scarecrow."

"No!" Jordan thundered. "I'm not leaving you here." He grabbed Vin by the arm to drag him along, but as he did, the arm dissolved into straw, tore free from the scarecrow's body. A monstrous horror welled in Jordan's heart. "No," he said, trying to catch the straw as it scattered. "No!"

The Vin-scarecrow, now one-armed, resumed his post. The guide gently pulled Jordan away. "Some folks been here too long," she said quietly, sadly. "They're part of the Hallow, now."

Jordan could see, now, the way the vines and grass crept up into the bottoms of Vin's jeans where his feet should have been so that he couldn't tell where the plants ended, and Vin began. Maybe he was all grass inside. The thought twisted Jordan's heart into an awful shape. The room filled with a faint shushing as a wind that shouldn't have been there whispered the grass, whistled through Vin's teeth. Jordan was afraid to touch him again.

"I'll come back for you," he said, and he almost believed himself. Numbly, he turned, followed his guide onward.

After a time, which Jordan had stopped trying to count, she paused, and he looked up to find an opening ahead, a staircase leading down, stone steps lined by stone walls, nothing like the staircase he'd first come up. "There you go," she said, "Stairs down." But she made no move to walk ahead of him.

"Are we going?" he asked around the ache in his chest.

She shook her head. "This is as far as I go, baby."

Jordan looked down the crumbling old stairs receding into darkness. This was what he wanted, wasn't it? There was no way back now: only forward. He went to the first step, paused, looked back at the woman who had taken him this far. "I never got your name," he said.

She grinned. "Sharon."

One proposition for the origin of consciousness is not from only a single level of biological organization, but as a result of the interactions between networks at different levels, in the form of fractal stacking. Not only, then, does the fractal network come into play as the basis of biology and natural selection, but also as the basis of consciousness, either natural (biological neurons forming a nervous system) or artificial (a computer simulation with neuron-like properties). One may then understand biological organization as a series of nested networks, wherein the units of one network are also their own networks at the next level down, and so on and so forth, replicating the same patterns at different levels.

—Jordan Robertson, PhD, from "Natural Selection, Allometric Scaling, and the Fourth Dimension of Life"

Jordan left Sharon and descended the stairs until he was deep in the darkness, feeling his way along the cool stone walls, with no sense of how far down the stairway went—only that it was long, long enough that he could no longer see the light at the top. But he couldn't go back, not now, not yet, not when Peter and Jermaine might be down here somewhere. When he found them, he could take them back up to Vin, take them all out of this place.

(—he knew, of course, deep down, that this was a fantasy, yes, he knew, but he wouldn't allow the thought to cross his conscious mind, for it kept him going, it kept him from unraveling—)

Here in the dark, the baby's crying grew louder again, echoing, endless. He pressed his hands over his ears, hummed, tried to ignore the invasive wail, but still it penetrated.

Jordan was all alone again, and his face crumpled with the urge to laugh or weep, because wasn't that simply his eternal mode of being? And hadn't he pursued a degree in biology as if it would bring him closer to other living things, as if it would make him feel less alone? Yet, that emptiness had never left him.

A part of him knew, somehow, that if his friends had grown old, they would eventually have grown apart, as friends do; they would have gone to different universities, pursued different paths in life, maybe called each other every few years to see how the kids and grandkids were doing... but it would never be like it was when they were young. When they were happy and perfect and inseparable.

He knew this, yes, but he couldn't help reaching back for it still—reaching back for them, for what he'd lost. Reaching for connection, for life. Searching, in his research, for an understanding of where it came from, where we came from, people, living breathing conscious people, from whom he felt so distant and alone. Consciousness seemed a burden that could only move in one direction, toward that infinite solitude of self, ever-complexifying and ever-further from any other conscious self, and ever more alone.

His laughter drowned out the baby's crying. And he thought he heard another's laughter, too, echoing with his own: the laughter of a young clown. He realized he was still carrying the bear, and, not wanting to see its accusatory button eyes if he ever found light again, he dropped it somewhere on the stairs, left it in the dark. His knees popped.

And then—he reached the bottom.

His feet made tentative movements forward, finding only flat ground, and like this he felt his way down another corridor, waiting always for the sudden drop of another step, until he saw the flicker of candles standing in sconces that mercifully lit up this dungeon, this parody of the living room somewhere far, far above, or perhaps the living room was merely a sketch of this ancient place, and perhaps it wasn't merciful at all.

(—and he thought but did not really allow himself to think that maybe consciousness itself was madness, or indeed that ever-complexifying consciousness was ever-madder madness, and he laughed and thought he could hear Peter laughing with him, though Peter was perhaps too young to understand, would be eternally too young—)

The room ahead was less than stone, older, built from dirt. Dirt and bone. But "older" held little meaning here. Maybe "older" and "deeper" were one and the same, the way it was to gaze out into deep-deep space, both far away and back in time. Maybe extrapolating backward was only yet another measure toward entropy.

The baby's crying shrilled and shrieked, and Jordan stumbled into the room, hands on his ears, wanting to cry himself, wanting it to be over and knowing somehow that it never would. Awful thoughts surged through him: he wanted to strangle this baby, he wanted to silence it for good, he wanted to bury it in the dirt. In all his years of teaching about the beauty of living things, he'd never thought himself capable of harming a child—had considered all life sacred—but this, this endless crying, did not seem sacred to him.

The walls seemed to ripple and move like worms, like the peristalsis of a digesting gut.

A shape scuttled across the floor.

He whirled to see it, grabbed a flaming sconce from the wall to light his way along the low dirt tunnel. Worms curled into figure eights at his feet. He pursued the skittering creature until he had it cornered against a wall where strange roots burst forth like dendrites, and the flame flickered over a face.

A face he recognized.

An adult, a woman, hunched on all fours, naked, jaw hanging open, eyes black, breasts sagging against the dirt.

Donna Martin.

Jordan raised his hands in a pacifying gesture, horrified, wanting to turn from her naked body parts that he and his friends had been so eager to see as children.

How long had she searched for her husband and baby, after they'd left? How long before she'd lost her mind?

Or no—not lost it. Given it up, perhaps, to the intricate workings of the Hallow.

Donna opened her mouth and shrieked—the sound of a baby crying, an awful imitation, wailing and bleating.

Repulsed, Jordan staggered away, heaved, let her crawl, spider-fast, into the darkness.

If animals are conscious, why not other things? Why not plants? Why not fungi? Why not computers, or trains, or houses?
—Jordan Robertson, from his PhD dissertation: "Is Consciousness a Biological Function?"

In the dark and the dirt, in the structure that no longer seemed anything like a house or, indeed, anything much like a familiar structure at all, that seemed to twist and reroute itself around him, Jordan found another child. One he recognized.

Tears spilled from his eyes, and he fell to his knees, which twanged in his ears like plucked strings.

"Jermaine."

He wondered if it was really him or if he had been subsumed, somehow, his consciousness chewed up and swallowed by the house, just another network inside of its veins and arteries and madness—but it looked like him. God, it looked like him, and it made Jordan feel both less alone and more alone than ever.

The boy turned, face pale as bone instead of the warm dark hue it had been in life and every other day except for that Halloween when his mother had painted it death-white.

"I'm sorry I left." The words ripped themselves from Jordan's chest. "But I'm here now."

Jermaine's breath hitched and his eyes focused. "Jordy?" he asked in a voice that Jordan so remembered, that felt familiar as home, which made more tears spill from his eyes, which made him think, for a moment, he could go backward.

"It's me," he gasped, not sure if that was even true anymore, if Jordy existed anymore, if he had been here for an hour or sixty-six years.

Somewhere in the distance, he could hear Donna crying like a baby, and somewhere else, he could hear clownish laughter.

It wasn't Halloween anymore, he thought—he had been here too long now, surely—but, at the same time, it was always Halloween. It was always the same moment, turned in on itself, wasn't it? All of time, all of space, folded inward like the gyri and sulci of a brain, making the conscious networks of themselves into units of a larger conscious network, of the house, which fed on their madness, which perhaps might someday awaken to itself, if it hadn't already.

Jermaine threw out his arms and Jordan went to him. They embraced, an old man and a boy, but Jordy thought maybe he was really only twelve again, had always been twelve, had always been here with them, had, in fact, stepped inside that bright foyer with them all those years ago, had followed them into the labyrinth, had never gone on to study biology and teach and retire, had never met Mike or Carl or John Jacobs, had only imagined, in the endless complexity of consciousness, his entire life out of the eternity here in Hallow House, but had always been here and always would, and had only wished, having gone with his truest friends, that he could have lived a full life apart from them, even knowing, deep down, he had never been able to escape the endless fractal paths of this endless house.

A gasp of air—Jordy turned, wondering if now would be the time, of all the infinite times he'd tried, that he might find the staircase up and out again—but Jermaine clutched him closer, stared with gleaming button eyes, opened his mouth of razor fangs, sank his teeth into Jordy's throat, and drank the halls and arteries inside of him, and drew him deeper.

Chapter Three

Nory's

BY MICHAEL J. MOORE

My walk has become pathetic, if I'm being honest with myself—I'm not always—more like a trundle, really. I don't need the cane. Yeah, I've used it since the surgery, and yeah, my hip aches something fierce, but it doesn't hurt any less when I'm hauling around this aluminum tube. Some years ago, I told myself I liked the feel of the glossy wooden handle against my palm, and it was probably true in the beginning. Over time, however, the muffled clank of its rubber-clad base against the pavement became like a third footstep. I suspect, at this point, I'd feel like an amputee without it. The only one who's ever understood this, is Dolores.

There's a group of kids at a bus stop on Main Street. Teenagers, I think, but who can be sure these days? Hormones in the groceries, makeup on the girls—even on the boys sometimes—and levels of pomposity that were unheard of in my day have made it increasingly difficult to differentiate the stages of youth roaming the streets of Anacortes. One of them has his pants around his rump, and half a cigarette between his lips. The other two, a boy and a short-haired girl, are sitting on the bench. I'm hearing snippets of their conversation as I approach, but not yet able to tell who's saying what.

"Where'd you hear that, dude?"

"It's not even true. Don't let him freak you out."

"If you don't believe me, Google it."

Traffic whooshes by, ushering the scent of saltwater into my nostrils. Seagulls shriek somewhere in the distance. Every town, I imagine, has a Main Street, but the one in my waterfront community has remained true to its name. Anacortes hasn't grown much since I was a boy (a very long time ago), and just about every major business can be accessed from the three-lane road. One end will dump you onto the highway, while the other stops at the marina. The kids at the bus stop are so close now that I can smell burning tobacco, and they're loud enough to extinguish any regrets I've ever harbored that Dolores couldn't conceive.

The girl says, "Even if it used to be a whatever—"

"Crematorium." The smoking boy seems to be enjoying himself. "It was called Nory's Crematorium, and after it shut down, the owner opened—"

"Whatever. Even if that happened, they wouldn't use the same ovens to cook—"

"I'm telling you, Google it. The place is famous for being haunted."

I'm making a point not to stare, but the girl's burgundy hair is cropped closer to her scalp than that of either of her male companions. My dear mother would have whooped my sister black-and-blue had she shown up to dinner looking like that, but times have certainly changed. Dolores would have said something to the effect of, "Oh Gene, don't be so damn old-fashioned." Then she succumbed to cancer—how many years ago? Most days I prefer not to remember—leaving me a lonely old widower.

Reaching up, I brush a few loose strands of gray hair behind my ear, a strategic misdirection to keep the kids from noticing as I slow down to eavesdrop. I'm trying to maintain a straight face but feel my lips tightening into a smug grin. I've known Fred Nory since he was swimming in mud puddles with nothing but a cloth diaper. Ages before he inherited his late-father's business.

The girl's on to me, though. She glances over, stares for longer than any child should be eyeing an adult man. The clown with his pants down blows a long smoke-cloud and smiles. "These days they have better ovens for cooking dead people, but back then they would use different ones—I think they were stone, or cement or whatever, and Nory figured out they were also good for—"

"I don't wanna talk about this anymore." The girl finally averts her gaze. "It's creeping me out."

The boy sitting next to her laughs like a hyena. "I told you not to listen to him!" Then the topic of Nory's Crematorium seems to evaporate into the late afternoon air.

Normally, I walk to Cypress, take a left, and circle back around. However, I think I'll pay the old cooker a visit. It's a few blocks up, where Main touches Spruce Street, and I imagine Fred will get a good laugh out of what I've just heard.

It was hot enough today to fry an egg on the hood of a Cadillac, and I'd be a fibber if I said the lingering heat seeping between my thinning hair isn't pleasant. I know this must seem a bit odd, but Dolores used to cup my head, and her hands were always very warm (notwithstanding the day I held one as she lay in her tan casket).

Once I've made it to the corner of Main and Spruce, the sky has begun to flush as the sun makes way for evening. Somewhere in the back of my mind, I'm aware it will soon cool down and I didn't bring a jacket. However, before I can surrender anymore of my focus to the weather, it's taken captive by a sign above the crematorium's door. Decorative red letters announce: Nory's Pizza Factory.

My knee-jerk reaction is to chuckle, as it seems I've fallen victim to some sort of a lark. Making my way through the lot—which is packed with vehicles—I step inside the old brick building, and my senses are greeted by a lovely array of spices, sauces, meats—do I even smell cheese? —and the low murmur of conversations. Mostly occupied tables are scattered before a checkout counter, behind which a pretty blond works a register. Countless eyes dart in my direction, as a familiar face approaches.

Without thinking, I say, "William," knowing how ridiculous this sounds because Bill Nory has been dead for years. The man flashes a set of pearly whites set within a gray beard and speaks so quietly only I can hear.

"Mr. Coldwell. Great of you to stop by."

Glancing around the dimly lit eatery, I tell him to call me Gene. People are staring. Pointing and whispering. With a great deal of effort, I suppress any contemptuous thoughts toward such an ill-mannered generation. Instead, I say, "You look more like your father every day, Fred."

"So, you've mentioned, sir. Would you care to take a seat?"

I tell him I think I'll stand, and then ask, "Am I succumbing to an early case of dementia, young man, or have you aged substantially in the past—"

"You visited last month, sir. I'd like to think I haven't aged too much since then."

"My apologies," I feel my brow furrow, "but this place? Your father's business—"

"The crematorium shut down ages ago." Fred's smile perseveres. "The funeral-home over on Birch handles all that jazz now with the use of—shall we say—more contemporary methodology. We were one of the last in Washington to use brick kilns, though. They were good for trapping gases released during the process, though it turns out they're also good for—"

I cut him off with a clearing of my throat. "Yes, I ah—I see."

Not taking the hint, he chortles, "Apparently, folks don't like their dead cooked old-fashion, but they prefer their pizzas that way. Are you sure you wouldn't like to take a seat, Gene?"

Ignoring the question, I step aside as a woman exits hand-in-hand with her young daughter. "When exactly did you close the—"

"You were one of our last customers, sir. Do you remember how long ago you—"

"No, Fred. Most days I—"

"—prefer not to. Of course. Then I take it you're not here because you're ready to accept that you're—"

"No." I shake my head. "You always were a hell of a salesman, Fred, but not today. I think I'll be on my way now."

I turn to leave, and he speaks to my back. "She's not out there, Gene. You can walk around this town for the next century, and you won't find your wife. She moved on long before you—"

"Thank you, Fred. Have a nice evening."

Somebody—a woman, I think, but who can be sure these days? —asks, "Mr. Nory? Who are you—" But whatever else she says disappears into a gasp that seems to fill the restaurant when I push open the door and step outside. It swings shut behind me, and all thoughts of Nory's fade like a ghost in the light as I return to my walk.

Chapter Four

Behold, Death Arrives, A Duet of Ash and Fang

BY JAE MAZER

Clips and clops carried Veronique over the cobblestone paths of Habitation de Québec, burlap sack in hand. Travel had been much easier before filling that sack with a week's worth of rodents and rabbit. Hidden beneath the cloak of bison hide she'd traded her mother's flageolet for—a horrible, shrill instrument Vero had no use for after her mother's passing—Vero floated the paths like a ghost, all but undetected save the racket of her blocky heels on the roan walkways.

Vero navigated the side streets, taking care to avoid the village square as if it were ripe with the black death, dodging notice best she could. Though stifling and rank with the smell of mildewed leather, the hide she wore masked her gleaming ginger hair and creamy skin; men either wanted to bed her or strap her to the stake. Papers flapping on the walls of the town hall bore the sketches of faces, each a warning. Executed. Cursed. Men and women, their eyes screaming for help.

Such a sigh of relief heaved from Vero's lungs when she crossed the threshold of the forest, the towering sugar maples whispering their welcome as she and the breeze passed deep into their embrace. It would be many kilometers before she was safely behind a barred door that prohibited visitors both fair and hostile.

The day grew dark, though the sun remained high in the sky; trees were what brought about this premature dusk, their gangly arms entwined overtop Vero's head, blocking the light of day. The stench of human toil and waste was replaced by dank decay and animal essence, the leavings of bovine and bird, rodent and canine abundant in this area of the woods that rarely tasted human flesh. But fear flowed through Vero's veins. The forest had a suffocating beauty that loomed in every direction, coating her sight in the glory of sparkling winter and filling her mouth and nostrils with the thickness of nature. It was intoxicating.

Muscles aching, Vero had no choice but to slow her pace lest she not reach the sanctuary before nightfall. *Better to be late than never,* she thought as she dipped her head and ploughed forward, wishing she had no mouth to feed. The sheer amount of food she had to carry to sustain him for a fortnight was more weight than a girl of her condition could carry without struggle.

The steeple of the church peered through the trees, its cross hanging haphazard atop the grey, rotting wood and weathered stone, acting as both beacon and sentry. It was easy to spy it from afar, even in melancholy weather, and its looming judgement kept ne'er-do-wells at bay.

Though mere steps away from the clearing encircling her abode, Vero slowed to a stop, silencing the dull thuds her shoes were making on the loam. She felt eyes upon her body, all over the flesh beneath the layers of her skirts. Holding as still as a mouse caught in a cat's breath, she hoped further notice of her presence would not be taken. She was not ready for him just yet.

A dozen pounding heartbeats passed before Vero summoned the courage to ignite movement again, her steps light and speedy, carrying her with haste to the chapel's entrance. She burst inside, dropped the sack to the floor, and heaved a pew with all her might, sliding it in front of the door to bar out whatever might want in.

From the other room, a cackle rose, mocking her. "Foolish little girl. You think wood will protect you? Spears and shields and God's grace will not protect you from your foolishness."

Paying no mind to the heckles from the room beyond the sanctuary, Vero gathered up the sack and its spilled contents, heaving it once more over her shoulder and slogging her way down the center aisle, peeking in the rows of pews to ensure she had no surprise parishioners come to worship or engage in activities otherwise unholy.

The kitchen and pantry were large enough to store food for an entire army. Methodically, Vero unloaded the food, orderly, neat, and tidy. The meat went in a salt box closet in the corner of the room, with ventilation sealed from the rest of the church that would allow the cold air access to enter and dwell. *Not that the meat needs to keep for long, but he might balk if it spoils even the slightest.*

After she put the food away, Vero swept and scrubbed all the surfaces, banishing spider webs and bunnies of dust for another day. It was an unnecessary task but one that kept things normal. Familiar. Like they were before. With chores complete, Vero retired to the living quarters behind the pulpit stage. The bedroom wasn't much, just a small, unadorned room with a single bed, but it was comfortable and safe. For now.

Vero untied her bodice and the many ribbons of her skirts, allowing all to fall to the floor, revealing skin so pale it glowed in the moonlight. With fluid grace, she dove under her blankets and tucked her feet under the moose hide at the end of her bed. As her eyes flickered like candles blown by the winds of sleep, a shape shifted in the corner, masked by the shadows of the night. Vero's eyes narrowed, seeking to focus on the misshapen movement haunting the corner of her room.

It was a young woman, hair black and patchy, white nightdress marred by the lick of flames. Her flesh was a sickly sheath of grey decay, and her eyes were mere sockets writhing with bloodworms and fire.

"Goodnight, fair Thérèse," Vero bade as she rolled over, turning her back to her departed sister.

———◆O◆———

"It's a fool's errand," Thérèse scolded, her voice thick with the wheeze of death.

Vero ignored her sister's taunting and continued to brush her own tresses with a boar's hair brush, another treasure her mother had traded dearly for at the Hudson's Bay Company when they perched beside the St. Lawrence the year before.

"It's maniacal, this plan of yours," Thérèse chided.

"What would you have me do?" Vero faced her sister, who floated in the corner of the tiny bedroom, crooked and broken. "You'd have me do nothing, I dare say."

"I'd have you realize they are futile, these flights of fancy. What do you hope to accomplish?"

"More than standing in a corner for the rest of all days," Vero mumbled, her mouth curling ever-so-slightly into a coy grin.

"I only linger so as not to leave you."

Vero examined Thérèse in the mirror. Her sister was but a wisp of what she once was; though the decay was stagnant, it proved increasingly difficult to bear witness to the nothingness that had replaced her vibrant, vivacious Thérèse. With thoughts of that loss came visions of their parents, Mama preparing the fish and Papa baking bannock over an open flame in the pit behind their humble cottage. So lovely were those days when the crisp kiss of winter hung like gossamer in the air. The rich bounty of their toils filled their home and bellies, and the music of Mama's violin filled their hearts.

Gone were those days. Taken.

"I know you suffer, sister," Thérèse said. "I know not how to remedy that."

"This idea will work."

"To what end?"

"Vengeance. I must try or submit to madness. My rage will consume what little is left of me. Of us."

In minuscule increments, Thérèse's mouth clicked shut, closing the cavernous black hole that emitted her croaking voice. She had no more to say, Vero supposed, and that was good. Vero had no more to hear this day.

Vero knotted her hair in tight plaits and pinned it atop her head, then went to the kitchen to fetch a rabbit. She had not yet dressed it, which was a chore but worth the effort. Meat was most ripe with blood exposed. She carried the rabbit by the ears out the back door, its body swinging to and fro. A light skiff of snow had dusted the ground during the slumber hours, leaving the clearing a sparkling winter wonderland under the pink morning sky. Vero begrudged disturbing the virgin snow, but there was work to be done.

Blade in hand, she set the carcass upon the chopping block and buried her knife to the hilt, tugging and tearing until the rabbit had been liberated from its pelt, its insides on the outside. The smell was putrid but inviting, a coppery stench not quite spoiled but less than savory. *I have a mind to spice this to perfection,* Vero thought, then thought better, Thérèse's voice echoing in her head; *"Be cognizant of where you dedicate your efforts, wee fille, lest you run out of efforts to give."*

With the rabbit butchered, Vero gathered her father's tools, sliding them back into the leather belt he'd made to hold such things—a convenience only a leatherworker could create. Vero once again thanked the stars she'd had the foresight to grab that belt and all its treasures as she'd fled the family home. She'd be terribly lost without those conveniences. On her own, she had no power. No strength. No ability.

The woods were quiet, nary a whiskey jack cawing or a marmot scuttling through the thick brush. It was sudden, that silence. Though the white noise of nature was something rarely noticed by Vero, its absence was a blaring alarm.

They were watching her again, those eyes—hungry, patient, and calculating. One step into the trees and those eyes would look no more. They would give into their feral, primal drive, and no sooner than she could turn to run, she'd be crushed between those massive jaws.

Though the pink sky was dissolving into yellow dawn, the forest remained dark. And in that dark, between the claws of trees, shone two glowing moons, yellow eyes that rose and fell with each of his breaths. Vero could see nothing more than eyes, though, buried in a mass of fur between the trees. There was no telling where beast ended and dark began.

Vero clucked her tongue and spoke with the softness of a faerie's waltz. "'Tis okay, mon amie. You are safe here."

Thérèse's voice cawed in Vero's head. *But you are not, little sister!*

"Come," Vero said, her voice measured, hypnotic.

The things it could do to you!

Vero took care to keep her movements slow and smooth as she scooped the hindquarters of the rabbit off the chopping block and waved it at the trees.

A huff, a puff, and the beast showed itself, first extending a single limb out of the cover of the trees, then another, until it stood tall and exposed in the light of day. It was the first time Vero had seen the beast in its entirety. During trips to and from town, she had seen the glow of its eyes and the blur of its coat as it whirred past her like a storm through the woods. But the behemoth that stood before her was like nothing she could have imagined.

Le Loup Garou was a folktale told to children at nursery school, a cautionary tale planted by parents and school mistresses to warn children of the dangers of sloth. A powerful, hulking biped, Le Loup Garou was a man cursed to werewolf form after failing to adhere to his godly duties. The beast and his pack were condemned by the church to wander the woods in want of the taste of death and suffering.

"And we have suffered much," Vero said as she tossed the meat into the snow.

Le Loup raised its massive snout and sniffed the air. With ribbons of drool swinging from its maw, it crouched to its haunches and consumed the hunk of rabbit in a single bite. Vero tossed another piece and hit the bullseye; the chunk of meat slid straight into the beast's throat without ever touching its teeth. Bit by bit, Vero fed the rabbit to Le Loup until only pink-tinted snow and the sickly smell of blood remained. A massive grey tongue lapped out of Le Loup's mouth, cleaning the black lips stretched over his sharp teeth.

For the briefest of moments, fear nudged Vero's stomach, clenching her bowels. The beast could be upon her faster than she could blink, if it decided to.

"But you know me, beast," she said, her voice monotone and calm. "We've been doing this dance for weeks, yes?"

Le Loup Garou swayed from foot to foot as if considering attack. With a bare hand, Vero reached out, wanting to make contact though she was still many meters from the beast, too far to touch. The beast startled at her movement and sprinted off into the woods, announcing his departure with huffs and grumbles.

It took a great deal of time to gather water from the pump to fill the bath but was worth every wasted minute. For a long few weeks, Vero had been trying daily to close the gap between her and Le Loup Garou, and she wanted to soak.

Vero lowered her ivory body into the water, the aroma of honey and lavender a welcome change from the stench of blood and carcass and decay. The candles flickered, then extinguished, leaving the bathroom in near total darkness. From the glint of the moon peeking through a slit of a window high on the wall, a pair of glowing red eyes rested upon Vero's naked flesh.

"Your appearance doused my candlelight, dear Thérèse."

"I worry for you, sister. You will never tame the beast."

"Oh, ye of little faith."

The rest of Vero's bath was spent in peace. Sated with the illusion of relaxation, she went to the bedroom, leaving a trail of wet footprints across the oak floor. From her spot in the corner, Thérèse reached for her sister, white fingers like snakes groping in the moonlight.

"Come to me," Thérèse pleaded. "I will give you the love you need."

"It is not love I seek. It is revenge."

"That makes you more beast than Le Loup Garou."

"So be it."

Thérèse wept, fat droplets of black tears rolling down her pallid, gaunt cheeks. "It will not put things back to the way they were."

It was true, Vero knew, but she didn't care. Seeing her sister's face, a mask of death, birthed a thick sob in Vero's throat. She remembered the way Thérèse's plump cheeks would press against hers when they embraced, the smell of cinnamon in her hair as they ran to the village to see if the toy maker had any ugly sticks for sale. Together they would sit by the fire at night, reading tales of the ocean, of Bonhomme, of little girls on great adventures.

Swiping away tears with her hand, Vero also swiped away the memories. For the time being. The memories and tears always returned, stronger and more painful each time.

Months passed, each with more promise. Now, Le Loup waited in the morning light for Vero to appear out the back door. It would sit beside the chopping block as Vero butchered the meat, its hot breath on her skin. Just that morning, Vero had been sly enough to cop a feel, brushing her palm over Le Loup's massive paw, careful not to slice herself on its razor-sharp claws. Le Loup did not pull away, but Vero dared not try again. Best to not push the limits, or she might find herself with an excellent view of the beast's stomach lining.

Excited by her progress, Vero reached the village in record time, anxious to retrieve another supply of meat. On the previous two trips, she had stocked up on squirrels and rabbits, so this trip was dedicated entirely to bigger blood and longer bone; she intended to up the frequency and duration of her interactions with Le Loup Garou. It trusted her now. She was close. So close.

With raccoon and beaver filling the pack, Vero made one last stop at the stables. The vendor was pleased when she saw the silver in Vero's palm and offered her up a live plump black goat in return. Vero tied a rope around the goat's neck and coaxed it through the street. Whether it bleated in protest or excitement, she couldn't tell. Unfortunately, the racket from her cloven-hooved offering drew the attention she so vehemently tried to avoid.

"Who's that?" The voice was callous and familiar, a memory of days long past but seemingly yesterday. "Drop your hood!"

Vero did not respond. She kept walking, tugging on the goat to encourage haste but to no avail. A goat will do only what it wants.

The voice boomed again, this time right above her. "You, there. I said show yourself."

Without waiting for her to comply, the voice swiped back Vero's hood with a meaty hand, exposing her face to the village. It was the Reverend, his black cloak hanging from wide shoulders, a crumpled bible tucked in the stained and sweaty pit of his arm. His brows furrowed together into one as he studied the face below him.

"Who are you, girl? Are you known to me?"

With every ounce of soul in her body, Vero willed her expression to stay faithful. She shrugged her shoulders and pouted her lips, trying to look as young and innocent as she truly wasn't.

"You are familiar," he said, stroking the mangy beard upon his face, "but I cannot place you." His eyes fell on the goat, who was bleating away, nonplussed by the interaction. "And what, pray tell, is this for?"

"Food, sir." Her voice was meek and her response too quick.

The Reverend's lips pulled back into a smile, revealing yellowed teeth packed with stringy sinew from a lavish meal. He was gross and fancy all at once. Rank body odour and hair slicked with grease, nose bulbous from drink and belly distended from gluttony. But that was nothing compared to the ugliness Vero knew resided inside this horrid man.

"Goat, eh? Odd meal, what with chickens around."

"I best be on my way," Vero said, drawing her hood. "Papa will wonder where I am."

"And who is your papa?" The Reverend grasped her arm, his fingers pressing into her flesh, she straining for her flesh to press back.

Vero couldn't contain herself. "None of your business!" Yanking herself out of the Reverend's grasp, she stumbled away, backing towards the edge of town.

He held her gaze, his eyes burrowing into her brain. "Be wary. You, a young girl child, wandering these streets alone, without father or husband, and with an animal such as this. One might mistake you for one of the witches we so eagerly seek to burn."

Rage roiled in Vero's belly as she turned away, rounding a corner, and dodging up and down paths so the Reverend would lose sight of her as she plunged herself into the forest. As if sensing the urgency as excitement, the goat trotted along behind her, choosing not to resist as Vero barreled through the trees, hot tears like rivers streaming down her face, a battle cry lodged in her throat.

It was time. Veronique would wait no longer. The Reverend had seen her, and even though she hadn't been recognized, he was in want of her now. And the Reverend always got what he wanted.

"Please don't." Thérèse clutched her chest, covering her quiet, shriveled heart. "Stay with me instead."

Vero finished knotting her hair behind her head and tied the strings on her woolen overcoat. "I cannot, dear sister. They took everything from me. They will pay."

"It will never right things, Veronique. Nothing will."

"Maybe so, but I must try."

For the first time since her sister had appeared, towering in the corner in the dead of night, Vero approached her. Thérèse reached out her boney hands and placed them on Veronique's cheeks. Vero did not recoil or resist. Instead, she stepped forward and draped her arms around Thérèse, feeling remnants of the plump, lush girl her sister used to be. They embraced, Thérèse pressing her cracked, cold lips on Vero's forehead, and Vero crying into her sister's ivory dress.

"This is not goodbye, sweet sister," Vero said as she pulled away from the stench of burnt flesh and decay. "We will meet again."

Thérèse's face contorted in a medley of fear and sorrow, and her body dissolved into ash, floating away on a frigid breeze that passed through the stone walls. Vero lingered in the corner where her sister's ghost once stood, now missing that presence as much as the living one. After a moment of grieving, she soldiered on, grabbing the sack of meat from the kitchen and the goat from the shed before joining Le Loup Garou in the backyard.

It seemed like only yesterday Vero had fled her childhood home. She remembered her screams echoing off the towering trees that pierced the sky. She had run until her feet bled, and vomited all the tears and snot she gulped down into her belly from hysterical sobs she could not control. Like an angel in waiting, the large cross of the sanctuary had appeared, granting her solace and security, if only for a night. But that one night had turned to many, and her life had begun again, this time with fevered purpose. The church was indeed a sanctuary, abandoned but blessed, a place no witch could ever hide, therefore a place no witch hunter would ever come looking.

Now, many months later, Vero traced the path back towards home. A mismatched caravan, Vero led the way, followed by the goat on his rope. Le Loup Garou brought up the rear, salivating but waiting patiently for Vero to grant him permission to consume the meal walking in front of him. Every so often, to ensure Le Loup's compliance, Vero would toss a smaller animal from her sack into the Loup's gullet, sating its need for another good while.

And a good while it was from the church back to Vero's old cottage. The last time she'd made this journey, though in the opposite direction, it had been in a panic, the trip completed at twice the pace. This time, she had companions in tow: a stubborn goat and a violent werewolf, both of which she had to handle with kid gloves. No matter, though. She had nowhere else to be and no one waiting for her.

Night had laid its inky shroud upon the land by the time the travellers reached the cottage. The sky was clear, granting the moon permission to illuminate the way to the front stoop so they wouldn't impale themselves on fallen trees. Dropping the goat's rope and leaving him behind, Vero entered her old abode. The door was still open, swinging, banging on the wall in a rhythm that reminded Vero of the way her heart thrashed in her chest on that last night there many months before. She did not want to cross that threshold, but her feet carried her forward, boots clip-clopping on the old hardwood floor.

Mold and vines had overgrown the walls, and food was spoiled in the pantry—there was no stench like that of a rotten potato, let alone the many sacks piled there. Emaciated rats scattered as Vero moved, passing by the kitchen, and pausing in the frame of the first bedroom door. The mattress was still there, covered in fabric speckled with wild roses, threadbare and fringed at the corners from the gnawing of wildlife. Thérèse's porcelain dolls littered the floor, seated around a stack of wooden blocks.

Vero imagined Thérèse's face, pink and plump, and could feel the breath of her voice as she sang lullabies while sparkling snow fell outside. They had been full of glee, playing with toys while Mama and Papa danced in the kitchen. After they were too tired to dance another step, Mama would take out her violin and stroke it with a homemade bow crafted from the tail hair of their dear horse, Celine, coaxing the strings and making it sing like an angel. And the aroma! The scent of freshly baked bread permeated everything in the cottage, welcoming all visitors within a ten-meter range. Vero could still remember the crackling of the fire, the way the flames reflected off her sister's dark hair as she twirled on her toes, dancing a pirouette worthy of a Parisienne stage.

Mama, with her doe-brown eyes and squishy hugs, always waiting for her daughters with a smile. And Papa, his strong arms, muscles rippling as he heaved the axe from the chopping block to cut another cord of wood for the winter.

That cottage had been happy once. Alive. Now it was a corpse, lifeless and cold.

Vero continued to the master bedroom with soft steps, as if she didn't want her boots to rouse the cottage itself. Her folks' room was at the back, with a large window facing the yard. The window provided the moon access to light Vero's way, reviving memories spent snuggling beneath the comforter with Mama, Papa, and Thérèse as thunder and lightning argued in the clouds above the forest.

There was no warmth in that bedroom now, only moss-covered walls and a mattress. The bedclothes were as neatly made as Mama had left it the day the Reverend and his men arrived.

Vero gazed out the window at the trees beyond. The makeshift scaffold still stood. Like gunshots, she could still hear the pounding of the nails as the men erected it while Mama screamed, and Papa yelled. The men's laughter was poison as they gathered wood from the shed and brush from the woods, building a pyre, and stuffing it with bits of moss and kindling to set it raging on that cold winter morning. Vero could still see those men, their faces greasy, their fat arms reaching, snatching her and Thérèse from their hidey-hole within Mama's wardrobe. Vero rubbed her arms, remembering the pinch of the meaty grasp of the man struggling to contain her as she wriggled and writhed. Thérèse did not fight but yelled for Vero to run, pleading for her sister's life.

Vero heard a great many things.

The pounding of the nails blasting like gunshots through the forest. The wails from Mama. The cursing from Papa. The crackling of fire.

And Vero felt a great many things.

The chafe of the rope around her wrists and ankles. The pressure of the thick pole they tied her so very tightly against. The sting of the cold upon her face and the heat of hell on the soles of her feet.

A cough drew her attention to the present. Not a cough. A huff. An expelling of air. Vero turned her attention to the hallway and the living room beyond. In her peripheral, inside the bedroom with her, her parents stood, black and tall as the ceiling, their bent and broken forms reaching for her. She didn't dare look but could see regardless, their solid white eyes glowing in the dark, spilling black tears down skeletal faces. No longer pink and plump. No longer warm and cuddly. No glee, no life. Mewls squeaked from Mama's throat, and blood spread like a blooming rose across the private area of her lace nightgown. Evidence of those men and their interference. Papa's face was a twisted sob, contorted in pain from his impotent panic and anger and shame. He could not save them, nor them, him.

The front door banged against the wood siding, startling Vero to attention. Le Loup Garou waited patiently for her just outside the cottage. The goat was untouched, as was the sack of meat on the porch. It was time to go. Vero stole a glance at her parents, at the strips of burnt flesh hanging from them like ribbons, at their black and bloodied faces and smashed shards of teeth. Those were not the parents she knew. Those were the parents the Reverend and his men created.

Vero would look no more. She walked down the hall and out the front door. Le Loup looked at her with watering eyes and mouth as she stepped out onto the porch, dipped her hand in the bag, and drew out a squirrel. When Le Loup finished his snack, Vero plucked the rope off the ground, led the goat around to the backyard, and tied it to the scaffold. Le Loup followed and tilted his head in confusion. Vero rapped on the ash with her knuckles, upsetting a cloud of death. She breathed deep and exaggerated, then tapped Le Loup's chest, repeating the motion two or three times before the beast caught on. With her toe, Vero disturbed the ash once more, and Le Loup breathed deep, mimicking her. It sniffed the air, tasting ash and death. As if a flame had lit in its brain, its eyes grew wide, and its jaw dropped open.

Vero was terrified when it stood overtop her, bending to press its muzzle into her chest and draw a deep breath. One final lift of his head and sniff of the wind, and it howled, a raspy, dichromatic sound that curdled Vero's blood and echoed through all of Quebec.

Vero whispered to her only friend, "They cursed my family, just like they did you."

Dropping to all fours like its distant kin, Le Loup Garou looked at her with pain in his eyes.

"Yes," Vero said. "The same man that cursed you burned my family. The same village that shunned us shunned you."

Anger flashed in Le Loup's eyes, then a wicked smile curled the corners of its mouth.

She offered the goat to the beast as reward, but Le Loup refused, his burning eyes and muscled frame aimed in one direction with one purpose.

Revenge.

Veronique did not leave the goat behind. She would not condemn an innocent animal to death as those men had done to her family. No animal, human or otherwise, should ever suffer that fate. Instead, the goat shuffled through the forest, though this time Le Loup Garou led the way with Vero and the goat close behind. Le Loup was determined, and for that, Vero was glad. She hadn't been positive that she could befriend such a thing, but this particular flavour of monster had not been born as such. The hatred of man had made him this way. And it was that same hatred, and those same men, that had turned her family to ash.

The trek to town did not take long, not at Le Loup's rage-fueled pace; Vero had to jog to keep up with the beast's loping strides. Sweat formed on her flesh, as it had the night she'd escaped, the chill deepening when the wind whipped up her skirts. Le Loup noticed her violent shivers and slowed its lope enough for them to walk side-by-side. She startled when it curled an arm around her and drew her close. He smelled like gangrenous meat but radiated heat like a wood stove, so Vero did not resist. He was wrapped around her like a brother, like she was draped with a living pelt.

They reached the village shortly after nightfall. Vero did not need to say anything. Standing on her toes as Le Loup crouched, she kissed his cheek and ruffled the hair on his head. "Merci."

It whimpered in response, then scampered off into the night.

Vero was done with sneaking. She marched into town with her head held high, her boots clipping and clopping a proud beat on the frozen cobblestone. She whistled "Nous N'irons Plus au Bois" as she walked, the shrill notes pinging off the buildings like balls of ice. When she reached the village square, she climbed up on the Reverend's platform and stomped her boot four times.

"Reverend!" she bellowed, her voice rattling icicles off the nearby market carts. "Care to come out and play?"

It wasn't long before pale faces appeared in windows. Soft steps padded from every direction, gossipers and looky-loos coming to see what all the fuss was about. The town had always hungered for drama, especially in the form of pain and suffering. The Reverend parted the crowd like the Red Sea, reaching his stage as more and more villagers gathered to gawk.

"What is the meaning of this disturbance?" he scolded. "Do you know the lateness of the hour?"

"The hour matters not," Vero shouted. "And since we are speaking of knowledge, do you know who I am?"

The Reverend studied Vero's face. A faint glimmer of recognition sparked, but then fizzled. "I have seen you around, yes?"

"You have seen me, Reverend. But you have seen many, haven't you? So many faces, so much death, you can hardly remember anyone at all."

The Reverend scanned the crowd—whether looking for her parents or for help, Vero did not know.

"You are but a child," he said. "Where are your parents?"

"At our cottage in the woods," Vero said. "Exactly where you left them."

"Where I left them?"

Vero spit her words like venom. "Yes, sir. Tied to a pole. Though you wouldn't recognize them now. You left before the fires had even reached their knees."

The Reverend straightened his collar and his spine, standing sure and proud. "Well then. I see why you are so sour, girl. Your parents were witches, were they?"

"So said you."

He dared to laugh, a smug sound that made Vero's skin crawl like restless maggots. "Many are angry at me for carrying out my God-given duties, but the witches must be stopped. Quebec must be cleansed—"

"My parents were no witches. My sister neither." Vero's voice was a steady crescendo, approaching a scream. "You are a murderer, nothing more!"

The Reverend looked at Vero's face again, this time studying her closer, his eyes squinted to narrow slits. "I *do* know you," he said, his voice barely a whisper.

One, two, three, four steps carried Vero to the edge of the stage, where she hunched to the Reverend's face. "As you should."

With a heavy sigh, Vero released the glamour, revealing her true self.

The Reverend recoiled as the illusion Veronique had cast melted like ice in the sunlight. She was no longer an ivory girl with a dusting of freckles and strawberry hair—a girl with the possibility of marriage and child. The creator of music and art. No, now she was a wretched thing, scalp burned bald, and face, a distortion of the beauty she once was. An ivory gown hung from her charred body in strips stuck to her oozing flesh. And her eyes were black as the night, sockets filled with smoke and rage.

"I was no witch either, but you burned me just the same."

Fear rippled over the Reverend's face, but it quickly turned into a hesitant smile. He touched the cross around his neck with trembling, crooked fingers. "You ... are not real. You are merely a ghost. You cannot harm me, foul thing!"

He swiped a hand out, striking Vero's flesh, but his fingers parted her as if she were smoke.

The crowd held their collective breath as Vero stood tall and whistled again, this time a call rather than a tune. "You have ruined so very many people, Reverend. Good people. Burned whole families at the stake, cursed innocent men for no good reason ..."

Vero crouched low and licked out, her tongue brushing the Reverend's lips as she spoke.

"Isaiah 8:19, Reverend. You are familiar, yes?"

He nodded.

"Well, I have altered it, composing my own version," Vero continued. "Would you like to hear it?"

He shook his head, his eyes wild, scanning the woods.

"They, the sinners, have no lights of dawn, yes ... because they cannot see through the ash from fires lit by the righteous."

Vero glanced down the cobblestone path that led into the woods. All those families he'd burned were dead. There was nothing they could do to him now. Nothing she could do, not in this form. It'd been a strain to carry on as she had been, hoisting meat and donning clothes. But those men he'd cursed ...

Howls brayed through the woods. The Reverend's lower lip quivered as his bladder let go, soiling the front of his trousers.

Like a shadow in the night, Le Loup Garou galloped down the path, his loping gait bringing him to the Reverend in four strides. There was no discussion, no negotiation, no final words. In one swipe of his massive paw, Le Loup severed the Reverend's neck, sending his head spinning through the air and down to the ground with a dampened thud in the crisp white snow. As blood spurted and spread in crimson fractals around the Reverend's final expression, Le Loup fell upon his body, plunging his muzzle through the Reverend's ribcage, and gorging himself on entrails.

Horror silenced the crowd; the only sound reverberating through the village was the squelching feasting of Le Loup Garou. It took a break from its meal to stand tall, its eyes meeting Vero's. She nodded, and Le Loup tilted its head back, opening his throat and howling to the sky. As he dropped and resumed consumption of his kill, the sound of heavy footfalls surrounded the village like a drumming circle, huffing and puffing and marching toward the villagers.

Vero spoke, loud and clear. "You have all been witness to inhumanity. You have said nothing time and time again. You laughed and pointed as your friends and neighbors were reduced to ash." Vero descended the stairs, her charred feet hissing on the powdery snow, melting it to puddles beneath her feet. "This town wanted a cleansing, so a cleansing it shall have."

Le Loup Garou, an entire pack of them, pounced in unison, filling the town with a chorus of gnashing teeth, ripping flesh, and cracking bone. Blood stained the winter, a canvas of white splattered with red, and steaming with torn meat.

As Vero walked the cobblestone path, her flesh swelled, color and fat returning, the charred flesh sloughing off and making way for her creamy skin to return. In the trees, Thérèse waited for her, her full peach lips stretched into a wide smile. She was as lovely as Vero remembered—lovelier, even—with her shining hair in plaits that cascaded down her ivory fur coat.

When Vero reached the trees, the sisters entwined their glistening fingers and walked into the woods, leaving the bloodstains behind for their sparkling white eternity.

Chapter Five

Hell Hath No Fury

BY DIANA OLNEY

Claire wanted to throw the flowers away the moment she saw them. Even before she found out where they came from.

But she wasn't sure why. There was nothing visibly wrong with them. She'd checked. Physically, they were completely unremarkable, just the standard rosy, red Hallmark cliché, nothing more. But she couldn't shake the sick, twisted feeling she got in her gut when she looked at them. The flowers seemed so ordinary, and yet they felt hostile, dangerous somehow. They were trying too hard to blend in, hiding behind their everyday appearance like a poisoned apple in some fractured fairy tale. Even now, she could sense them silently judging her, their tiny dewdrop eyes drinking her in from their conveniently central vantage point on the table. Granted, she was the one who had put them there.

Claire stepped closer, inching into the kitchen. She was probably just being neurotic. That was nothing new. These days, her conscience was working so much overtime, it would likely go on strike soon.

Or maybe it'll quit.

Claire certainly hoped so. She could use a break. But she wasn't going to count on it.

She sighed and reached across the table, careful to avoid the bouquet as she hunted for her cigarettes. Just being near the roses made her uncomfortable, so she couldn't risk touching them. With bated breath, she worked her way around the glass vase, retrieving her pack of Lucky Strikes.

I need all the luck I can get.

The cigarette was just what she needed: a friend to light her way through the darkness when no one else would. It wasn't the best choice of companion, considering the content of its warm, smoky embrace, but Claire didn't mind. Friends were in short supply lately, so she'd take whatever comfort she could get.

She exhaled, watching as a cloud of effervescent cancer flew from her lips, metastasizing in the air around her. It tasted delicious. Plus, the smell of the tobacco almost overpowered the pungent floral odor filling the house. That alone seemed worth the health risk.

Those flowers fucking reek.

They really did. It smelled like she had invited the entire Nordstrom fragrance department into her living room.

Try the new and improved Chanel Rouge! Now infused with the sweet scent of asphyxiation!

She almost laughed out loud. *Almost.* Usually, Claire's sense of humor never failed her, but after the week she'd had, it hurt like hell just to smile. So instead, she focused on her cigarette, blowing a smoke ring right into the face of her unwanted guest. And as her billowing breath enveloped the vase, she swore she could see the flowers shrinking inside it, trembling in fear as their rosy cheeks faded to gray.

That's better.

Still clinging to her cigarette, she turned away from the roses, making a beeline for the kitchen window. The bouquet was hidden, for now, but its bittersweet stench lingered on, trailing behind her like a living shadow.

Claire shook her head. She had enough of those already. These days, her every breath was haunted, filled with the ghosts of all the words she wished she could say.

I'm so sorry...

She flung open the window, welcoming the sound of the urban sprawl outside. Then, she leaned into the frame, hoping the symphony of street noise would drown out her unwanted thoughts.

And that goddamn smell.

For a moment, it almost did. The world beyond the window was louder than life, crashing down like a tidal wave onto her tiny apartment. Here on the outskirts of Seattle, there was no such thing as peace or quiet, especially not at this hour. Every day, the streets filled with creatures of all shapes and sizes, swarming the sunbaked pavement as they cursed the afternoon traffic. Some were trapped in the rolling tide of gridlocked cars in the street, while others wove in and out of the intersections on foot, scurrying like rats in a maze. It was rush hour on Lake City Way, and that always made for solid entertainment.

Never a dull moment around here...

That was certainly true. At first glance, these people looked ordinary enough, but you never knew what the weirdos around here were really up to. A closer look would reveal quite an eclectic cast of characters—they had everything from workaholics to stoners to reincarnated rock icons here.

I met "Jim Morrison" on a bus once.

He wasn't much of a singer though.

That had been an interesting day. One of many, actually. But for Claire, that was a different time. A different life, almost. Back then, she'd only been in the city for a few months, and every moment still held the promise of redemption, a chance to turn her life around. But there were no second chances now.

Claire frowned, staring longingly out the window. She would have given anything to go back. Hell, she'd scrape the slate clean till her fingers bled if it would give her a shot at a do-over.

But it won't.

She took a final drag from her Lucky, letting its trail drift into the clouds of exhaust outside. The city was running on fumes today, and so was she. Even without a cigarette in her hand, her life was moments away from going up in smoke.

Claire leaned forward, tossing her cigarette into the empty flower box beneath the window. The garden out there used to be pretty, but there wasn't much beauty in it now. She could thank her landlord for that. Fall Pines Apartments wasn't big on amenities, so when the caretaker quit, the foliage had fallen into decay, withering beneath the trash and debris cast off by careless pedestrians. But Claire couldn't really judge them. She was just as careless as they were.

Maybe I should throw my bouquet down there.

That wasn't a bad idea. If she didn't want the flowers, they had no business being in her home.

With a heart heavy sigh, Claire abandoned the window, returning her attention to her colorful guests. But they didn't seem quite as vibrant now. Their faces looked a little pale, as if they knew she'd been plotting their demise. She stepped closer, studying their expressions, and for a second, she felt a little guilty for being so cruel to them. Perhaps she would change her mind and invite them to stay. Perhaps not. But either way, they had some explaining to do.

Claire bit her lip, staring down the bouquet from across the table. She still didn't want to touch it—the single time she'd handled the cold glass vase had given her an instant chill—but she no longer had a choice. She had to know where the roses came from, and there was only one way to find out.

"Who sent you?" she whispered, searching their faces for an answer.

The flowers did not respond. This did not come as a surprise to Claire. Her imagination was running wild today, but not wild enough to spend the afternoon talking to plants. Though a small part of her—that must be the crazy part—wished she could. For if the flowers would just speak for themselves, they could help her make up her mind.

With a trembling hand, Claire reached across the table, slowly scooting the vase closer to the edge. Then, she took a long, deep breath and dove in.

Maybe I have a secret admirer.

That was doubtful. Admirers were scarce these days. Though she did have plenty of secrets. She'd been collecting them for a while.

But they're out now.

Claire sighed as she parted the slender stems of the bouquet, careful to avoid the thorns. Every branch had a bite, but their teeth were so well hidden, she'd never noticed them before. Apparently, the roses were better at keeping secrets than her.

And they know it, too.

As Claire moved closer, hovering over the vase, she could almost hear them laughing at her. But she couldn't blame them. The roses had their flaws, but she was the one lying in bed of thorns. And there wasn't much point in trying to get out. She had nowhere to go.

Nowhere but down...

Claire forced her hand deeper, and the flowers shuddered, shedding petals like teardrops onto her fingers. But she didn't feel bad. They had plenty to spare. By her count, there were two dozen roses crammed in the vase, yet there was still no sign of a card. So, maybe there was nothing to find, after all.

Nothing...

And no one.

A few minutes later, Claire was ready to admit defeat. She needed to know the truth, but the flowers were no help. In fact, they seemed to be going out of their way to hide it from her. That, or they just wanted to get under her skin. And if that was the case, they were doing a damn good job of it. The sensation of their slick, waxy leaves was making her flesh crawl, like the lascivious touch of an unwanted lover. It was nauseating, almost as much as the smell, and if she didn't get some air soon, she was going to lose her lunch. But just as she was about to give up, something sharp pricked her finger, piercing her skin from inside the vase. She winced, assuming it was a thorn. Yet, as she pulled her trembling hand from the bouquet, she saw that it was not.

There it is.

Finally. With a sigh of relief, Claire reached back in to retrieve the envelope. It was wedged deep in the vase, hovering just inches away from the water. The card had probably fallen during delivery, yet still, she got the feeling it didn't want to be found, as if it had been hidden there on purpose.

But it did have her name on it. Along with several drops of her blood.

No sense crying over a paper cut.

Clutching the card to her chest, she hurried into the living room, hoping to read it in private. That was easy enough. There was no one else there, after all.

She planted herself on the couch and inspected the envelope. There was a thin trail of red running down the middle, bisecting the paper. It looked like an incision, the kind made by a knife or a sharpened scalpel. Claire counted to three and tore it open, digging her fingers into the wound.

What the Hell?

Claire gasped, staring at the single sentence written on the card. The words stared back, glaring in all capitals.

This can't be real...

But it was. As she ran her hand along the oversized text, tracing the lines of each letter, the words leapt off the page, their sharp edges slicing through her already scattered thoughts. Suddenly, Claire felt like she was literally losing her mind, strapped to a chair in some archaic asylum while men in white coats cracked open her skull, performing an impromptu lobotomy on her frontal lobes.

If only.

At this point, that kind of ignorance sounded like bliss. But unfortunately for Claire, there was no such escape. The tears were coming now, trying to wash away the script, but they couldn't. It was written in permanent ink.

Claire leaned back, letting herself sink into the sofa. Then she dried her eyes, watching as the last of her tears fell onto the card. It didn't say much. There were just three words, but not the ones she'd spent the last week hoping to hear.

"Enjoy your gift!" the script proclaimed, punctuating itself proudly in the center of the plain white paper. But Claire wasn't enjoying it, not one bit. And that was thanks to the name at the bottom. A name that never should have been there at all.

Rebecca.

"Becca..."

Claire paced the room, wandering aimlessly as she whispered the name under her breath. She'd been doing this for a while. She wasn't sure how long but judging by the lengthy trail of foot prints on the carpet, and the pile of dead cigarettes in the ashtray, she knew she should probably stop. But she couldn't. Not until the mystery was solved.

"Shit," she grumbled.

There. The cycle was broken. But still, she couldn't slow down. There were too many unanswered questions keeping her up. As she circled the room, she could almost see them, hanging in the air like clouds. And there, in the eye of the storm, was the biggest question of all.

When she'd first received the roses, Claire had wracked her brain, making a list of suspects. Given her current status of Universally Spurned Social Pariah, it was pretty short—mostly family members, maybe a co-worker or two. But, of course, she couldn't really see her fellow record peddlers at Platinum Vinyl shelling out for two dozen roses. They barely made enough for the bus home. And her parents never sent her flowers, not even on her birthday. Plus, these ones were a little over the top. Red roses were a romance staple, which automatically ruled out most of her list. Claire only had one old flame, and that fire could not be rekindled. She had already tried, and failed, at least a dozen times. Over the last week, failure had become her new MO.

And it's all my fault...

Yes, it was. She'd dug her own grave, and now, it was too late to crawl out. Which was precisely why the name written in that overly casual card made no sense. Rebecca would never send her flowers. Not after what she'd done.

Claire sighed, lighting another cigarette. She'd been through some bad break-ups in the past, but her fallout with Becca was another story. A story that began with the sweet, tender melody of a classic love song, and ended on a painfully sour note. But for Claire, the story was far from over. She'd lost the love of her life, and after a loss like that, everything else was just an epilogue.

But don't forget the twist...

Claire shuddered. If only she could. But whether she liked it or not, that horrible moment would be with her forever. There was a shadow over her heart, and each day, it spread, infecting her days like a disease. But she had brought it upon herself. She'd let that darkness into her life, inviting it in through the front door.

Multiple times.

And she'd enjoyed it, at first. But the fun didn't last. Bad decisions could only feel good for so long, and eventually, Claire's darkness came back to haunt her. She'd tried to get rid of it, but not fast enough. Becca saw her shadow, and after that, everything faded to black.

Aside from the spray paint on her car, which was neon yellow. She'd tried to scrub it off, but it always returned. So, she had no choice but to accept her new title, announcing herself to the world as a Cheating Whore.

Claire stopped in the center of the room, suddenly dizzy. All this chain smoking was starting to catch up with her. Maybe she should cut back, before she ran out of breath—for good.

That's what I deserve.

Probably. She had enough sin under her belt to guarantee a ticket to Hell. And if she had the guts to use it, she would.

But she didn't. Outside of her penchant for toxic chemicals, self-destruction wasn't Claire's thing. That was Becca's flaw, if she had one. Her ex-lover was as close to perfection as a woman could get, but she didn't seem to see it. Or maybe she did, but she didn't want to be perfect. That's why she had to give herself a few scars.

But now, Claire couldn't even judge her. After all, her wounds were self-inflicted too.

She bent down to put out her cigarette, crushing the embers into the pile of ashes on the coffee table. Then, she let herself fall, collapsing onto the sofa. At last, the fire inside her was starting to die down. There was only a single flame left, slowly burning a hole in her heart.

Though perhaps, Claire thought to herself as she slipped back into the soft embrace of the cushions, that was part of the problem. Her passion burned so bright, she'd let it blind her, feeding the fire until everything in it went up in smoke. And here, in the aftermath of that fateful inferno, she was all alone, clinging desperately to the charred remains of her world. The days were long and hot, and the nights were even hotter, spent tossing and turning in sweat soaked sheets that writhed like snakes around her limbs. Sometimes, she laid awake till dawn, wondering if Becca was thinking of her, speaking her name to the darkness just as she had spoken hers.

Maybe. But only until she gets that tattoo removed.

Claire shivered, gazing down at the faded lettering on the inside of her arm. Even up close, it was out of focus, blurring at the edges like an old photograph. That was normal for a tattoo, but to Claire's tired eyes, it looked as if the ink was starting to bleed, running through her veins in search of a way out. Nevertheless, she refused to let it go. It was a beautiful memory, one she hoped would never fade as much as the tattoo.

But she hadn't forgotten yet. In her mind, that day was still crystal clear, much more than this one. It was her first anniversary with Becca, and by the end of their romantic evening, she and her pretty paramour were so love drunk, they'd wandered into a classic couple's cliché: a tattoo shop. At first, they toyed with the idea of getting matching tramp stamps, but the artist, a cute girl with a significantly less cute number of facial piercings, said names made the best statement. So, the girls went for it, writing their love letters in permanent ink. Claire wanted her tattoo on her chest, for obvious sentimental reasons, but her other half had a better idea. "We wear our hearts on our sleeves," she'd said, smiling that perfect smile of hers. Claire had agreed, but secretly, she didn't like seeing her name stuck in the middle of Becca's collection of hesitation marks.

Bet she has a few new ones now.

She probably did. That was one of many reasons why Claire couldn't sleep at night. In all the years they'd spent together, Becca had never actually attempted suicide, but her history was enough to give Claire nightmares for life. In her mind, every new cut or bruise was one more step in a dance with death that would one day sweep her sweetheart off her feet—for good.

But Becca was obviously fine. Fine enough to be sending roses to her adulterous ex-girlfriend.

Claire looked over her shoulder, eyeing the flowers suspiciously. If they really were from Becca, she might want to check them for explosives.

Or poison.

No. That was crazy talk. Time to reel that imagination back in before it ran out of control. But regardless of what her conscience had to say, Claire couldn't ignore the insanity of this whole situation. She still loved Becca, but after what she'd done, it was far too late to kiss and make up. So, in what world—*what universe*—would her scorned lover send a super-sized bouquet of roses her way?

A parallel dimension.

Where she's decided to forgive me.

Claire shook her head. The existence of such a place was doubtful. The last time she'd tried to apologize, she'd earned herself a black eye, followed by a violent verbal assault, the final battle of a war she had no hope to win. Still pouring her heart out through her tears, Claire had retreated, making her escape with her sinful tail tucked between her legs.

After that, everything went quiet.

Claire had to hand it to her. When they were together, Becca wasn't much of a fighter—she never argued, not even when Claire forgot her birthday—but post break-up, she went in guns blazing. First, came the screaming expletives, punctuated by a well-timed slap in the face, and then, the silent treatment. Claire tried everything she could think of to get Becca's attention: tears, gifts, grand gestures inspired by eighties movies—she'd even tried her hand at writing a poem—but it was no use. After five years of complete and utter devotion, her sweetheart wouldn't even take her calls. Dozens of desperate voicemails and texts went unanswered, piling up like bodies in a mass grave out in cyberspace, until finally, she gave up.

I'm gonna have to call her now...

Claire bit her lip, already itching for another cigarette. Her phone was right there on the coffee table, waiting for her to make her move. But as much as she was dying to call Becca, just so she could hear her voice again—even if it was just a recording—part of her was afraid. But who could blame her? The last time they spoke, all Hell broke loose, releasing an army of angry spirits. And unfortunately, those demons were still here. Sometimes late at night, Claire swore she could hear them, creeping around the apartment until even the skeletons in her closet were scared to death.

So, what are you going to do then? Sit here, staring at the phone all day?

She leaned over, gazing longingly at her cell. The voice in her head made a very good point. She was standing on the brink of a serious downward spiral and doing nothing wasn't going to keep her from falling in.

Okay ... But this isn't going to go well.

Claire reached for the phone, holding her breath as she plucked it from the table. Then she stood, studying the room. She would make the call, but she wasn't going to do it in here. Not with those *things* watching. The roses may have seemed like a white flag, but whenever she looked at them, she could see their true colors. And they weren't pretty. Every flower in that vase was an open wound, a bruise that was just waiting to bleed.

Claire sighed, wiping the sweat from her brow. She was painfully aware of how nuts she sounded, but it wasn't as if she could do anything about it. In fact, that was probably why Becca had sent the damn flowers. Because she knew how easy it was to get into Claire's head.

Love makes you do crazy things.
Even when it's over.

Gripping the phone in her hand, Claire sat on the bed, counting the fibers in the carpet as she tried to work up the nerve to make the call. She was up to one hundred and twenty. But her confidence was still in the single digits.

Finally, she shifted her gaze, turning to face the mirror on the adjacent wall. Her reflection was a mess, but a pretty one. She'd had a rough night, even before today arrived in all its bizarre and terrible glory. But now, as she soaked up the last of the sunlight streaming in from the window, she was practically glowing. Her blue eyes were filled with tear-stained stars, encircled by a frame of dark lashes so they wouldn't fall. She still hadn't put on any real clothes, but sitting there in her tiny black nightgown, she looked kind of sexy, like an alluring silhouette in a dark window. She was a beautiful disaster, a literal shadow of her former self. Sadness suited her, she supposed.

I guess this is my new look.
Heartbreak chic.

She squeezed the phone, wrapping her hand around the hard plastic until her nails dug into her palms. It stung, but only a little, and only for a moment. She tightened her grip, then, slowly, she began to soften, uncurling her fingers. It was now or never.

Claire kept her eyes on the mirror, watching herself in the glass as she flipped open her cell. She traced the pattern of familiar commands on the keypad and held it up to her ear. Then she stretched out on the bed, and her reflection did the same, filling the frame on the wall. But outside of the glass, she was just as empty as before.

The phone rang, chirping in her ear.

She held her breath, waiting for an answer. Though she still wasn't sure if she wanted one.

Her cell continued its song, humming the same stale note. Though suddenly, Claire swore it was growing louder, shouting at her through the tiny speaker. By the fifth ring, she could feel the sound rattling her bones.

It doesn't matter. She's not going to pick up.

Two rings later, the phone went quiet. Then the voicemail clicked on. Claire's heart raced when she heard Becca on the other end of the line, promising she'd return the call as soon as she finished the last episode of *Lost*.

Claire shut the phone, then threw it forcefully onto the bed.

Damn it.

She sat up suddenly, rising like a ghost from the tangle of sheets beneath her slender frame. Then, she cocked her head to the side, giving the phone a judgmental look. She'd never even finished Lost. She and Becca were supposed to watch it together, and she couldn't enjoy it alone. Now she'd never find out what those numbers meant.

Or anything else.

She stood and went for the door, then backtracked to grab her cell. She wouldn't be calling Becca again, but she still wanted to keep her phone on her.

Just in case.

Back in the kitchen, Claire clung to the window, watching the sun make its slow descent across the horizon. The streets were less crowded now, gentle rivers flowing beneath the heavens. Passengers and pedestrians drifted along, driven by the current, and the pavement glistened, collecting the last of the light. As Claire gazed down at the sidewalk, the cracks seemed to shiver, branching out like ripples in a pond.

It was a beautiful evening. But she knew it wouldn't stay that way. The streetlights would burn all night, but soon, the sky above them would fade to black. This close to the city, there were never any stars.

She turned around, grabbing her pack of Lucky's from the table, and the roses swayed, quivering as a gust of wind blew into the kitchen. It was surprisingly strong, for a summer breeze. Claire lit her cigarette while the flowers watched, still shaking. But then a second later, they settled back into place, holding their heads high above the clouds.

Claire stared into the smoke, looking for answers. But she got the feeling there were none to be found. This all felt like some sick, twisted game, a wager she was born to lose. But she didn't want to play anymore. She couldn't, because someone else kept changing the rules.

But she still didn't know who. This puzzle was missing so many pieces, she'd never be able to see it for what it was. The card she'd received with the flowers was blank, aside from the text she'd already read, and she didn't recognize the handwriting. She assumed it had been filled out by an employee, but there was no business name listed, no phone number or even a logo. And, of course, she hadn't received any calls. But maybe, she thought to herself as she studied the smug faces of her mysterious guests, maybe it didn't even matter. What difference did it make where the flowers came from? They were here. They'd done their job.

Claire stumbled forward, leaning on the edge of the table. Suddenly, she could barely stand up. Her heart was too heavy, begging to be released from the weight of this day.

I need a drink.

Normally, Claire wasn't much of a drinker. Not since her early twenties. She'd spent most of her college years partying, doing jello shots and keg stands while she poured her wasted dreams down the toilet. Hence, her illustrious career in secondhand vinyl. But after everything she'd been through, she deserved a distraction. Or two.

Claire took a drag from her cigarette, then sat down at the end of the table, keeping her distance from the flowers. The sight of them still made her nervous. Beneath their pretty petals, they seemed to be hiding something, as if they had another part yet to play in this story. But after a few drinks, she'd forget all about them, erasing their rosy faces from her memory. Besides, she could use some real company. Claire only had one or two friends left, but she knew where to find them. It was karaoke night at the Alcove, the bar down the street, and her buddies never missed a chance to steal the spotlight. Especially her coworker, Cory. She was quiet, at work, but once the drinks were flowing, she was a rock goddess, belting her heart out like Janis Joplin—before the drugs got to her.

Welcome to Woodstock... 2009.

Claire chuckled, laughing in spite of herself. Since Becca dumped her, she'd been so heartbroken, she'd forgotten how to have fun. But tonight, maybe she could remember. After all, her guilt would still be there in the morning.

She yawned, stretching as she stood from the table. She was exhausted, but that wouldn't stop her from going. She needed to get out of the house. And out of her head. Just for a few hours.

And a few minutes later, she was ready.

Claire stood in front of the bathroom mirror, inspecting her work. She still didn't look her best, but a little make-up and a new outfit went a long way. Gone was the dark shadow from the bedroom, replaced by a luminous vixen who almost had her shit together.

Almost.

Claire nodded her approval, watching as her reflection sparked up a cigarette. Then, she darted down the hall and out the door, disappearing in a puff of smoke.

She took the flowers with her.

The evening was a disaster.

Though not at first. When Claire arrived at the Alcove, she got everything she wanted: a strong drink, good company, and some wild entertainment. The second she saw her friends on stage, singing an awful rendition of an even more awful eighties ballad, she almost lost it. But she didn't. She didn't want to ruin the moment by laughing. So instead, she danced.

And she smiled.

She kept smiling for hours, thanks to the bartender. He had a heavy pour, but the martinis tasted so light, Claire felt like she was walking on air, free from the weight of her sorrow. Though it would return soon enough. She'd left her worries at home, and they were still there, waiting. All of them... but one.

The flowers were gone now, buried deep in the dark, filthy depths of an industrial sized dumpster. And there they would remain, rotting with the rest of the garbage.

Where they belong.

Claire smirked, smiling to herself as she made her way down the street. But her smile didn't last long. She was halfway home, following the dimly lit path back to her apartment, but the night had taken a much darker turn hours ago.

And, as usual, it was her fault.

She should have seen it coming. This city was full of restless spirits, but of all her old haunts, the Alcove had the most ghosts. And they weren't very friendly—once they saw her.

Assholes.

Claire sighed, staring down at the sidewalk. She'd made a lot of enemies lately, but the creep she ran into tonight, a human wrecking ball by the name of Scott, was arguably the worst. He was one of Becca's best friends, but he'd always had it out for Claire. Even before the break-up. So naturally, he'd been the first one to turn on her, running his big mouth all over town. And based on the lengthy list of profane nicknames that had come out of it, Claire suspected he may have had something to do with the obscene graffiti painted on her car.

Among other things.

She grimaced, glancing down at her ruined clothes. When Becca dumped her, she'd been labeled a whore, but after the beer shower she'd received at the bar, she literally smelled like trash. Maybe she should throw herself in the garbage, too.

No...

She shook her head, fighting a fresh batch of tears. Normally, she didn't care what Becca's idiot friends had to say. But this time, they'd said too much.

Don't listen to them...

You know they're full of shit.

Maybe. Maybe not. Scott was a skilled liar—he'd flunked out of law school but kept his degree in bullshitting—and he had a twisted sense of humor. But none of this felt like a joke. Before he'd poured his pitcher of Corona all over her, she'd seen the look in his eyes. The look that said he was telling the truth.

Claire sighed. She didn't know what to believe. Becca had her problems, but she'd never tried to commit suicide before.

At least she didn't succeed.

But according to Scott, she got pretty close. Apparently, Becca downed enough beta-blockers to knock out a whole SUV of pill popping soccer-moms. But luckily, he found her in the nick of time and rushed her to the hospital.

Or so he says.

Claire shivered as she crossed the street, clutching her damp jacket. She didn't know if it was her fear or her wet clothes, but she was glad she was almost home.

Claire stood in front of the door with her hands over her mouth, holding back a scream. It was working, so far, but every time she tried to swallow her terror, it came back up again, burning like fire in the back of her throat.

Then, all at once, it was released.

Sixty agonizing seconds later, Claire found herself lying on the pavement, gasping for breath. She'd already regurgitated her entire bar tab, yet she still couldn't seem to keep anything down. Not even air. Her insides were begging to come out.

Fuck.

Steeling herself against a second wave of nausea, Claire froze in place, praying she could hold it together. Luckily, she did. A few minutes passed, and gradually, she began to feel like some semblance of herself again. She sat up carefully, moving in slow motion. Then, she reached into her pocket for a cigarette. As she lit it, she kept her eyes on the pavement, staring down at the filthy dregs of her evening.

She didn't want to stay there, huddled up next to her own vomit, but she was afraid to turn around. She was afraid to see the thing behind her, the thing that had been waiting on her doorstep, hiding in the shadows.

But it wasn't going to leave. Not on its own.

What the hell is going on?

Claire had no idea. But she knew what she had to do. So, she tried for a moment to calm down, finishing her cigarette. Then, she forced her aching body into action, pulling herself to her feet. Her legs swayed beneath her, threatening to give out, but she didn't let them. She couldn't. Not until her task was complete.

She turned around, and the world turned with her, trapped in a drunken spin cycle inside her corneas. And there, in the center of her downward spiral, were the roses.

They looked like they'd been expecting her.

As she bent down, wrapping her hands around the vase, the blossoms blushed, their vibrant petals unsoiled by the events of the evening. Claire tightened her grip, holding the bouquet at arm's length while she carried it down the sidewalk. With every step, her pulse pounded, beating a desperate warning into her ears. She tried not to listen. The less she thought about what was happening, the better.

Just wait until it's over.

And soon, it would be. The dumpster was right around the corner, ready to receive her offering. She held her head high as she made her way there, trying not to inhale the bouquet's sickeningly sweet odor. She didn't want to throw up again.

Please... let this work.

Praying to whatever gods were watching, Claire counted her steps as she made her way across the parking lot. The vase was heavy in her arms, heavier than it should have been.

But she wouldn't have to carry it for long. It was time to take out the trash, in...

...three...

two...

one.

Harnessing the last of her strength, Claire lifted the bouquet up over her head and tossed it into the dumpster. The vase sank like a stone, crying out as it hit the bottom.

CRASH.

Claire listened closely, waiting. Then, once it was quiet, she walked away, retreating into the silence.

That night, as she slept, Claire had another visitor. When she closed her eyes, drifting into the blank space behind them, her old flame was there, burning deep in the darkness.

Claire should have been happy to see her. Becca was her dream girl, after all. But there was something wrong with her. And even in her sleep, it didn't take Claire long to figure out what it was.

Her fire was dying.

Claire froze, watching in horror as her lover's light began to fade, shrinking into the distance. But Becca couldn't leave. She was bound to this place, tied up in the fabric of someone else's nightmare.

Mine.

Claire shuddered, holding back tears. There was no point in crying now. Her beloved's fate was already sealed, wrapped in chains that were creeping across her skin. But when Claire looked closer, she saw the truth. The shackles on Becca's body weren't just moving—they were *growing*, rising up like smoke from the shadows. And as they grew, they blossomed, sprouting dozens of blood red petals.

This is it.

Claire was afraid, at first. But then, she remembered something. She remembered she was asleep, miles away from these imaginary monsters. That left her two choices: she could run, and try to wake up, or she could stay, and put an end to this nightmare. Maybe for good.

So, she ran. She ran right into her sweetheart's arms.

Well, she tried. But Becca's arms were a little occupied at the moment, buried beneath the layers of vines that were tangled in knots around her limbs. She couldn't even speak, thanks to a snaking tendril that had covered her lips. But as Claire rushed in, trying to free her, she could feel her lover's tears, flowing down like tiny rivers.

"It's okay," she whispered. Even though it wasn't.

Becca might have nodded. It was hard to tell.

Claire grit her teeth, returning her attention to the task at hand. Not that her hands were of much use. The plants were strong, far stronger than she'd expected. And their bite was deadly. She grabbed a fistful of vines, pulling with all her might, but they pulled right back, sinking their teeth into her skin. Claire winced, pushing through the pain, but she was getting nowhere. Every second, Becca's bonds grew tighter, cutting deeper into her tender flesh.

No, please... no...

It was a losing battle, but Claire kept fighting, trying desperately to rescue her sweetheart. Becca was bleeding now, and so was she. Not that she noticed. Blood and tears looked almost the same on the scarlet faces of the flowers.

She tried to not look at them, but she could still feel their eyes on her. For even here, in her dreams, the roses were always watching. Watching, and waiting.

But they wouldn't have to wait much longer.

Within minutes, Claire's hands were tied, bound by the same chains as her beloved. But she didn't give up. She kept pushing, thrashing against them with all her strength, until at last, she overpowered one of her enemies. The vine snapped, ripping in two, and she pulled her hand free, then started work on the other, clawing at the green serpent coiled around her wrist. Meanwhile, Becca was still trapped, withering inside the bars of her prison. But Claire wasn't about to leave her behind. Once she cut herself loose, she would save her sweetheart. Then, she would wake up.

Or so she thought.

A moment later, she was almost free. But just as she broke the last of her chains, she felt another creep up her shoulder, wrapping itself tightly around her neck. She leapt back, trying to escape, but it was too late. By the time Claire reached for the vine, clawing at the thorns wedged in her skin, she was starting to fade, disappearing into the dark. And so was everything else. Around her, the world was turning black, shrinking into its own shadow. Claire tried to scream, but when she opened her mouth, something held her tongue. It was soft and almost sweet, yet it tasted rotten. She reached in, grabbing at the thing, but it was already gone, sliding down her throat and into her stomach. She couldn't see it, but she knew what it was.

Even as she slipped away, she could still smell the roses.

When Claire awoke, she was falling.

But only for a moment. She cried out, fighting the air as it dragged her downward. Then her body hit the floor with a hollow thud, smacking into the hardwood.

She gasped, and her lungs filled with fire. Everything hurt. But she was alive. She was awake. The nightmare was over.

"It's okay," a voice said. "I've got you."

There was a face too. A woman's face, hovering like an angel above her.

Claire tried to speak, but words escaped her. Instead, she looked around, watching as her surroundings slowly came into focus. But there wasn't much to see. The whole room was white. White walls, white floor, white ceiling. A blank canvas.

She took a deep breath, glancing back at the angel. She was wearing white too, apart from her name tag, which was grey with black lettering. Claire's vision was still a little blurry, but she was pretty sure it said "Sally."

"Don't worry," the angel said. "Help is on the way." Then she reached down, wrapping her hands around Claire's throat.

Claire squirmed in her grasp, trying to get away. But she was too weak. Every bone in her body was screaming, begging her not to move. And as the angel's hold grew tighter, stealing the air from her lungs, she remembered her dream. She remembered that she had no hope.

But then, something strange happened. The angel—or Sally, according to her name tag—suddenly let go.

And she was still smiling. Claire trembled beneath her, wondering what had happened. Then Sally showed her.

Slowly, she pulled a long, slender piece of fabric off Claire's neck. Claire looked down, trying to figure out why this woman was taking her scarf. But it wasn't a scarf. She knew that.

"It's alright," Sally cooed, unraveling the last length of the tangled cloth. It was a bedsheet, stark white, just like the rest of the place. But it was something else too. As the fabric swayed, dangling from her hands, it looked just like a noose.

What the Hell...

Claire shook her head, staring in disbelief. No. She would never try to kill herself. Let alone hang herself with a homemade noose. But there was someone who might. Someone she still held close to her heart.

"Becca...?" she whispered.

"Oh, honey..." Sally sighed, her round face flush with pity. "No. Becca isn't here."

"But..."

But, what?

Claire sat up, prying herself off the floor. She looked past Sally, studying the emptiness around her. There was more to this story than what she was seeing. She could feel it, buried beneath the ache in her bones.

Sally reached out and grabbed her arm. "Careful, honey. You really shouldn't move. Not until the doctor arrives."

Claire ignored her, slipping out of her hands. "What about Becca?" she demanded. She knew Becca wasn't here, without even knowing where *here* was. But she didn't like the way Sally had said it. Or the way her eyes were misting over, filling with familiar clouds.

Sally shifted her gaze. She seemed uncomfortable. "She isn't here," she repeated. "You remember."

She was here...

...but she's gone.

Claire frowned. She stared up at the ceiling, counting asbestos stars. Yes, she remembered. But not everything. The story needed an ending.

She returned her attention to Sally.

"But I've been here for a while," she said. "Haven't I?"

Sally nodded.

Claire looked over her shoulder. Behind her were more empty walls, a bed—minus a sheet—and a small nightstand. But there, in the corner, the white world was stained, blooming with color.

"Who sent those?" she whispered, eyeing the roses suspiciously.

"The flowers?" Sally asked.

"Yes. The flowers."

"Oh... those have always been here, sweetie," she said gently. Tears pooled in her eyes, sparkling like dewdrops. "They're not real, you know."

Chapter Six

A Halloween Ghost Story

BY CHRISTY ALDRIDGE

"It's not fair!" Kenzie whined. She was standing in the doorway of her mother's closet and wasn't very happy about what was going on. This was evident by both the whiny nature of her voice and the scowl on her face. She crossed her arms to be sure her mom knew she wasn't pleased. She was on the verge of a full-blown attitude.

"Life isn't fair, honey."

"This is worse. You're ruining my life," Kenzie reminded her.

Her mom looked at her from the rack of shoes she was standing in front of. Her face was a clear sign that she thought Kenzie was over-exaggerating. And maybe she was, but it felt the same either way. It was ruining her life. Or at the very least, ruining her night and at sixteen, that felt equal.

"Your life won't be ruined by one night. You know what could ruin your life though?"

Kenzie was already rolling her eyes. She knew exactly what lecture was coming and she was already annoyed by it. She was tired of hearing it told to her in some variation for the last week.

"Getting drunk and getting into a car accident. You and your boyfriend could have really hurt someone or even killed them, Kenzie. I don't think it's unreasonable that you should be grounded for drinking, but driving too? You're lucky you still have any privileges," her mother reminded her. "My mother would have beat me till I couldn't walk and then ground me to my room for months other than school and church."

"It was one beer, mom. One! And I wasn't even driving," she told her.

"That doesn't change anything," her mom said, looking at her again. "I could overlook a beer. I could even overlook a couple. I know what it's like to be a teenager, but you got into a car with someone that was drunk. Don't you know how dangerous that is?"

Kenzie shot her mom a scornful look as she crossed her arms tighter. "It's not like he was plastered. If that nosy old biddy would have just minded her own business- "

"You're lucky it was her car he almost hit bringing you home. You're even luckier that she didn't call the cops. Anyone else and they might have called them, but she decided to tell us and let us handle you," her mother answered.

"Yeah, and now she's my warden tonight."

"You realize how dangerous that was, don't you? You could have been killed. And because you haven't realized that, that's why you're being punished tonight too. Your dad and I would have been willing to let you have Halloween to hang out with your friends if I actually thought you'd learned your lesson, but you still think it's nothing. So, you're going to put on your costume and you're going to give out candy."

It was quite literally the worst punishment her parents had ever inflicted upon her. Yeah, maybe she shouldn't have been out drinking a beer with her boyfriend, Will. She probably shouldn't have gotten into his car when she knew he was drunk, but more importantly, she shouldn't have got caught. That was always the solution to doing the thing you weren't supposed to. Don't get caught like an idiot. Because getting caught meant that your parents would ground you. Because some parents still did that. Some parents were lame and still chose to do things that were punishment to their children.

Her parents did that. She had been grounded for a week and it was looking like she would continue to be grounded for even longer. For one beer.

Well, one to their knowledge.

But she didn't want to call them to pick her up. Will didn't seem too bad in her opinion, so she risked him taking her home. But he was drunker than she'd judged and ended up hitting Mrs. Rochelle, their neighbor's, car. The damage wasn't anything, but the way he fell out of the car and reeked of alcohol, Kenzie knew she was in hot water. Mrs. Rochelle practically ran to her parents to tattle on her. In doing so, she was the reason Kenzie's night was ruined.

Her parents decided that Kenzie should pass out the candy for Halloween this year. They had already moved her from her school and friends over the summer to this new town and this new house. And not just any new house. The group of kids she'd become friends with told her the house was empty for years because it was creepy. Will joked that it was the Addams family house and that embarrassed her.

Still, they had their nosy neighbor keeping an eye out on Kenzie as she did this. The same neighbor that was responsible for her punishment. It was like they were enjoying all of this just so they could go to some stupid Halloween office party. As if people over forty should celebrate Halloween to begin with. Kenzie didn't think that if you were over twelve you should celebrate Halloween.

It was literally the stupidest holiday to exist. The only good thing about it was getting to dress up in something sexy and no one really said anything. She had planned to go to her boyfriend's house with some friends and dress up as a sexy cat. Will was going to be a punk from their parents' day.

Complete with eyeliner and no shirt. She'd been looking forward to that and it was about the only thing that could change her mind that Halloween wasn't stupid.

So, her parents decided that because Kenzie hated Halloween so much, and because they wouldn't be home to give out candy like they did in their old house each year, Kenzie should have to stay home and do it instead. It was a cruel punishment, and she swore that she would get her parents back for it.

"It's bad enough that now I'm going to be a loser for not being able to hang out with my new friends because you want me to give out candy to some snot-nosed little brats. But to put a cherry on top of my horrible life, you're going to make me wear that stupid costume too?" Kenzie complained.

There was a slight smile on her mom's face. "The costume will humble you a bit. And it's my way of making sure you don't have your boyfriend over," she said.

"I could still invite him over," Kenzie said defiantly.

"And risk him seeing you in that old hag costume?" she asked, smiling again. "I know you, Kenzie. You'd rather deal with handing out candy to snot-nosed brats than have your boyfriend see you when you're not 'cute'."

Kenzie frowned, crossing her arms even tighter. Her mom had her there, but she wasn't going to concede. This was cruel and unjust punishment. Making her deal with these tiny children and their stupid superhero costumes, making her have to sit on the porch all night in the cold just to pass out little pieces of candy to children that did nothing to deserve them. Candy that was going to rot their teeth and make them fat. Candy that they literally had to walk to earn. It wasn't right. It wasn't fair.

But her parents were stupid anyway. That was all she thought now. At this point she couldn't stand them. She hoped they got food poisoning at their precious party. It would serve them right for treating her the way they did.

She was sixteen. She didn't even like dressing up when she was a kid, and she didn't understand why she had to dress up in order to pass out candy. And she didn't understand why she couldn't wear the costume she had picked out for tonight. Even if she hadn't been grounded, it became easy to see they wouldn't have approved of it either. But she would have worked past that and changed somewhere else.

But not tonight. Her parents decided that she had to be a witch. A lame and stupid witch that wore a long black dress with long sleeves, and an ugly pointed witch hat. They even tried to make her wear a fake nose that tied around her face, but Kenzie would not accept that. Even if they made her look frumpy and stupid, she was not going to be completely ugly.

"Go get dressed," her mom said. "I still have to get my costume on."

Kenzie rolled her eyes. She wasn't going to win this argument. She hated to admit defeat, but it was looking like she would have to hand out candy in her stupid witch costume.

She left the closet and stomped to her room. If she had to do it, she was going to make it very clear she wasn't happy about it. They would get no kind words, no smiles, and no joy from her. Only attitude. What more could they do? Keep her grounded even longer?

The costume was hanging on the back of her door, ugly crooked, wart nose and all. She snatched it from the hanger and undressed. She stood in front of her mirror and looked at the shapeless costume. She couldn't remove the scowl on her face as she examined it from every angle. It was ugly and unflattering.

Her cat costume also hung on the closet door. It was pleather and lined in fur. A leotard with a deep plunging neckline. It would have accentuated all of her best assets.

This one hid all of them. With the gray wig and hat, you almost wouldn't know she was sixteen and not sixty. This was the best part of her punishment to her parents, made aware when she went downstairs, and her mom had to cover her mouth to keep from laughing.

"I'm glad you think it's funny," Kenzie said.

"You will too, one day," her dad said, snapping a picture with his camera.

"I'll never forgive you for this," she warned them, hoping it might appeal to them and their compassionate side. Hoping they'd tell her they were joking and let her off the hook.

Instead, her dad looked at her more seriously. "That attitude needs to go now, Kenzie."

Kenzie rolled her eyes.

"We're not stupid," her mom interjected. "We're not blind either. We know you're just upset about the move here. We both understand that it was a big change and happened so quickly, but we deserve a little more respect than this."

"What about me? I had to leave my friends! You took me away from them and then punish me when I try to fit in with the people here. I'm just trying to fit in," Kenzie told them and felt tears spring to her eyes. She hadn't realized how much it had bothered her about moving until she said it out loud.

But it appeared her parents had noticed before her, because they both looked sympathetic.

"There's better ways to fit in than that, Kenzie. It's about being safe. You just have to be smarter than that next time. You would have been in less trouble for calling us because you'd been drinking. I would have even been proud of you for taking responsibility for making a dumb decision and not making it worse. But if you'd had been killed because you got in the car with him and he was drunk, or worse, he'd killed someone else, that could have ruined your life," her mom said.

"We're not completely unreasonable. We just want to keep you safe," her dad answered.

She knew that. She really did. She almost hated knowing that because it made her feel guilty to hate them. It was easier to pretend they were awful, not that they loved her and were trying to keep her safe.

"If you handle tonight like an adult, we've decided we might let you off next week. But I'm going to need a hug first. As a sign of good faith, you know."

Kenzie considered this. There was a football game next week that she could go to. Probably a little party after. If all she had to do was pretend for a few minutes now, and hand out candy until she ran out, she could probably stand it. Her freedom was more important at the moment.

She moved forward and gave them both a hug. When they squeezed back, she knew they loved her. She wished they didn't so she could hate them, but she knew they thought they were protecting her. It seemed a little hypocritical, knowing that her dad was probably going to get wasted at this office party, but that was a problem for another day. She knew the situation was different.

"We'll be back around midnight. When you run out of candy, you can have the rest of the night to yourself, but no one is allowed over, and you're not allowed to leave. The neighbor will be watching over the house, but I'm trusting that you'd like to end your grounding, so you won't have to be watched," her mom said.

Kenzie nodded, twisting her mouth ruefully. "I'll be good," she answered.

"Doubtful, but we'll take it," her dad said with a smile.

Kenzie managed a smile.

"Be good, kid," her dad said, giving her another hug and heading out.

Her mom pushed the wig hair from her face and sighed. "It's just one night," she reminded her. "Make the best of it and it'll be over before you know it."

Kenzie nodded and gave her a hug, but she was still bitter. A punishment was still a punishment, deserved or not. Even if she knew it was actually just, it still sucked. Her plans were still ruined. Her night was still going to be boring. And Kenzie was still annoyed by all of it.

As her parents left the driveway and headed out of the neighborhood, Kenzie turned on the porch light and grabbed her bowl of candy and chair. She made herself comfortable at the door and then waved once to the neighbor across the street that was waving from her door. Kenzie might see her parent's side, but Mrs. Rochelle was still on her bad list. She was the one assigned to be her guard because she was the only neighbor her mom had really spoken to in the few months since they had moved in. And because she was good at tattling on her to her parents.

Her bowl of candy wasn't huge. It was a fake, plastic cauldron. She figured she'd be done in an hour or so but was surprised when trick or treaters weren't coming to her house as often as she thought.

The town wasn't huge, but that wasn't the problem. The issue was that a lot of kids, especially those on their own, were avoiding her altogether. They would look at her, look at the house, and then run along to another house. Until the first set of trick or treaters came up, she'd almost began to wonder if this was part of the punishment. She couldn't run out of candy if she didn't give any away.

The first set of kids were siblings, it seemed. Both dressed as angels, and they looked identical. But their mom came up with them to get candy. Kenzie tried to smile and be welcoming, but both of the little girls looked terrified to get close.

"They're just scared of the house. Some kids at school told them it was haunted," the mom told her, rolling her eyes at this. "Little kids making my job harder. There's nothing to be scared of. See, she's a nice witch and the house isn't scary."

The children were not willing to trust her. They got closer, but only long enough to get their candy. Kenzie had to get up to make sure it didn't fall on the ground.

As they left, Kenzie looked at the inside of the house. Sure, it wasn't anything new and modern, the house certainly had some personality, but it wasn't the scariest thing she'd ever seen. Yeah, it kind of felt like the Addams' family lived there before her parents started renovating it, but it was slowly growing on her. It seemed silly that anyone would be scared of the house just because it looked older than the other houses.

A group of kids dressed as princesses and superheroes came up to her a little while later. In a group of four, three looked hesitant while one, the tallest and likely the oldest, looked excited. He was also the only one dressed differently. He was a zombie.

"See, she's a fake witch!" he told the other kids. "A witch doesn't live here, I told ya."

Kenzie smiled a little, hoping to ease the kids' fears, but they still looked wary.

"Trick or treat," the oldest said. The others sort of mumbled it, but they looked uncomfortable. They looked ready to bolt at any moment, just like the twins from before.

Kenzie reached into the bowl and handed each a handful of candy. They accepted it graciously but didn't move. They were equally as scared as they were fascinated.

But as before, the oldest was the one to speak. "They're just scared of the house," he told her. "They thought a witch lived here, but I knew one didn't."

"No, no real witches here," she told them, smiling, but they still looked scared.

"See? I told you guys, it's haunted. Ghosts, not witches," he told them.

"I'm afraid to burst your bubble, kid, but no ghosts either. It's just an old house," she told him, but he definitely didn't look convinced.

"My brother told me about the ghosts. That's why no one has lived here for a long time. He said the people that moved in were probably weirdos," he said.

Kenzie frowned. "Tell your brother to choke on a di-"-" she stopped herself, biting her tongue and trying to smile. "Choke on a duck. It's not haunted. It just looks creepy."

"So, you haven't heard anything scary? Like gunshots in the middle of the night?"

"Nope."

And that was the truth. The house looked creepy in Kenzie's opinion. It was older, in need of new paint and windows, but her parents had been restoring it. It was coming along better than when they'd first moved in, but the slightly creepy appearance didn't tarnish the inside. Kenzie hadn't experienced anything weird or spooky because those things weren't real.

"My brother said it was haunted by a husband and wife. They were hanged to death," the zombie kid answered.

"I think your brother was just trying to scare you," Kenzie answered. "There's nothing scary about this house. It's just a house, just like the rest of the ones on this street."

She could see the other kids loosen up a little. She was sure the older kid had been scaring them with ghost stories all night. He'd built up this house to them because it looked a little scary. He was having his fun and she'd eased their fears a little.

Honestly, she was happy to do so. Part of growing up was realizing things were often not as scary as other people said they were.

"Sure," he answered and rolled his eyes. "Just don't run out of candy before the kid comes."

"What kid?" she asked.

He smiled. "The one they were hanged for. The ghosts that haunt your house. They killed their own kid," he said.

"I'm sure they did. What does this kid look like?" she asked, entertaining this ghost story.

"Oh, you'll know him. He wears this old, papier-mâché mask and carries a potato sack. His mask looks like a pumpkin, but he wears old, tattered clothes," he said.

"Let me guess, he's a ghost kid that was killed on Halloween?"

"Yep!"

Kenzie rolled her eyes. "And what does he do if you don't have candy? Kill you?" she asked.

He shrugged. "Probably. But no one runs out of candy to find out."

"Did your brother tell you this story too?"

"Yeah. He's seen him before."

"I'm sure he has," Kenzie answered. Being an only child, she'd never had to worry about being told stories to scare her from some older sibling. She didn't have to go to these houses and look stupid for believing ghost stories.

One day, this kid would learn. He'd realize his brother just wanted to scare him and maybe he'd be a better kid.

Or maybe he'd be just like his brother.

"Well, just make sure you don't run out of candy. It won't be pretty if you do. Come on, guys," he said, and started walking away.

Kenzie rolled her eyes. It didn't take her long to realize he was trying to scare her the way he'd scared those other kids. If he couldn't get her with the ghosts in the house, he'd make up some other ghost to scare her.

But Kenzie wasn't the type to get scared. It was one of the reasons she detested Halloween. It was a silly night of people trying to scare other people for their own sadistic enjoyment. That wasn't fun. It was cruel. And the only good that came from it was being able to walk away with candy.

After them, more trick or treaters started to come. Most seemed curious. Some were babies carried by their parents that paid no mind to the house or her. Because they were adults and just wanted to get back home and eat the candy their little babies couldn't eat. Kenzie respected the parents that were trick or treating for infants. They were the biggest hustlers, getting candy for a baby that couldn't eat it.

Kenzie wasn't as annoyed as she thought she would be. Some of the kids were loud and annoying, but mostly it was just little kids that wanted to show off their costumes and get a little candy. They talked about how scary she looked and asked her repeatedly if she was a real witch. After a little while, she even began to play along and tell them she was.

Only, they wouldn't look afraid when she said it. They would be excited.

When Mrs. Rochelle walked over with her own child, Kenzie faked her brightest smile and handed her candy. The little girl was cute, but Kenzie decided Mrs. Rochelle would forever be the enemy.

"You can run back to daddy, sweetie," she told the child. She then looked at Kenzie and smiled. "I wanted to come see how you were doing. Your parents told me you just had to finish the bowl and then you could have the rest of the night."

"Yep."

Kenzie wasn't going to be overly respectful to her. Maybe she'd report that back to her parents, and she'd regret it then, but this woman wasn't getting a 'Yes ma'am' from her lips.

"Looks like you're almost done," she said. "You're free to come over to our house when you finish. My son has a few friends over that I'm sure wouldn't mind an extra face."

Kenzie smiled tightly. She knew Mrs. Rochelle's son. A pimple faced nerd that quoted Star Trek and hung out with likeminded weirdos that dressed up as their favorite characters for conventions. The last thing she wanted was to involve herself with them.

"I'll think about it."

Mrs. Rochelle nodded. She seemed to quickly realize that this conversation was going nowhere. Kenzie was being a brick wall on purpose.

"You do that," she answered, then nodded toward her house. "I'm going to head back now. You be safe."

"You too," Kenzie answered.

She didn't expect for Mrs. Rochelle to stop again and look at her. The look was one of sympathy and Kenzie wasn't sure how she felt about that or the words that came from her mouth.

"I'm sorry about getting you into trouble. I see a good kid, and I would hate to know I didn't say something, and you had gotten hurt. I'm sure moving to a new place has been stressful, trying to fit in, but you'll find your place. I just hope it's with people that don't lead you down the wrong path," she said.

Kenzie hated that she suddenly felt bad. She felt seen. She didn't want to like her any more than she wanted to see reason with her parents.

"I know. I'm sorry about your car," she said, finally apologizing.

"You didn't cause any damage really. I was wanting to put in for something newer anyway," she said with a smile. "I'll see you around, Kenzie."

She watched her walk back to the house. She still wasn't a fan of the woman, but she didn't hate her quite as much. At the end of the day, she was an adult, and they were usually annoying anyway.

She focused back on the trick or treaters again. She was finally beginning to see less of them. That was good. That meant the night would be over soon. She could go in and have time to herself. Maybe she'd watch a movie or take a long hot bath. She was actually thinking about getting into the Halloween spirit and watching a scary movie. Maybe a little fear was good for a night. She would be home alone and that might even make the experience a little fun. It seemed silly, but no one would be around to see her scared out of her mind like a twit.

The phone inside began to ring. Kenzie's cell phone was somewhere in the house and had been since the night she'd gotten in trouble. The house phone was usually reserved for things involving her parents, or it would be her parents.

Kenzie left the bowl in her chair and walked inside to pick it up from the receiver.

"Hello?"

"Hello, my ghoul-friend," a familiar, but surprising voice said from the other side.

"How did you get the number?" she asked her boyfriend, surprised, but pleased that it was him calling her.

"My parents wrote it down in the address book when they called last week," he said.

Kenzie frowned. She wasn't sure if she liked his family keeping her family's number. That meant they could start talking, and she and Will might get in a lot more trouble about things. It was never good for your families to speak to each other.

"You still handing out candy?" he asked.

She had told him about the punishment at school earlier that day. His parents had taken away his driving privileges, but that was the extent of his punishment. He wasn't happy about it, but at least he still had a life at the moment. Had she been driving drunk, her parents would have been worse with their punishment.

"Yeah, I think I'm getting close to being done though," she told him.

"What time do your parents get home?"

"They said around midnight."

He was silent for a moment, then lowered his voice just a tad to say, "Maybe you should sneak out and come hang?"

Kenzie laughed. "You want me to stay grounded until college, don't you?"

"You could do it," he assured her. "My house is only a few blocks away and it's only nine. We could chill out and watch a movie or something."

She wasn't stupid. Yeah, she made some stupid decisions sometimes, mostly because they were fun, but she knew chilling and a movie was the last thing he was thinking about. They'd start making out and then maybe move farther. Kenzie hadn't gone that next step with him yet, but she was sure it was only a matter of time before they did.

Not that she was sure she wanted to. This moment was one of many that was starting to nag at her.

"You want me to go out this late and walk to your house? Alone in the middle of the night? On Halloween?" she asked him, a little surprised that he would suggest it.

"It's not that far, Kenzie."

"But it's also not safe," she told him, surprised that he didn't seem to understand the point she was making. "Besides, if I just get through tonight, my parents are going to let me off the hook soon. I'd rather not risk getting killed or grounded again."

He was silent. When he spoke again, his tone was completely different. "Fine. I'll just see if the guys want to stay over instead. Maybe invite Maria, too," he said, his tone flat, but she knew what he was doing.

A kid came up to the door and Kenzie smiled tightly at them and pointed at the bowl. "Get as much candy as you want," she told them. She then turned around to turn her attention back to the phone. "Maria was over?"

Kenzie had been dating Will for about two months now. He was cute, liked, and with the crowd of kids that made her feel like she wasn't a loser. This meant sometimes there were pretty girls he hung out with, and that was fine, but he teased and taunted her about Maria in particular, a girl he'd dated before her. He knew she was jealous of her.

And any other night, she might have done what he wanted and risked getting hurt or in trouble. Because she didn't want him to leave her for an ex. Because he was her boyfriend.

But tonight, that thought didn't seem so appealing to her. In fact, she was beginning to wonder if being his girlfriend was even worth all the trouble. Maybe her parents were right. Maybe even Mrs. Rochelle was right. Maybe being 'cool' wasn't as good as she thought, not if it meant dating someone willing to risk her life and taunt her with an ex because she wanted to be safe.

"She is. I told you I was having a little Halloween bash, but I told them that we were going to cut it short because I wanted to hang out with you. But since you don't want to- "

"I don't."

"What?"

Kenzie gripped the receiver and took a deep breath. "I don't want to. Actually, I'm pretty sure I want you to go hang out with Maria instead. Because you're single again," she told him. She hung up and released the air she was holding.

She could not believe she had just done that.

A part of her suddenly regretted it. A part of her felt powerful for doing it. A part of her even wanted to tell her parents that she had. They hadn't said anything, but she could tell he wasn't the type of guy they wanted her to date.

School would be weird come tomorrow, but maybe that would be okay. Maybe she would even take Mrs. Rochelle up on that offer and hang out with her son and his friends instead. Maybe she'd make new friends. Maybe the possibilities were limitless now.

When she turned around to go back to her candy, she realized she had just run out. Now that her official punishment was done, she was free. She was seriously considering going over to the neighbors. End the night on a good note. She'd hang out with them and not break into her mom's wine stash. She'd actually make her parents be proud of her and realize that she was responsible.

But as she stood to turn off the porch light and end her punishment, one last kid stood in front of her. She didn't know how she didn't catch him coming up the walkway, but he scared her.

"Sheesh, kid! Quiet much?" she asked.

The kid didn't say anything to her. He just stared at her with his bag out, an old potato sack. He was dressed as a pumpkin, but his parents didn't do a very good job with it. The mask was disproportionate to his small body and the paint against the paper was faded. He was barely orange at all. His costume was the same way. It hung loosely on him and looked uncomfortable. There were holes and tatters, like it was moth eaten.

She looked out to see the idiots that would make their kid go out like that, but there were no parents waiting for him. The only people on the sidewalks were parents that had children and were headed back to their cars.

"Where are your parents, kid?" she asked.

He looked up, like he was looking at her second story. Then the kid shook his head and held out his bag again. He shook it at her, to make it clear that he wanted his candy. It seemed a bit rude of him in Kenzie's opinion.

Kenzie showed him the empty bowl. "Sorry. You're late. I'm all out of candy," she told him.

He looked into the empty bowl. When he looked up again, he shook his bag again.

"I don't have any candy. You have to go to the next house," she said.

He began to stomp his feet, shaking his bag at her, but not making any sounds. He wanted his candy, but Kenzie had nothing to give him. It was getting close to nine and most of the kids were heading home. She peered out the door to see that the porch lights were going off too.

When she looked again, she felt stupid. She began to smile. "Okay kid, you got me. You need to go find your friends now," she told him.

She knew it was the kid from earlier. The costume was too on the nose for it to be a coincidence. It was probably him and his brother trying to scare the new girl. They waited until she got up to go in and then got dressed in the costume to scare her.

But the kid in front of her tilted his head like he was confused. Kenzie had to admit he was good. He hadn't giggled or broken character at all. He was committed to his stupid role, but Kenzie was ready for the night to be over.

"Look, kid. Halloween's over. It looks like you have candy, so go home," she instructed him. "You've managed to scare me. See, I'm scared."

She waved her hands a little in mock fear, but he didn't move. He just held out his bag and shook it at her again. This time with a little more force.

"I can't give you what I don't have. And you don't deserve it anyway. Now get going," she ordered him.

At this point, she was tired of the charade. At some point, you had to learn when to pull away from the prank. If it wasn't working, you stopped before it became annoying, and it was becoming annoying very fast.

She turned around to turn off the light. If he wasn't going to leave, she was going to leave him on her doorstep. She was sure the neighbor would see them if they didn't leave her alone. She was going to go inside and call her to make sure she knew but was stopped by the child screaming into her ear as he jumped onto her back.

"Get off of me!" she screamed, but it wasn't doing her much good. The bag the child had was going over her head and being pulled tightly. Her screams were muffled, and she was more concerned with getting the bag off of her head before she suffocated. She could feel the candy being pressed against her face as he pulled tight, determined to hold the potato sack as tightly as possible.

But the child wasn't letting up. He was choking her even as she fell to the floor. When she was on her back, he was on her chest, sitting down as he pulled the bag around her throat just as tight as he could.

Kenzie could feel the candy inside the bag being smooshed under her head. But her biggest fear was the tightness around her throat. She was starting to feel the effects when the bag suddenly loosened, and someone was pulling it from her head.

"Kenzie?" Mrs. Rochelle, the neighbor, said in concern. She lifted the bag from her and helped Kenzie to her feet. "What's going on?"

"Where's the kid?" Kenzie asked, struggling to regain her breathing.

"What kid?"

"The kid that was strangling me. He was dressed like a pumpkin," she told her. Mrs. Rochelle just stared at her. Kenzie was feeling angry. "He was a short little kid dressed like a pumpkin and when I told him I was out of candy, he tried to strangle me!"

Mrs. Rochelle suddenly relaxed. She even laughed. "That old story? You got me. Happy Halloween to you too," she said with a smile.

"What in the world are you talking about?" Kenzie asked, outraged. "I'm not joking. And it wasn't a story. He was here."

"The ghost kid that kills anyone that doesn't give him candy on Halloween? That story has been around for as long as I've been alive. I didn't even think you kids knew about that anymore," she answered.

"Yeah, I heard about it earlier from some kid. And then he came back and tried to strangle me!" she told her.

"What kid?" Mrs. Rochelle asked, suddenly more concerned.

"He was with a group of other trick or treaters. They were princesses and superheroes. He was a zombie. He said his brother told him that this place was haunted," she told her.

Mrs. Rochelle rolled her eyes. "That sounds like Kit and his older brother, Marcus. I wouldn't put it past them, honestly," she said at first, but Kenzie watched as she suddenly went into deep thought. She shook her head as she narrowed her brows. "But Marcus picked them up about an hour ago. I watched them leave after they stopped by my house for candy."

"Obviously, they came back then. Because that kid tried to strangle me," she told the neighbor.

"They're a little rough around the edges, but I doubt they'd come back to strangle you over some Halloween prank. And I didn't see anyone running off when I got here."

"You honestly think I just tried to strangle myself for attention?" Kenzie asked.

"I'm not saying that," she said. "I'm just trying to figure out what happened."

"What about this stupid bag? I mean look at!"

And they did. The bag was old, but she guessed that didn't mean much. It was a potato sack. Kenzie had never seen one in her life. But Mrs. Rochelle seemed to give it a closer look. Like it meant something. She was staring at the design on the front, something Kenzie hadn't paid attention to until now.

It was painted, hand painted, from the looks of it. There was a picture of the house she was in now, but the land around it was bare. Tilled for potatoes, by the family on the front holding an arm full of potatoes. It said 'Parker's Potato's and more' on the bag in faded red letters.

"Parkers," she said slowly. "But they haven't been around for at least a hundred years. They were one of the first families to set up shop here, but they were hanged."

"Hanged? For what?"

Mrs. Rochelle seemed to turn white. "Killing their son," she answered. "I'm going to call your parents."

Kenzie nodded as Mrs. Rochelle went to the phone. She looked down at the bag and felt a small sting of pain as well as fear. She picked up some peppermints from the entry way and put them in the bag too. Then she sat it at the door. It wasn't Halloween candy, but it was something.

When she turned around to go to Mrs. Rochelle, she heard the faintest voice behind her. "Thank you," he whispered, but when she turned, he wasn't there.

But neither was the bag.

Chapter Seven

Mine

BY MATT SCOTT

"I sit in this study pondering my fate and am left only questioning my legacy. What a funny thing fate. What an odd desire is legacy. 'Oh, look, look at how the mighty have fallen.' That's what they'll say in the papers. 'Look at poor old Bartholomew Bishop. Taken down by a house full of specters.' They've been waiting, the newspaper men; watching, hoping for this moment. The vultures are circling, to be sure. They'll say, 'he's too frightened to leave the house that's keeping him held fast.' They don't know, nor could they ever. The House of Bishop is not scared. House Bishop will tremble before me. House Bishop will...did you hear that?

"He's at it again. The specters haunt me night and day and I fear they are done with me as well. They are driving me mad. I only know that...there they are again. Do you hear them? See? There, just down the hall. The racket of dead men. The clangs and clatters of the discontent, aye, that it is for sure and for certain.

"But I say this, the House of Bishop still stands even if its master cannot. Master. Yes. Yes. I am the master of this house. I, and I alone, am in charge of my destiny. I alone...alone."

Jubal Bishop built the settlement of Bishops Cove, in 1809, with his own two checkbooks and a bunch of cheap, almost slave labor. He was 27, from Boston, and already a self-made man through some clever business dealings with some less than reputable Italian gentlemen. He pushed, shoved, and backstabbed his way to the top, clawing tooth and nail, stepping on anyone that got in his way. Before the age of thirty, Jubal was a millionaire and headed west.

The property Jubal began developing sat atop a sea-cliff along the northern Oregon coastline. It was almost a hundred feet above the water, the cliff faces a brilliant pink against the pacific sunset.

The manor was a sprawling ten-bedroom affair on three levels built out of granite blocks and old growth timbers. It was complete with servant's and guest quarters and a stable. In between was a beautiful courtyard separating them from the main wing of the house. It faced the ocean, overlooking Woebegone Bay, and was the biggest structure at the time for two hundred miles.

Jubal Bishop was a ruthless man, a petty and petulant man. He was used to getting his way. When his estate wasn't being built fast enough, work schedules were "adjusted" to have round the clock shifts working on his brainchild, the center piece of his new empire, even if that compromised health and safety. To him, his workers were his property; they had a job to do and so were not afforded the same measure of care that some other workers might have. They were dogs, and as such, were treated like it. In all, three workers gave their souls to the project, to Jubal.

Bishop Manor was a gaudy structure looming large over the small village of Bishops Cove. It had started as a trading post to do business among the fur trappers and loggers but now had a school, a church, stores and a governor, Jubal Bishop. He ruled his pocket kingdom with an almost authoritarian bent. He set trade hours, curriculum in the school, prices in the stores, rented land and buildings out to the people that slowly began populating Bishop's Cove. And then soon after, within a matter of a decade, it was all gone.

In 1814, the residents of the Cove advanced on the estate, with the intent of ending the governor and his oppressive rule. They marched in the dead of night up to the manor. They wanted Bishop, and they were going to have him.

They turned the horses loose and ran them over the cliff into the sea below. Then they burned the stables to the ground before heading into the main estate to fetch its lord and master. They wanted nothing left of the evil old house.

They set fire to the rest of the house, but it wouldn't burn. They found Jubal hiding in his expansive study surrounded by books and ledgers. They dragged him outside and hung Jubal out front as the house smoked, and wailed, and moaned.

Most of the folk headed elsewhere, nary a charge brought upon anyone, for all had heard of Bishop's Cove and the evil hand that held it. A curse was laid on the property. Because it didn't burn, wouldn't burn, only a Bishop could live there. What was once a testament to his power, was now a monument to their family's doom. The house would always let Bishop be.

After that, the property passed out of the bloodline for a few decades as French aristocrats and British officials tried to live there, only to die violent, tragic deaths. The locals knew the history of the house and warned all that stayed there, but colonizers are not known for rational thought, or their openness to communicate with indigenous populations. And so, they were met with the specters and spooks that now occupied Bishop Manor.

Then, in 1851, his nephew Bart had the good fortune of being the recipient of a rather advantageous legal windfall leaving him in possession of Bishop's landing and its grounds. The news was fortuitous as Bartholomew had just married and the couple were expecting their first child in the spring of the following year. And so, the newly wed Bishops headed west to live in their familial estate.

"Be gone, Jubal. There is nothing left you can take from me, save my life, and you will have it soon enough. Be gone, and be quiet, foul specter. I am a Bishop, Goddamnit. A Bishop..."

Bart and his new bride, Cassandra, lived happily and prosperously, for years. Bart was a lawyer by trade and was well respected around the area. Folks knew the name. They hadn't forgotten, but they knew Bart was not his Grand Uncle. He was a learned, capable, fair, and just man. And a family man, at that.

In 1852, the couple welcomed into the manor their first child, a boy. They named him Clay. Another boy, Gregory, followed two years later, and a girl, Katherine, the year after that.

"Howl, and puff, and beat on your chest all you want, you old bastard. You will not take me from this chamber to rattle around for eternity in this house with you. I am the master of this house. And I will leave it when I am good and ready, Uncle. It's mine now. For decades now, you rotten, debaucherous son of a bitch. Howl all you want. You can't get in. Howl..."

It was 1860, when Clay first saw the ghost of Jubal Bishop. And as boys do, Clay was apt to tell his pa about what he had seen. And though Bart had known about Jubal and the curse, he was certain that if there truly was a ghost and the place was haunted, then surely a specter could do no real harm. And he told the boy as much, assuaging his young fears.

Ten years later, the old bastard killed the fresh-faced young man.

Clay had fallen from the terrace outside his bedroom to the cobblestone courtyard below, breaking his neck on impact. How he fell was up for debate. Cassandra was convinced it had been Jubal and his hateful town folk spirits that conspired together to murder her poor Clay.

Two years later, Gregory died choking on a chicken bone in the kitchen, sneaking a taste before supper. He collapsed onto the floor, and slowly suffocated to death, while the family was seating themselves.

Upon her 18th birthday, dear sweet Katherine was getting ready to meet her beau when she fell from the top landing of the stairwell, down the staircase, cracking her skull and breaking her back in the process. A week later, Cassandra shot herself in the mouth, after drawing a bath and leaving a mop and bucket beside the tub.

"I've rattled around in this old house alone now for ten years, you old coot. Ever since you took my Cassandra away from me and her children away from her. You and your curse. Bah. I am your curse now. The bane of your existence, old timer. Be gone now. Be gone, now, with the house you coveted. Be gone and go back to hell where you belong."

As soon as Bart finished screaming into the empty chamber, the very moment, the floorboards erupted beneath his feet in an ear shattering explosion that rattled the timbers. The upheaval sent splintered pine up through his slippers and into the bottoms of his feet. He screamed out again but this time he had laughter in his voice, a kind of lightness that he hadn't known for years. It was working. Jubal was scared.

An instant later, the floor disintegrated. The implosion propelled him up, and back, six feet off the floor, his body, a rag doll, flying against the far wall of the darkened study. The high ceilings were lost in shadow; the area before him, a gaping wound in the heart of the manor.

The library in disarray, Bart lay in a heap beneath a portrait of his beloved Cassandra. Dazed and dizzy, he was determined for this to end. The haggard old man struggled at first to get upright, to gather the cords, and the plunger box and take care of this infernal place, once and for all. In a matter of seconds, he was up on his knees, pulling himself forward, hastily.

The entire manor shook, slate shingles fell from its immense peaks and dormers, from the towers and turrets with its tangential runs and perpendicular intersections. Its moorings in the stone vibrated against the cliff walls as the growling and churning grew louder still.

Its cornerstones, and courtyards, began to crack and crumble around him and stones the size of carriages fell from the east wing of the estate. Jubal was trying to take back what belonged to him, but the deal had already been made. A Bishop, and a Bishop only, could live in the manor, and Bart was a Bishop, by god, and there was no running him out. Jubal could spit, and groan, and throw a fit, but he would not be allowed to take anymore.

He slowly made his way to the hall, circumventing the chasm in the middle of the room, crawling over broken boards and shredded planks, his hands bleeding from pokes and rips, tears and gashes. Below, far beneath the bedrock of the manor, beneath the water, the fossils, the oil; below that, the darkness gurgled and growled.

He fell to his stomach when he reached the hallway, his arms too weak to hold him up any longer, his legs too unsteady, his feet a symphony of pain. At almost seventy years old, Bart had learned a thing or two from this old house: if you're going to be trouble, go all in.

The sound from the pit was getting louder and closer, and still, Bart willed himself down the passage, toward the staircase. If only he could make it to them. With each labored breath, he propelled himself further down on his belly, one arm grabbing, reaching out in front of him, finding anything to latch onto. Clawing with broken fingernails. Inches. Feet. Almost there. But the thing in the pit was almost out. He could now hear scraping along the stone walls below, perhaps Jubal was still deep inside the sea wall, where his power dwelled down past hell, and all its minions. Jubal was almost out, and Bart was out of time.

He craned his neck to look behind him, his hands on fire, his feet numb, his heart pounding inside his chest, grey whiskers covered in blood and sweat. And yet, as he saw the clawed hand of one of Jubal's arms breach the top of the pit, clawing at the dismantled flooring above it, Bart smiled and roared laughter out of the fat belly on which the old timer crawled. It made his head hurt, and he squinted as his vison blurred, then went wavy, but yet he smiled, a grin of a man who was in on it. He knew the joke, even if no one else did. It was a good one too.

Bart wrapped the two wires around the terminals on top of the wooden plunger box and sat up as best he could.

He was at the landing. He faced the study from which he had just belly crawled all those many yards. His back to empty space, nostrils choking with the stench of whale oil and sulfur, Bart, and the thing from the pit locked eyes. He was certain it, too, was smiling. As they watched each other, Bart pushed the plunger down, and the entire manor exploded from the bottom. Bedrock hurled into the ocean below, the top of the house ripping off in a maelstrom of kinetic energy. Wood and beams and tiles and trusses splintering in the background, the foundation cracking, faltering, giving way to the immensity that sat atop it.

Bart hurled himself backwards down the stairs to the vaulted floor below. On the seventh step down, he broke his back. On the ninth, his jaw and all his teeth. Five steps before the bottom, Bart's neck snapped at the fourth cervical vertebrae. The sound echoed along the lower chambers.

The growling came to a crescendo, becoming so loud the whole estate was bathed in a wave of energy, white like lightning, crackling and electric. The massive arms retreated back inside the pit, deep down below the cliff, beneath the water and the rock of Bishop's Cove. What was once a study, a place of learning, of exploration, of acceptance and understanding, was now no more than a bombed-out husk of what was. That section of the house, the study, and the rooms on the two floors below it, caved in on itself, filling the tunnel with house, mountain, and Bartholomew Bishop, of the Boston Bishops.

Chapter Eight

The Dare

BY TONY EVANS

"This is it? This is how you aim to scare me?"

Tim stood at the end of the long driveway looking back at the trees as they arched over its entire length, shielding it from any remaining vestiges of sunlight the late October evening had to offer. One eyebrow cocked, he turned and faced Gina with a look of arrogance that only a teenage boy can show. She was, after all, the girl who'd thought it wise to bet against the new kid, to dare him he wouldn't do something so simple. The one thing she didn't think to take into account, though, was that when you're a new kid in a new town...you have to look arrogant and cocky, and you can't turn down such an easy dare.

"Yeah. This is it, all right. The Baily House."

The two of them glanced up at the structure, a combination of bad lighting from the setting sun mixed with a chilled autumn breeze playing a dangerous game with the shadows around its gables. The way they moved, flittering about on the edges of the walls, the silhouettes of leafless limbs dancing around with each gust, all of it gave the impression that the surrounding forest, the house itself, even, was alive.

Tim grinned, tilted his head to the side. "Oh, I get it. This is supposed to be a haunted house. That's it, right?" He nodded, ran one hand through his hair. "Look, I don't know what kind of stories you guys have around here, folktales or legends or whatever, or what you normally do to haze the new kids on the block, which I obviously am, but I can guarantee you one thing..." He paused for a moment; his eyes wide with confidence as he gauged Gina's reaction. Her attention was still on him, so that was a good thing. "If this is the best you've got, you might as well just give up now and concede defeat, because this," he gestured toward the house, "just ain't gonna cut it. I mean, come on. Aren't we a little old to be afraid of haunted houses and ghosts? I don't even believe in those things, girl."

"Well," Gina said, a wry smile stretching across her pouty lips, growing larger as she thought through her words carefully before speaking. "First off, I never said I was trying to scare you. All I said was that most people around here are too scared to go inside. I don't care if you're scared of this place or not." She took a step closer to him, one hand fiddling with her thick, auburn curls, the other stuffed in her hip pocket. "And neither does she."

Tim could feel his heart rate increase as Gina closed the distance between them, the slow, steady thump in his chest becoming more frantic and fast paced as a myriad of hormones filled his bloodstream. She was very pretty, after all, and he wasn't used to such pretty girls giving him the time of day. This, he both realized and was extremely grateful for in this moment, was one of the few good things about changing towns and schools as a teenager. It was like a fresh start, as stupid as he knew that sounded. Nobody knows you and most people show an interest, for one reason or another, at least initially.

"She?" He looked around at the other kids standing idly behind Gina, trying to see if this she she'd spoken of was present. From the expressions on their faces, those Tim had chalked up to as stupid fear and nervousness, he could tell that wasn't the case. These kids were nothing more than the few in town who weren't too scared to come along and see if he would really carry through with it.

"Yes. She."

He waited for her to continue, to elaborate a bit more on this subject, but nothing came.

"And secondly," Gina continued, "the deal, if I recall, was that I'd go out on a date with you...if... you survive a walk-through of this house. Gotta go in, check out all the rooms, and come back out."

She took another step toward him; they were almost face to face now. He could smell the sweet scent of vanilla around her, a scent that instantly pulled him in and took his mind to much better places.

"Well," she said, looking up at him as she lightly bit her lower lip. "What do you say, new kid? You think you can handle that minor little task?"

Tim chuckled nervously, his confident demeanor starting to wane. Not because of the house or the dare. No, not at all. He wasn't worried about any of that. It was just a house, and nothing more. The only difference in this one and any other he'd ever set foot in being that this one was vacant, or at least it appeared to be. None of this bothered him.

The other kids staring at him, though, that made him slightly uncomfortable. Just standing there like a bunch of robots or mannequins, their eyes fixed on him. What were they doing? Why were they even there? Were they just a bunch of losers from around town wondering if he was actually gonna go inside?

And then there was Gina. She was definitely making him nervous, but in a different way. In a good way. She made his blood hot, made his stomach shaky and swirly and weak.

She made his heart race. She excited him, and he loved that feeling.

"What do I say? Am I up to the task?" He looked to the other kids again. All of them just standing there, motionless, their mouths hanging open as if they were nothing more than braindead zombies. Tim shook his head, their rudeness sickening, the thought of how scared they seemed to be of this house so foreign to him that he couldn't even comprehend it. "I say, hell yes, I'm up to it. Let's go!"

Gina's mouth opened slightly, her tongue sliding between her ruby lips, moistening them, an act that sent Tim's heart into overdrive. "You're sure, then? You're sure you wanna go inside? Once you say it, there's no goin' back. That's just how it works here, okay?"

"Huh? What do you mean, that's not how it works? I'm not sure I follow."

Gina smiled, licked her lips again, leaned in closer. "I just wanna make sure you're up for it. That's all. I mean...you certainly...look like the kind of boy that can handle himself."

He squinted his eyes as if studying her, the way she moved, the small little subtleties in her expressions driving him wild, and suddenly whatever it was she'd just said was forgotten. He thought about the consequences of what was about to happen, those of their agreement. If he could pull this off, and surely to God he could – after all, what's to walking through a vacant house? – then she'd most certainly be the prettiest, most attractive girl that'd ever given him the time of day.

I got this, he thought. Piece of fuckin' cake.

"If it means going out on a date with you, absolutely. This'll be no problem. I'll go in and show you, girl. This place ain't nothin'."

"Let the record show," she said to the others, "he's agreed to go inside."

The others whispered to themselves, their dull and emotionless expressions changing to those of genuine interest.

Tim chuckled, slightly surprised. "What is this? Am I on trial or something? Let the record show? What's that all about?"

One side of her mouth curling up just a bit more than the other, Gina placed one hand on his cheek. "Oh, it's nothing. Just something we do. You've got this, remember? Piece of cake," she said, turning to grab a flashlight from her backpack. "I'm guessing you don't have one, since I don't see a pack or anything on you?"

Tim was silent for a moment as his mind went through what was happening. 'Let the record show' and 'that's just how it works here'? What was that all about? He certainly wasn't afraid of a so-called haunted house, but something definitely wasn't right. They were acting strange, regardless of his beliefs on the afterlife.

"Well?"

"Oh...uh, a flashlight. No. I don't have one."

"Didn't think so." She walked to the other kids and said something to them in a low voice.

"Hey," Tim started. "What are you guys talkin' abo—"

"Well," Gina said, turning back toward him, cutting him off. "Are you ready?"

"Oh, uh...well...sure. I guess. You're coming too?"

"Well, yeah. How else will we have proof, silly?"

Tim grinned. "Proof? Proof of what?"

"Proof that you went in, of course."

"I mean...I'll be right back out."

"Oh, yeah. Right. Well, this is just sort of a tradition we have, the way we do things. You understand, I'm sure. We don't much like breaking tradition around here."

Out of nowhere, the gears clicked in his mind like a well-oiled machine. Proof! Of course! There's someone in there waiting to scare me. That's why she's going in. She's gonna make sure they find me and probably video it all. It makes perfect sense.

"You about ready," Gina said, interrupting Tim's thoughts.

Tim smiled and nodded slowly. "Absolutely, girl. Bring it on."

She gestured toward the rusty iron rod fence at the end of the drive that separated them from the house. "After you, then."

"So," Tim said, stopping to place his foot on the first step up to the porch. "Do you do this to all the guys that aren't from around these parts?" He turned back to Gina, who was following immediately behind him, and grinned.

"Do what? Bring them out here? Or do you mean let them take me on dates if they survive?"

Tim cocked an eyebrow, amused at her response. "Either or, I guess?" Grabbing the handrail, he shifted his weight forward onto the first step. "Is that an admission that you do bring lots of guys out here?"

Gina laughed, her sarcasm on point. "Oh, absolutely. The problem is, though, that none of them have taken me out yet, because none of them has ever made it out of the house."

"Oh? You must be a regular little black widow."

Gina's jaw dropped. "Well, now...a sharp tongue and a sense of humor, huh? You really are something special, aren't you?" She slapped him on the arm playfully.

"Yeah, that's what they tell me. And by they, I mean my momma. She tells me that all the time." He faced the house again and started toward the door. The steps creaked and groaned under his weight as he pushed on to the second and third ones, and for a moment, it wasn't clear whether the old wood had enough strength left to hold their weight.

As they made it up onto the porch, the first thing he noticed were the windows. There were two of them, one on either side of the door, each covered in a thick, milky-white film from what had to be years neglect. Tim reached out and wiped at one with the cuff of his shirt sleeve, but it was no use. The substance had long since dried and become a permanent fixture on the window.

"Jesus, this place is a mess. What's the story here?"

"Story? What do you mean?"

"Every haunted house has a story. This place is supposed to be haunted, so what's the story? What is it, people were murdered here? It used to be a funeral home? Name any other typical haunted house tropes and insert here." He walked over, placed his hand on the doorknob, and gave it a jiggle. To his surprise, there was no resistance. "I guess we just go on in, then?" he asked, pushing the door open.

The pungent smell of rotting wood and mildew passed over them as a rush of stale air was forced from the house when the door flung back. Tim raised his arm to cover his face, the dust riding on the breeze making him cough.

"Holy shit," he said, waving his arms back and forth as he tried to waft the mold ridden allergens away from his nostrils. "And I thought the outside was bad!"

"Yeah, I could've told you it wasn't much better in here," Gina replied. "I figured you'd have enough sense to figure that one out. The whole house is in pretty bad shape."

"Got jokes, huh?"

"I'm just sayin', it's in pretty bad shape. And, as far as the story goes, this really isn't your typical haunted house. You see, there wasn't anything horrible done here, no bad deeds or old funeral homes, and it wasn't built on top of some sacred burial ground or anything."

Tim stepped inside, careful not to trip on any unseen objects in the dark and unfamiliar room. "Really? Doesn't sound like anything too scary or haunted to me, then. What makes it so special? I mean, if nobody died here, or there wasn't some horrible act committed or something like that, why's it haunted?"

"Here," Gina said, turning on her flashlight and handing it to him. "You need this more than me."

"Oh, thanks." He took the flashlight and shined it around the room. "It's dirty as hell, that's for sure, but other than that, it doesn't look too scary."

"Right. This room isn't, at least."

Tim paused for a moment, turned back to face Gina. "This room? Oh, I see. So, there's only one room that's haunted? Is that the deal here? Was somebody tortured there? An old woman left to die or something?" He turned around and continued inspecting the room, walking toward the staircase. As he aimed the light's beam up and down the steps, something caught his attention. "Are those...footprints?" He knelt down to get a closer look.

"Something like that," Gina said. "The spirit, if you want to call her that, is sort of confined to one place. She likes it there, feels at home there, you could say."

Tim was halfway up the stairs now, stopping on every step to take a closer look. "Are you seeing this, or am I going crazy? These are footprints, right?" He stood up and placed his foot over one, matching almost flawlessly. "Nobody lives here, do they? Maybe there's some homeless person staying here."

Gina laughed. "There are no homeless people staying here. They wouldn't last a night. She's very hungry. Always hungry."

His attention fully on finding out where the footprints went, Tim wasn't really processing what was being said. "But...these are footprints. They have to be, right?" He looked at them, a trail leading from the front door to at least the top of the stairs. Footprints, impressions pressed into a thick layer of dust that covered the rest of the floor. "That has to be what they are, but who's are they?" As he reached the top of the staircase, he saw that they continued down the hall, stopping in front of a room at the end of the long, dark corridor. "It looks like they go to a room up here. I bet there's someone staying in there," he said, walking down the hall slowly toward the door.

"It wasn't original to the house. That room, I mean. It was an add on. According to the story, the wood used to build it came from an old oak that used to set at the top of the hill out back. They say that that particular tree was used as a hanging tree, and unfortunately, it was used to hang her. They said she was a witch, you see? But she wasn't. That didn't stop her from calling on Satan right before she dropped to her death on that tree, though. She cursed the town and swore her revenge, and they say that Satan gave her powers. Only thing is, she's tied to that tree, which is now in the walls of this room. He gave her powers, though. Strong ones. Powers over this town, ways to keep us under her thumb, her control. But she's not a person anymore. She's a spirit...a dark one. Like I said, it's all really unfortunate."

Almost to the end of the hall, something Gina said finally had enough force to catch Tim's attention. He stopped, staring on at the door. He couldn't take his eyes off of it. Something about it made him want to look, made it nearly impossible for him to take his eyes away from it. Gina's words hit him too, though. Something she'd said hanging on a ledge in the corners of his mind. Her? Her who? Hungry? What does that have to do with anything?

He shook his head hard. "Wait...what? What were you saying? I'm sorry, I didn't catch what you sai—" A sharp pain radiated into the back of his head, sending him collapsing to the floor. His vision blurry, he thought he caught a glimpse of a short, cute girl above him for a brief second, and the only person he could think of in that moment was Gina. "Hold on...whas—" he mumbled, as he saw the young lady raise a foot into the air and bring it down on his face.

When Tim woke up, he was lying on a hard surface in a dark room. He could smell the mildew again, stronger than ever now, the feeling of something tight against his wrists and ankles registering immediately.

"Wh...what the...hey! Hello? Gina? Somebody? What's going on? What is this?"

A metallic sound rang from his left side, and suddenly the room was filled with a bright light as a door opened.

"Goddamn," he shouted, the beam of light shining straight into his eyes. "Gina? Is that you? What the fuck is going on? If this is some kind of fucked up prank, you better stop it right now! It's not funny!"

"A prank?" Gina said with a laugh. "Oh, I wish it was a prank. But, unfortunately for you, it's all too real."

He tried to toll over, but the restraints on his limbs prevented any movement. "What the fuck is going on?" he yelled out as he started to cry. "I didn't do anything to you!"

"I know, Tim. I know you didn't. You see, though, you and your mom are new in town, no relatives that know where you are. You're an only child. It's really easier when they're like you. A lot less to worry about in the long run."

"What are you talking about," he shouted, tears flowing freely now.

"Listen," Gina said. "For what it's worth, I really am sorry about this. It's not like I have a choice in any of it. I really did like you. You seemed like a good guy, and you really do have a great sense of humor."

"You don't have to do this, though! Just let me go, please?"

"I do have to do it. I'm the only one who can. She won't tolerate anyone else. She's my great-great-grandmother, after all, and she barely tolerates me. I've helped her spill so much blood, Tim. Too much. But she has to eat. She has to. If we don't feed her...if I don't feed her, well...she'll come for us. The children first, then the parents. She doesn't care about anyone. The forests will die, there won't be any more crops. I tried to tell you before, she's very powerful. You found the footprints of the others we brought to her. Those that we fed to her. I thought you were gonna walk on in here without any trouble. But you started thinking, and we couldn't have that. There's just too much to risk for the town. It's the whole, 'sacrifice one for the good of the many' argument. You understand, I'm sure. You're a smart guy."

"No! Let me go!" he screamed, snot flinging from his face as he shook his head wildly. "Let me go now and I won't say a thing! I swear!"

Gina laughed, then checked her watch. Ten twenty-four. "I'm sorry. I don't mean to laugh. It's just that, I can't let you go, and I really want to."

A dark shadow filled the room, despite the beam of the flashlight shining into it. At first, Tim thought that someone else with another light was on his other side, but when he turned to look, there wasn't any other light there. Instead, against the wall where Gina's light shined, a dark mass began to spread. It looked like a shadow, but it was forming on the wall itself, spreading to places where the light didn't touch. It was darker than the night, something that, in spite of everything else that was happening, gave Tim a very unsettling feeling.

He turned back to Gina for one last attempt at begging to be set free, but she was gone. In her place sat a chair, the flashlight sitting atop it, shining into the room. Tim slammed his head against the floor and stared up at the ceiling. The figure from the wall, the inky blob was above him now, and it was taking the shape of a woman. There were no features, no eyes or mouth, just a coal black mass, something that looked like the shadow of a shadow, if such a thing existed.

There was no sound to it, no smell, just an eerily calming movement, graceful almost, as it glided across the surfaces of the room and took its final humanoid shape. Tim was crying uncontrollably now, his words lost in a jumble of strange sounds that no person could comprehend. He looked up at the ceiling, watching as an even darker blob took form in what could only be the face of the shadowy figure. He opened his mouth to scream, to cry for his life again, but that cry would not come.

As he took in one deep and final breath, the newly formed mouth of the shadowy spirit opened wide and fell from above, consuming Tim in one swift motion.

Chapter Nine

Cries of the Night

BY GUY QUINTERO

The wineskin flew across the shack, deflating as it impacted the wall, and plopped on the dusty floor. Matilda rushed over, her thin legs shuffling through the constriction of her tight gown, worn and bearing a myriad of brown and tan stains.

"A harlot like your sister!" Gregor snapped. "Dragging your steps like I don't know. When I send you to fetch me swig, you do it an' ne'er lookin' one o' them denizens in their eyes! Ya hear me, Matty?"

"Yes, Pa." Matilda's eyes found the old wooden bucket lying near the hearth's crackling embers. "Pa?"

"What? Did'n I tell you sumfing to do already?"

"We talked last season about gettin' me a new gown. This one is becomin' tight, wearin' thin. And there's the stains—"

"Yea, them boys are goin' to be starin' 'arder now that your figure is settin'. Okay, next season."

"But perhaps we can take some of the coin from your daily swig and—"

Gregor's bulbous frame sprang forth, hurling a bowl. Thudding echoes of wood boxed into Matilda's ears as she ducked. Graying remnants of porridge sprinkled the young woman as she cringed. Matilda sprang up and scampered from the shack. The wineskin flopped about in the grip of her pumping arms. Her chest heaved and a cool burn invaded the tiring lungs. The door's thin frame slammed, with thunderous rattles reverberating in the distance behind her.

And he wonders why Tabby ran away years ago. Just get the swig so he passes out and leaves me be.

Images from long ago flooded Matilda's vision, washing away orange hues from the setting sun, and the rustling foliage.

Across the way appeared the once-familiar presence of her mother, Gwen. Wrinkles pinched with spite as the woman stood glowering at Gregor, who stood in the shack's doorway. Thick blue swelling bloomed over the woman's right eye, and a line of blood trickled down her cheek.

Matilda stared back, her wide and watery eyes pleading. Calloused hands latched on to the back of the girl's neck, as she reached out for her mother.

"You want to leave, chasing new cock, s'all well and good," Gregor announced. "The girl stays with me."

"You damned beast!" Gwen screamed. "Don't you be pretendin' you have their best interest, like some lovin' papa! I'll be back for Matilda. Not goin' to let you ruin her life like you ruined Tabitha's."

"If anythin's goin' to be ruined, it's the other side of your face if you don't get from here, harlot! Head to the tavern and take your chances finding someone who'll take a used-up bitch like yourself. Get back inside, Matty! Now!"

"Curse you, bastard!" Gwen spat. "The lord says let justice be mine and I beg him that you be shown pain a hundredfold for what ya done to us! One day, vengeance will come callin' for you, Gregor!"

"Ha! Begone, cunt!"

Matilda had waited, but Gwen had never come back.

The dusk breeze lifted the curtain of memories. Forest-flanked cobblestone roads materialized with receding cries. The cold road pressed up through her worn shoes as she hastened on.

If only I had your courage, Ma, and Tabby. Missing you both so much these days. But... Yes, Pa will likely be ready to sleep by the time I get back. I'll hand off the swig and make myself scarce until he passes out. Almost there. I wonder if Tim will be at the tavern again.

Matilda smiled with timid hope.

A billow of smoke rose above the trees, fading into the stars that twinkled in the night. Shivers rushed through Matilda as she approached a domicile with a thatched roof. A stone chimney rose to its apex, expelling the aroma of roasting chicken, entwined with the savory tang of garlic and basil. Buildings lined beyond her view, their alleys diverging along the thoroughfare.

Laughter and conversation grew as the distance closed. Matilda arrived at the porch where patrons sipped and guzzled from mugs. When they lifted their heads, their greeting smiles were covered in white foam.

A boy stood from the crowd near the door, wiping his hands upon a stained apron as he saw her approach. "Matty!" The boy waved. "You're a sight!"

There he is. Act normal. Calm. Well spoken.

"Good evenin,' Tim." Matilda smiled, walking among the tavern-goers, and ducking a raising mug.

"Your father is needin' a refill?" Tim winced.

"Yea..."

"He hasn't touched his tab in over two fortnights. My pa is getting a mite upset about it. Well, not a mite. He is right upset."

"Please, he's in one of those moods again. If I go back empty handed, it'll get ugly. Just half a swig to put him on his arse and outta my way?"

"Fair enough, Matty. Anything for you."

"You're so good to me, Tim. Thank you."

As they entered the swinging tavern doors, a glower met them from across the vast room. Matty saw a wizened man's face draped in a mane of gray and white. Wrinkles scrunched around his narrowing eyes and lip-raising sneer. A nod of disapproval met his son Timothy's firm glance.

"Pay no mind to him, this one is on me," Timothy muttered. "I'll be the tavern master soon. He's barely able to keep the books in order."

"His looks aren't the ones bothering me..."

Matilda's gaze shifted away from the wide-eyed lecherous eagerness of faces glistening with sweat from the field's toil. A tug on Matilda's attention shifted her focus. With a head turn, she glanced over to meet a man's gaze.

Those eyes of his are like the emeralds Gregor goes on about. So beautiful. He knows I'm staring.

Matilda's eyes locked with his dark ones, dilating as a connection sizzled between them. Her admirer remained unblinking. Raven locks fell about the man's chiseled face, contrasting with his ivory skin, and narrowing into a strong jawline. He wore a shirt with a frilled collar, fitted to rise high along his neck. A link pulsed with the rhythm of their heartbeats, tethering her intentions.

She turned back to Timothy and the bulging wineskin sloshing as he returned it, but she glanced once more to the man, before looking away.

That man is quite handsome. Can't stop staring for the life of me. I'm acting like a jezebel, as Father Morris accuses. Curses.

"They know a good thing when they see it." Timothy delivered a warm smile. "We'll work out your father's tab later. Our long friendship is worth more than copper. Things are going to be different now that I'm stepping up, Matty. I'm not a boy anymore. I'll be sixteen come winter."

Timothy... I want to tell him. But...

"I-I..." The world pulled away, save for the view of her mind's eye, etched with the man's stare.

"Matty?" Timothy followed her glazed expression to the gentleman in the corner. "Oh. Fancy that one, huh? Looks like nobility. I can tell you this much. He dropped some coin on a flagon of wine that he never touched. Wasteful if you ask me."

He's looking back! His stares haven't waned. Am I ready for a courtship? Yes! I'm a woman now. Gregor's drunken slurs can't keep me shackled forever. Just look at him... That man is so handsome... Look at his dress! The coin he must have... along with those eyes... I can't. So much is happening right now. I'm all over the place! Too many thoughts coming in at once! Get a hold of yourself, Matilda!

Matilda stepped away from Timothy. The tavern-keep sighed, lowering his head, and nodding with reluctance as she closed on the stranger. He looked away, murmuring, "Can't compete with that kind of dress and coin."

What am I doing? Just sauntering over in shameless fashion...

With each step Matilda took, the warmth of the hearth faded to the chill of the unknown. Her gaze pulled away, searching the cracks along the support beams, then the doe-skin mounting a back wall.

No! No! No! N—

Her view fell back upon the man in front of her.

Matilda lowered her face, pulling her smile from immediate view. "I beg your humble apologies, m'lord. I don't know what came over me—"

"Nonsense," the gentleman answered with a smirk. "I hoped you would come, madam. I am Sir Gabriel, and I am honored that you have accepted my invitation. Please have a seat."

"Thank you, sir."

"Gabriel, please."

"As you wish." Matilda swallowed back the rising exuberance, lowering her gaze to the table. "Gabriel."

"I tire quickly of pretenses, my dear. You are a lovely damsel. Your outfit, most generous, reveals your svelte and youthful figure that pleases me."

The silver tongue of a rake! Gregor's cursed habit has a led me to chance. Could I hope for more than being the half-starved prisoner of a failed brigand?

"So, let us cease the dallying," Gabriel continued. "You are young but of breeding age. Do you come here often?"

"Only to fetch my father's swig."

"I have your word that you have not consorted with the denizens of this establishment?"

"Never, sir."

"Not even the one who admires you."

The noble's glance guided Matilda's gaze to Timothy.

The barkeep paused in his business of running flagons of ale to tables beckoning with outstretched hands. After a deep sigh, the young man's eye contact broke from Matilda and Gabriel, remaining steadfast on his craft.

"He's nice. Our families are close. His father and mine used to... work together. Mine squandered his earnings, while Tim's father invested in this place. But that's the problem—"

"Timothy's familiarity makes his ties brotherly to you."

"I never thought about it that way before. I guess you're right. This may sound awful. I see myself as more than being a tavern-keep's wife. I feel my life has a greater purpose."

"You have ambition. I respect those notions and appreciate what comes with it. That kind of efficacy isn't commonplace among the peasants."

"Pardon me, m'lord. What does efficacy mean?"

"It means you are a rare delicacy. And I have chosen well."

Gabriel's hand reached for the woman's, passing over her thin fingers with a slow caress.

A smile blossomed over Matilda's face, flushing pink. A calamity of falling mugs and flagons echoed throughout the tavern as they bounced across the floor, rolling away. Red eyed and swelling with tears, Timothy stared at them before he sloshed through the puddles of liquor and hurried out the door.

"See what I mean?" Gabriel smirked.

"I— Sorry, but Tim—" Matilda muttered.

"Don't be." The noble took Matilda's hand, guiding her from the table. "You need not apologize, my dear. Take the things you want in life. Remember that lesson."

As Gabriel rose, men dressed in long black coats stood with him. The tallest carried a grim countenance through scars that striped his brow and chapped lips. Light reflected from the shine of his bald head and the golden emblem of a dragon over his right eye patch. Gabriel exchanged nods with the man. Members of their party ushered aside the other patrons, creating a walkway for Matilda and her benefactor.

"This way, my dear." Gabriel's whispers flowed to her with clarity through the commotion.

"As you wish, m'lord." Matilda's grin widened, feeling everyone's attention upon them. *So dreamy, everything is dull... am I sleeping? Any minute, I'll be awakening to Gregor snoring like a boar.*

Cobblestone debris cracked and skipped under the wheels of an approaching carriage. The vehicle's ostentatious bench curved up and outward along the sides, flaring like wings.

Matilda was guided up the steps, the carriage shaking with heavy footfalls as Gabriel followed and sat across from her. Through the window, dreary bloodshot eyes from the attendants gazed incuriously. Gabriel tugged frills of silk and velvet to cover the window, concealing them from the outside world.

Matilda stared at the double black motif, recalling the glazed look from the servants.

Pa spoke about that look. That defeat in the eyes of the noble's servants. Always looking so tired. Likely why he never did an honest day's wo-

The loud pop of a cork stole her attention as she jolted on the thick wool cushion.

"Oh, my!"

"My apologies for startling you, my dear." Gabriel poured glasses of red wine. "But what kind of a gentleman would I be, if I didn't arrange for proper refreshments to celebrate?"

It's happening! Yes! I am to be his! Matilda's thoughts fluttered back to the wineskin, which should've been weighing her hands. She had left it back at the tavern. *Never again will I fetch from that awful place. May Gregor's stomach devour him with the pain of its absence. I can imagine his groans right now, holding his belly and wailing to the air for a relief that shall never come.*

Matilda smiled, accepting her glass by its thin stem before clinking it with her benefactor's.

"A toast."

"My lord?"

"A toast to benefactors and arrangements of passion."

"Indeed, my lord." Matilda glanced away, shrouding her blush.

"Don't hide your smile." Gabriel reached out. "Your shyness is adorable, but your smile is a delight to behold."

"As you wish, my lord."

"Gabriel," he corrected.

A mouthful of red wine swirled over her tongue. Salt and copper whisked down her throat, the liquid thick to swallow.

Gabriel gulped down his serving. The smile vanished from his face as he leaned back, examining her with an unblinking focus.

Another sip and a pungent bitterness rode hard on her tongue, stinging at tastebuds with an alarm racing in her mind.

Tension melted as rippling currents blurred her view. The glass slipped from her hand, bouncing on the floor, its stem snapping and base rolling away. A crack extended from the rim into the cup, where the sloshing contents seeped into the floor.

Jolts of unease raced through Matilda. She tried to rise but sank into the cushions. She reached up, her vision blurring as her eyelids fluttered closed.

"Gabriel..." Matilda's lips drooped, her words dragging in weariness. "What have... you... Why?"

The green luster of Gabriel's eyes receded into the shadows. What stared back was the nocturnal sheen of a predator, seething before Matilda as the remnants of her consciousness drifted into slumber.

"Perhaps, fate would've dealt us an idealistic pairing, had we met in another lifetime," Gabriel whispered. "Alas, I serve another lady; one who can be very demanding and even more unforgiving."

Darkness engulfed Matilda's view. She stood before an ocean of pitch black. Trembles spread from her feet into her legs. Deep breaths of anxiety pulsed through her bosom. She clutched at the material of her dress as she saw thin white lines in the gloom, topped by a bouncing bulbous glow. They advanced rapidly along the edge of her view.

What was that? Where am I?

Tightness wrapped around Matilda's arms, constraining them to her sides. Lithe pale legs wrapped around her with the cold hardness of their chitin layers, bruising her delicate skin. A force pulled her from the nothingness she stood upon, submerging her into the warm embrace of waves. Liquidity pooled around Matilda, rising to her neck with its thick presence.

I see a...

Twinkling lights amassed like stars overhead but faded to the blind embrace of slumber. Pain streaked down her forearms, diving into her wrists. Skin unzipped with a gash from her wrists upward. Cold steel drove in swift motion, carving into the thickness of her arterial walls.

They're killing me!

Warmth spilled from her twitching arms, flowing into the waters around her. Heartbeats slowed as an empty chill embraced Matilda's core.

So cold...

The beating in her chest became a faint whisper and faded out.

Matilda ascended from the wetness, reaching toward the flickering candles encircling the area. She peered down at the white marble squares, clouded with blemishes of pink. A tall silhouette stole her attention. It was Gabriel.

Who is that man? What is this place? How did I get here?

Blurry memories of the tavern resurfaced. Images of Timothy's agonized gaze while she fawned over Gabriel raced through her mind. *What have I done? None of this was supposed to happen... I wanted to tell Tim... the truth about how I feel... I wanted to marry him... he loved me despite everything, reminding me that I was still pure in the Lord's eyes, even if others would turn their noses at me. He'll never speak to me again! God help me!*

Gabriel nodded before kneeling, pressing his nose to the floor, the knife he wielded clanging with the rushed movement. Hinges whined from the opening of double doors. A woman sauntered inside, wearing black robes that hugged tight on her sashaying hips. Onyx strands of hair flowed down her back, with a few locks draping over the pallor of her face. Her feral yellow eyes fixed upon Matilda's limp body.

"The hunt went well, my mistress," Gabriel announced. "Please accept this humble quarry, this pure vessel to feed your magnificence, to extend your reign."

Matilda gazed down, seeing her own lifeless shell hunched within a large white basin. Rose-tinted water surrounded Matilda's bare frame, spreading from the life fluids escaping her wrists. A dullness possessed her limbs, growing pale as the marble floor.

That's... me...

The master tossed back her robes, approaching the basin. Smudges clung to the ivory souls of her feet, staining them pink. Chiseled muscles flexed with a cat-like elegance as her weight poised on the balls of each smooth step. The mistress's rippling abdominals tightened as she raised her hands.

Matilda's view traced the woman's movement to the ceiling. Stretching above them was a vast skylight, displaying the visage of a man standing over another with a stone raised for a killing blow. On the flanks of the image was a shepherd fleeing out of view and a bushel of corn opposite.

"I hunger, my child," she announced, sniffing deep into her button nose. "You've done well. I can smell the innocence from here."

"Twas nothing, my lady. It took longer than I had expected to find a pure soul. All expended effort is worth seeing you so pleased, my sovereign."

"Your successes continue. After I have completed my rejuvenation, we will discuss your ascent into the blooded ranks."

"It is all I have ever wanted."

The sire raised her alabaster leg, stepping into the crimson water, lowering her body. Gentle currents carried her hair, writhing like serpents as it floated around her. Dropping back, the woman disappeared into the depths of red.

Gabriel's fist tightened and shook with anticipation. The words of his mistress echoed in his mind. He thought of long and polished dinner tables. Chattering vapid nobles with their white wigs surrounded him. Sneers and smirks were shot at them, as he basked in the presence of the pale foundation caked over their faces. It was a pathetic attempt to mimic their masters, the true aristocracy of the night.

A torrent of water expelled from the large basin, raining over the floor in a shower of red. Screeching cries resounded through the area, ringing into Gabriel's ears, ripping him from his reverie.

"Countess! My lady! Please, what is the matter?" Gabriel asked, rising from his station, and stepping back.

Delicate hands of porcelain white gripped at the basin's rim. Skin and bone stretched with audible tension, until her fingers tripled in length. Sharp tips of yellowing claws punctured through her clear nails, pushing out and away the remnants of soft meat until thick leathery skin remained. Sloughed flesh from the countess' digits rolled down the side of the basin, plopping to the ground in a bloody heap.

The mistress gazed to the pane above. Her twitching black pupils dilated, encompassing her eyes with the radiant sheen of a nocturnal predator. Another bellowing cry left the distended jowls as images transported her vision to memories not her own.

This girl is not pure! The countess screamed into her own psyche.

Impact from a fat fist struck hard across her face. The countess keeled over on hands and knees. Blood swelled in her mouth with coppery bitterness coating her tongue. Two jagged articles shifted in her mouth with a familiar hardness, radiating agonizing sparks from bleeding empty sockets. Grime entered her vision from the floor she beheld. A fierce kick to the abdomen sent her wrenching downward, her mouth agape. The dislodged teeth pelleted from her cries, rattling against the floor.

"You ain't gunna leave me," Gregor cried out, his breath carrying the taint of liquor. "Learning to read, so you can leave me?"

"No, I swear, Pa! I just wanted—" Matilda's words left the countess' lips.

"This is what cunts are good for!"

"No, please!"

Gregor positioned behind her upon his knees, taking the girl's hips. She reached back, trying to paw him away, before a thudding blow sent her face reeling into the dusty ground. His plump hands reached for her gown, pulling it overhead. Gregor's warm and clammy body pressed to hers, his rasping breaths grew heavier with anticipation. Hard thrusts jerked the countess' view. Her psyche pulled away, back to the basin within the echoing chamber. Gregor's loud and breathy groans clung to hear ears. The countess willed away the connection, but his husky voice lingered with her.

"Gabriel!" the countess screeched.

Long fangs protruded from her parting lips. Large, rounded ears stretched from her head. Dark black sinews peeled from her back, stretching into membranous wings that draped the basin. With a mighty thrust of her wings, the countess propelled from her watery confines. She descended upon Gabriel, slamming the man on his back. Sharp talons pierced through his clothing, puncturing his arms with ease. She tightened the grip upon him, peeling away skin and meat, greased with blood. Vital fluids pooled underneath her whimpering minion.

Gabriel shrank into the ground, turning his face away from the cold breath expelling carrion reek. Dagger-like teeth flashed from a cavernous mandible, with laces of saliva quivering through the countess' bellows. Gusts of primal rage fluttered Gabriel's locks along the ground, pulsing on the muscles of his grimacing face. He dared not turn his head to the ire of her deathly gaze.

"You incompetent wretch! The offering was not a virgin!" the countess roared.

"No, that can't be! I searched her soul during the seduction, gazed into her during that incessant bantering, and found it pure. I read her aura as I subjugated her to my will. This was the perfect morsel, innocent, and judging how she dressed in form fitting attire, ripe for subjugation. The energies of her death were permeated with innocence!"

"She was violated by a lowly slob!" Fangs bared close to Gabriel's neck. "Now that experience resonates through my essence! I can feel it! All of it!"

"Mercy! I plead for mercy, my sire! I remain your humble and loyal servant! I do not understand how I failed to read her aura!"

With quick and pounding steps the fiend left its pounce, scampering on all fours. Gabriel peered over to his mistress' eyes, seeing trembling hate. Another screeching howl emanated from her quaking jowls, extending to the heavens with her glare. Gabriel cringed in place, limbs shaking, mouth dropping.

The abomination extended her mighty wings and with a hard thrust, propelled into the air, shooting up through the stained glass. A rainbow of shards descended into the basin and pelted the ground, leaving it sparkling with debris.

Guttural cries resounded through the night, calling from the manor, trailing over the treetops with magnificent haste. Peasants woke, trembling in their blankets. Families huddled together, locking doors, fetching swords and pitchforks. Fearful gazes peered from windows throughout the province, staring into the clouds and stars. High they pointed, their eyes following growls and roars, cloaked within the shroud of night.

Hawkish vision gazed down at the details of the forest. Leaves, branches, and bushes formed with crisp edges traced in hues of gray. Streets and buildings carried the aura of the moon, framing the world below in the mistress' baleful glower. Over the tavern she passed, where the final inhabitants staggered outward, only to freeze in place upon the porch, searching upward for the creature sending their hearts racing.

Matilda's whimpers rose like a symphony in the countess' psyche. Pain shot between her legs as innocence was torn away. Memories of wineskin carrying treks directed the fiend to a hovel appearing between a break in the trees. Her long-curved claws reached out as she closed upon it.

Gregor looked up to the ceiling of his home, shaking, sobbing as the bestial roars grew louder. His sausage-like fingers clenched the stained sheets while he squirmed upon the bed. Sharp pain arose in his chest from the quaking heartbeats that swallowed away stomach aches from a dry evening.

"No!" Gregor sniveled. "I'm a good man now! I gave up my outlaw days!"

A thunderous impact exploded through the roof. Straw rained down within the home. Howling winds washed through the area, snuffing out the hearth's blaze. Its breaths rumbled before Gregor, his eyes tracking the growls into the fog of dust. Glowing yellow eyes opened with thin serpentine pupils fixating on the man. The hulking figure coiled before leaping forward.

Claws met Gregor, running through his tender and jiggling flesh with the ease of a carving knife. Talons sank into his bulbous gut, pulling away in one stroke. Steam rose as warm innards spilled out, exposed to the evening cold seeping into the hut. Blood streamed and urine expelled, soaking into his pants until they withered around his kicking legs. Sharp pain rose into his chest, his mind drawing a blank as twitching overcame him. Growls rumbled over him; the vibrations coiled with seething fury.

"This is what men are good for." Matilda's voice entwined with the creature's snarls.

The salivating terror stomped, her heel driving hard into Gregor's kneecaps, bending them as they crunched within the socket. The bedframe cracked, its legs snapped, sinking into the ground with a shudder. Gregor's lower limbs rolled as they flopped independently from the rest of his writhing frame. The flopping skin wobbled like a sack, bagging the shattered contents within his leg.

"Matty... Is that you in there? I'm sorry! I'm sorry, baby!"

"Matilda is no longer!" bellowing winds from the beast announced. "There is only pain!"

Vice-like clutches wrapped around Gregor's ankles. A mighty heave of her powerful wings brought the mistress back into flight. Her wailing quarry swung about in her grip, the agony of his broken limbs surging throughout his convulsing body. Juices of red and brown spilled from the flap of skin that once held his abdomen closed. His innards sloshed outward, spotting the road below with long stretches of intestines and life fluids.

Cold crept into Gregor. The concert of wails between him and the beast faded into white noise. Pressure from the wind filling his ears subsided. The eruption within his chest released him from the pain of a slow gutted death. Light washed over the man, erasing the night. Matilda was before him, reaching out to the center of his chest. The energy from her touch seized his heart.

"I forgive you, Father," Matilda said. "Because I refuse to let you have power over me. But the countess isn't so merciful. If only you could see how clear it looks from here. I'm afraid you will never have that opportunity. So, this is my last errand for you."

His daughter vanished, and the night returned. Gregor clutched his heart, as his body seized up. Darkness swallowed his vision. The cold embrace of death numbed his torment.

She was the better than all of us, Gregor thought as the life force drifted from his vessel. *Why did I do those things? So much regret now...*

Within the darkness, yellow eyes opened, fixing on his floating presence. More appeared as he wandered deeper into the obscurity. Bestial cries resounded throughout the vast and unseen landscape. Dread trembled through Gregor as the denizens closed fast to his position.

Chapter Ten

The Feeding

BY D. E. GRANT

Selene opened her eyes only to be greeted with total and complete darkness.

How long have I been here, she thought to herself. *A day? A year? A thousand years?* Selene was uncertain. As a nigh-immortal being, time held no restraints on her, as she recounted the countless years of her existence, the passage of time, landmarks of history and those she loved and lost as each one of them shed their mortal coils. Being a creature of the night, she was unmoved by the utter darkness that seemed to embrace her; in fact, she was completely at home in it. She was, at first, unsure of her whereabouts until she felt the immediate surge of power the moment, she touched the chilled, damp soil beneath her. She felt her strength from the connection between her, and the handful of dirt, and those of her kind.

Selene caressed the soft satin lining of the box she was in before she removed its lid and rose out of it. Her bare feet touched the cold stone floor as she padded through the darkness and navigated down the hallway. The woman grew more familiar with the twists and turns among the maze of corridors as Selene now remembered the many times, she effortlessly wandered these darkened and unlit halls. With each step, Selene became more in touch with herself and who she was, an undead creature of the night. While some would call her a nightwalker or bloodsucker, Selene was certain of her identity, that of a vampire; a being who needed the warm nectar of human blood to maintain her life force. Forced and forged into the world of vampirism at a young age, Selene grew to embrace the ways of immortality in darkness and hunting for fresh victims to satisfy her seemingly unending urges.

As Selene was certain of what she was, there was also another part that existed inside her that was intensified by her connection to Mother Earth and the forces of nature. Two halves of the same coin that often came into conflict. For untold years, Selene learned to harness the powers she possessed from birth. With a crescent moon on her right cheek for a birthmark, Selene was taught to be a powerful spellcaster from her mother, as she was trained by her mother before her. On her Ascension night, Selene was given her Token of Power, a pure silver dragon pendant. With it, she could summon her silver dragon familiar Wyldfyre, her pet and confidante, who also occasionally serves as her eyes and ears. Her pendant gleamed in the midst of the consuming darkness as she reached the door of the crypt that contained her.

Selene walked out into a moonless and starless night, almost as abysmally dark as her sleep chamber. She turned to face the small building, spoke a few words of an incantation, and suddenly, several trees appeared where the building once stood, and blended in with the surrounding forest. Selene's attention then turned to the sound of chanting a short distance away. She moved stealthily towards the source of the sounds and the sight of a huge bonfire in a nearby clearing. Upon her approach, Selene spied several hooded figures gathered around the fire, chanting, and motioning skyward. As she neared the group, she recognized the words spoken and the reason for both the words and the gathering.

Selene entered into the clearing and the chanting momentarily ceased.

"Lady Moondragon," said one of the cloaked figures to Selene, "it is an honor to have you join us here. As you know, your coven has gathered here for hundreds of years on the longest night of the year in celebration of the Solstice and to renew our strength and powers from our goddess Arianrhod and connection to nature."

"I am well aware of this yearly gathering," Selene answered. As she was having this conversation, Selene became aware of two other things: her growing, gnawing hunger and sensing of others swiftly approaching the clearing through the shroud of trees.

Before Selene could react or warn her fellow necromancers, the attack had begun. Creatures from all sides leapt from the darkness to attack the hooded worshippers. The assault was swift and brutal as the vampires quickly swooped down upon the unsuspecting and surprised group. While some tried in vain to cast spells to protect themselves, it was already too late for most of the group that had surrounded the fire in peace and joy.

Screams of pain and horror echoed throughout the forest as throats were torn and necks ripped open. The strength the witches sought from their goddess and ritualistic worship evaporated quickly in light of the vampires' unrelenting attack. Fear ran rampant as no one was spared from the savagery and viciousness of the onslaught.

In the light of the blazing fire, Selene saw copious amounts of the victims' blood spurting into the air as the vampires began to feast. Beings bound by the dark desire for blood greedily partook of the free-for-all as they drained the vibrant lifeforce to add to their countenance of the undead.

Selene stood in the midst of the battle between death and undead life and watched the spectacle of the destruction happening around her: the rumbling hunger within her growing into a roar. Her pale flesh, devoid of her own flowing blood, became even paler as she witnessed the overwhelming slaughter of her kind. As suddenly as the attack began, it was over, and the screams were silenced. All that could be heard around the dying bonfire were the hungry sucking and slurping sounds of the vampires drinking in the last drops of their victims.

"Here's one that almost got away," one of the vampires, named Jared, said to Selene as he roughly pushed a young man to the ground. He trembled at her feet and immediately, Selene felt the excitement from his fear. "Probably was going to inform the Council of Witches about what happened here, even though word will get back to them soon enough. You know they'll be coming."

"I'm expecting that," Selene answered as she touched her silver pendant and whispered her familiar's name. A small silver dragon materialized, and soon, Wyldfyre's glow cut through the darkness.

"You know what I need from you," she said to the petite dragon as she pointed towards the mountains on the other side of the forest. Wyldfyre blew a puff of smoke and belched a small ball of flame as it flew off in that direction. Selene then turned toward the trees, waved her hand and her illusion faded, once again exposing the entrance to her resting place.

"Secure him," Selene said to Jared as she surveyed the clearing where the witches had gathered. In the light of the dying embers of the fire, Selene checked among the strewn and discarded bodies and retrieved anything she could use against the upcoming battle. Those magic-users who were not completely drained of blood became beholden, and forced into loyalty to Selene, who added to her horde of bloodsucking spellcasters.

Selene followed the last of her people into the crypt, and once inside, was again reminded of her gnawing hunger. It came back with a vengeance after the excitement of the ambush subsided.

Selene looked upon her hopeless victim and potential meal as he was hung upside down so the blood would rush to his head. Selene reached out to feel his pulse pound in his throat, which pleased her greatly. The warm throbbing of his pumping heart brought a smile to her undead heart. He squirmed against her cold touch which only served to heighten her anticipation of what was to come.

"Why," Selene's prisoner asked, "You are one of us, a witch from birth! Why commit this sacrilege against your own kind?"

"There is so much you don't know about me," Selene said sadly, in the midst of the silence of the nocturnal creatures that filled the burial chamber. "I am a witch, of course, of the royal order, marked from birth and destined to rule. What you may not know is that I was offered as a sacrifice from my people to the vampires, to keep the peace between our warring factions. On a night much like this one, I was made something else, became someone else."

Selene ran her tongue along his neck to feel his rapidly throbbing pulse. She relished the delicious taste of his fear and nervous sweat. The vampire-witch paused to continue her story, despite her nearly overwhelming hunger for the young man's rich blood.

"As I learned the way of the vampire and grew stronger in their ways, I came to realize I was unique, the first of my kind, born to rule over witch-kind, created to reign as queen of the vampires. I am the best of both worlds, so why shouldn't I rule over both, combine them, create a race for myself?"

"The Council will stop you, traitor!" the man yelled out into the darkness.

Selene again took the young man's face in her hands and shouted, "I'm not a traitor!" Her voice echoed loudly within the chamber walls. She paused and allowed the man to twist out of her grasp. Through Wyldfyre's eyes, Selene saw thirteen figures clad in black approaching her position. The Council of Witches, she thought, then turned her attention back to the man hanging by his ankles.

"The Council is coming," Selene said to everyone in the room, "coming to fail, and they will fail. Every one of them will fall under my sway and become my subjects! I will be where I belong as ruler of the darkness!" Cheers filled the chamber and Selene told the young man, "But you will not see my ascension."

As Selene's fangs penetrated his flesh, blood spurted onto her pale lips and she licked at it, sensuously, savoring every drop of its coppery taste as if it were one of the gourmet meals, that she used to consume. Now, Selene's only hunger was for the taste of a warm vein beneath her bite. Her thirst is satisfied solely by the thick, life-giving sustenance that flowed into her mouth. The helpless man twitched, and convulsed, as Selene deeply drank of his blood, feeling his essence strengthen the vampire.

His movements of resistance ceased as the final drops of his blood flowed through Selene's fangs. The vampire wiped her lips when she was done, satisfied with the drained corpse's ashen face in her hands.

With one hunger satiated, Selene turned to face her other hunger, that for absolute power. Through her familiar's eyes, Selene saw the Council of Witches arrive at the blood-soaked clearing where the massacre took place. The scent of death rose high, permeated the air, and mixed with the smell of burning wood. Through Wyldfyre's eyes, Selene could see that the witches had surrounded her crypt and were ready to attack.

"Selene Moondragon!" shouted one of the black-robed spellcasters, "Come out and face your elders!"

Selene emerged from her crypt flanked by several of her followers. "I have no elders!" she shouted into the dark, "You lost that place when you fed me to the vampires! Now, we're going to feed on you all!" Selene touched her talisman and whispered one word to Wyldfyre: "Attack!"

The dragon swooped down behind the unsuspecting witches and breaths of fire, engulfed two of the Council witches in silver and black flames. Their robes blazed under the night sky as they attempted to cast spells to extinguish themselves. Two other magic-users spoke a few words, and a crescent of dark blue lightning shot from their hands and severed the heads from the bodies of three vampires. The blood from their decapitated bodies spurted into the air and the acidic fluid bubbled, boiled, and corroded the ground where it landed.

Selene and her fellow hybrid vampires scattered in all directions to take the battle to the witches who were seeking vengeance against the renegade.

Selene moved quickly as she took on a nearby black-hooded figure and each cast a spell. Both Selene and her adversary fell to the ground from the impact of their magics, but they recovered quickly. As the spellcaster rose to face Selene, the vampire was surprised to see her opponent's face.

"The Queen Mage," Selene said, as the two women circled each other, "and my mother. The woman who used her daughter as a pawn in her game with the vampires!"

"It's me, daughter, and I am still The Queen Mage Minerva, your mother, Selene. You don't have to do this!" she responded. "Come back home and let's work this out. Please don't make me fight you!"

With heated venom in her voice, Selene said, "You didn't 'work things out' with the vampires, did you? You just give them your daughter, right?"

Minerva admitted, "I had to make peace with them! We had been at war for nearly three hundred years! We nearly wiped each other out of existence and the only way to stop the carnage on both sides was by the blood of my first born. I did it to save all of us!"

The savagery of the two battling factions continued around the women as the blood of both the witches and vampire-witches were shed in such large amounts that crimson pools formed where the combatants fell.

"And now, I'll do what I must to save MY kind! It'll be a pleasure to drink every last drop from your wretched body!" Selene yelled at her mother as she lunged towards her.

Minerva quickly cast a spell on Selene that temporarily stopped the charging woman in her tracks. "I don't want to hurt you, Selene," she said as she approached her daughter.

"But...I...want to...hurt...YOU!" the younger woman shouted as she broke Minerva's spell and countered with one of her own. The elder warded off the spell and Selene summoned her familiar to fight with her. Wyldfyre swooped down towards the woman who attacked its master.

The Queen Mage was suddenly aware of the creature's approach and with a wave of Minerva's hands, Wyldfyre exploded in a bright ball of blue and silver fire.

"AAAAAHHHH!" Selene yelled out as she saw the destruction of her dragon. At the same time, the pendant around her neck immediately turned unbearably hot searing the image of the dragon on her skin.

"What did you do?" Selene gasped as bits and pieces of Wyldfyre rained upon her. "You'll die for that!" Selene hissed at her mother, "Better yet, I will make you serve me for all eternity!"

Selene and Minerva continued their personal battle as the casualties of war mounted. They traded spells, and counter-spells, with neither gaining an advantage. Minerva had experience on her side, but Selene's hatred, and fierceness, began to wear down the elder.

Then, as Minerva deflected a fireball Selene sent her way, the vampire-witch took advantage of the distraction, rushed her mother, and pinned her hands to her sides as they fell to the ground with Selene on top.

Weary of the fight and her personal struggles, a defeated Minerva said, "I yield, Selene. The fight is over. Look around you, daughter. We're all that remains on this field of battle. Is this what you wanted?"

Selene looked around at the costs of the battle, at the recompence for rebellion. Twisted heaps of the bodies of the Council Witches could be made out in the fading fire that surrounded the women. Severed heads of Selene's hybrid horde were scattered near and far throughout the clearing.

The prodigal vampire-witch looked down on her mother, and Minerva seemed to smile, hopeful that Selene learned the error of her ways, but her smile was short-lived.

"No, Mother," Selene said, "this is not what I wanted. THIS is what I wanted!" With that, Selene sank her fangs into her mother's throat and began to drink from her. Unseen by Selene, a solitary tear fell from Minerva's right eye as her lifeforce was being drained from her. Blood trailed down Minerva's neck as Selene felt the Queen's heartbeat growing weaker until it beat no more.

Satiated and victorious, a smug smile crossed Selene's face as she wiped the final few drops of her mother's blood from her lips and rose from atop the body. To prevent her from turning, Selene found a nearby branch and drove its pointed end through Minerva's heart, ensuring her eternal death.

In the middle of the theater of death, Selene noticed the sun beginning to rise. As much a vampire as witch, she stepped over dead bodies and avoided pools of the combatant's blood, on the way to her coffin until the shroud of darkness covered the land once more.

"We must do this quickly," said one voice, "the sun must not catch you here."

"We will. Don't worry," another voice said.

Two figures moved quickly and quietly through the elaborate network of hallways until they reached Selene's burial chamber where her coffin lay.

"Careful now," one voice whispered into the darkness, "she might not have succumbed to sleep just yet. Ready? We must be quick and leave no trace of our presence here."

The two grasped the coffin lid and slowly slid the heavy stone lid off. Selene was in it, having indeed, already fallen asleep. Remnants of Minerva's blood still stained her lips.

"Ready?" one voice said, pulling a long stake from within the folds of a robe and poising the tip over Selene's heart.

"Ready," came the reply. A small sledgehammer appeared in the hand of the other and connected with the stake that was steadied over the vampire-witch's heart.

"AAAAAHHHH!!" Selene screamed as the stake was being driven through her chest. The pained-filled roar that came from her echoed through the halls of the empty chambers, now her permanent home. She reached out towards her murderers but just barely grazed their robes. Black blood filled her mouth, only allowing a muffled gurgle to escape her throat. Selene twitched once, twice, and then moved no more.

"Now to make sure, we must cut off her head, so she can't come back," one voice said, bringing a large, sharp blade into play.

Selene was held by her long raven-black hair as her head was separated from her body and carefully placed in a knapsack, to avoid any of her blood getting on them.

"There. It is done. There will be peace between our peoples once more," one voice said. The knapsack that contained Selene's severed head was held high in front of them.

"We must hurry," the other voice said, as they hurried out of the crypt, "the sun has nearly risen. You will die if you can't make it home."

"My son," one cloaked figure said, "I will make it home in time to rest. The night was long, but successful. Your curse of bloodlust has been broken by Selene's destruction."

"Yes, father," said Jared, who removed his hood from his head, "it was indeed successful."

"You will one day have your own clan and keep the treaty between the vampires and witches. We cannot have another like Selene again," the grey-haired elder said to Jared. He turned towards the mountains beyond the clearing then spoke again. "With the Council all but gone, you will be needed to take your rightful place by my side."

"Yes, father," said Jared, and with that, the pair disappeared from sight just as the sun rose over the horizon.

Chapter Eleven

Belladonna's Curse

BY DANIELLE MANX

Halloween. All Hallows Eve. The time when the veil between worlds lifted, spirits roamed, and all things were possible. At least, Grace Pringle hoped so. Her life depended on it. Literally. Cancer had ravaged her body, and brain, making her feel like a walking corpse.

On this day, kids dared to challenge the spirit world, wearing costumes of witches, vampires, and zombies with cries of 'trick or treat,' but really, all they wanted was a handful of candy corn or Reese's' Peanut Butter Cups. Grace felt the sardonic smile on her lips at that thought. As if the spirit world would be so easily satisfied with that. If only.

Tonight, was the night. The time was right. She had researched it all so carefully. As a seventh daughter, and a seventh-generation witch, when Grace found out about her diagnosis, she'd immediately tried more holistic methods to cure her body. When those failed, she succumbed to the endless train of doctors, surgery, chemo, and radiation. All she had to show for it was nausea, exhaustion, and hair loss. Not even witches could cure disease. They were human, after all. No one could live forever, but this body-switching spell was the next best thing.

She smiled again as she heard the squeals of delight from Trick-Or-Treaters. The sounds danced on the wind along with the scent of dried leaves: The russet, crimson, orange, and lemon-yellow leaves made a motley carpet, littering the ground. Aromas of cinnamon, apples, nutmeg, and pumpkin sang a song of autumn baking and made appetites stir.

She felt alive in the briskness of the October air. Sweater weather and Halloween, in particular, refreshed the skin and energized the spirit. Everything was waking up from summers lethargy for one last romp before winter approached. It had its own special magic. Everything in life did. As a witch, Grace knew how essential settings were for casting spells.

And it didn't get more perfect than Pringle House. Grace's three-story Victorian home that she had turned into a bed and breakfast. Even though it stood on the beach, it made the perfect backdrop for all seasons. Proud and stately, like a military officer's dress uniform, the ivory-painted house with turquoise trim boasted gables, gingerbread architecture, and a widow's walk. The front porch was a thing of beauty. A wooden swing guaranteed to inspire reading and relaxation. And now, a scarecrow perched there with crows, hay bales, and Jack' O' Lanterns--a pumpkin's version of plastic surgery. Those with artistic talent and imagination carved entire pictures on them.

Surely, Grace could have the same treatment as a silly old gourd.

Pringle House was decked out in Halloween splendor, including animation, smoke machines, and a light show. Her lavish decorations made an irresistible stopping point for Trick-Or-Treaters and passers-by.

As it should be.

―――――◆◊◆―――――

She needed all the help she could get. And Grace Pringle was no ordinary witch: The family lineage stretched to Europe and beyond. Ancestors sailed on the Mayflower and blissfully escaped that Salem hysteria simply by common sense, keeping their heads down and minding their own-- with a bit of foggy magic thrown in. She had learned the craft from childhood and later from her mentor, Old Melinda Gregg. Filled with tales and folklore, Grace had learned there was magic all around, in the simplest of things. Herbs, nature, water, and all the elements. White magic.

As a Hecatite Witch, she was unique. Grace had honed her powers to a stiletto sharpness. Through study, practice, and guidance, she'd learned it all. Halloween brought out all of it. Good magic, wicked magic, and all the grey shades in between. Grace felt her oily stomach churn again. Sinking to her knees and pulling her hair back, she made it to the bathroom just in time.

She'd been around death before. Old Melinda and her parents, friends, and loved ones had passed away. Some passed in pain, some in peace, and Grace had shed plenty of tears over them all. She felt the depression and the sadness. And mostly felt what a tremendous waste it all was; these vital people so ravenous for life were no more. Now, facing her own mortality, she felt the emotional agony more than ever.

Not for the first time, Grace prayed to the gods and goddesses for healing. For a way to keep living. She wasn't ready to give up just yet. At 36, she still had so much of life to learn, so much to teach, and to savor. Her nieces and nephews were so quick and bright. She couldn't let all that magic and knowledge go to waste.

She loved them. Little Arron liked how she made up games and funny faces; Jessica roared with laughter at how her aunt encouraged her to go higher and higher, as far as she could. The kid was fearless, Grace thought admiringly.

"Today the swings, tomorrow, the presidency," she'd encourage her. Grace so wanted to be around to see it. And then, there was Alex, her constant kitchen companion, where they made beautiful concoctions together. Her throat swelled at the idea of missing another moment with all of them, and she swallowed the lump in it.

With this spell, one could invariably see several centennials and millenniums if they performed it often enough. The future was just so much fun, Grace thought. And such a marvel. Just look at all the improvements and enhancements she had seen already. And there was so much more to come. Frantic excitement eagerly boiled inside her.

And what about love? At her age, she wanted both passion and the quiet contentment of having another person with her. Marriage. Someone to laugh with, someone to share life with her, to create a family with her. Screw sitting around and decaying, Grace thought. She wanted to embrace all life had to offer.

The time was right. Every instinct in her body knew it. What was more, all her research confirmed it. She dissected her magic books, studied the moon and tides, and examined the Autumnal Equinox against her own history. It all related to the same thing: on October 31st, underneath the full moon, she could have eternal life if she followed the steps carefully.

Well, sort of. The closest anyone could come to it. She just needed another body to keep going. *Please, oh please,* she thought. And Grace wasn't a woman who begged for anything. She would even retain her powers. With the sounds of the wind in the trees and violent crashes of the waves from the sea outside, she smiled, it was time. She had even discovered the ideal person for the body switch: an author by the name of Joshua Fisk. Grace poured the sacred lavender and rose sands around her, then placed the crystals, herbs, and tapers within the circle.

Here in her sacred space, in her sacred circle, she began the first part of the spell. All things that welcomed and beckoned. Scents and vibes that encouraged people to linger and stay. She lit the tapers before she arranged herself in the middle of the circle sitting cross-legged. It was no accident that Grace dressed in her most powerful dress that was both sexy and potent for both the woman and the witch.

Grace took a deep breath, trying to control her racing heart. Over the lit candle, she intoned: "Hear me, Aphrodite, Goddess of Love and Beauty, grant me what I seek... Hear me, Hecate, Goddess of all magic, hear my plea." She sliced the tip of her finger, drawing blood and adding a few anemic-looking drops to a simmering cauldron. At length, she grabbed a long-stemmed red rose out of a nearby vase, plucked the petals from it, and continued the chant. "Here me, Hecate, to you I pray..."

From the street of the historic district, Joshua Fisk sighed as he noticed the ivory home in the distance. Pringle's Bed and Breakfast looked just the same as every other B&B to him. Shit, he bristled. Jack had promised him a haunted house where he could write his next thriller, due out before he knew it. His fucking editor had threatened him with no more advances unless he showed results of written pages.

"Not one more damned dollar," Jack had bellowed. So far, he hadn't written one thing, and he needed the quiet and the inspiration. They couldn't all be as easy as *Belladonna's Curse*.

From this angle where he stood, it had tidy, sheer curtains at the opened window and a front porch.

Cute. But nothing that screamed "haunted" to him. It looked like every other cardboard-cutout historic home in Cape May, New Jersey. The widow's walk on top of the third story looked interesting. He'd fucking give Jack a tongue lashing when he got settled. But he was being impossible. He was immovable on the deadline, and Fisk wondered if the publishing company was getting antsy about him.

Fisk felt his head squeeze as if it were being pressed in a vice. Christ. He needed a good drink or two to knock that headache out. And for some dumbass reason, the woman lived on the beach. Oh great. He hated the feel of sand in his shoes. And seagulls? Yuck. Messy goddamned things. Ms. Pringle was probably some retired old woman living out her dream of living in a beach house after her husband had died. Boring, boring, boring. He'd seen this all before.

Plus, they all were such meddlers. They were all busybodies, always getting in his face. Fussing. It was impossible to get any work done at all.

As he made his way to the porch with his bags, he nearly collided with some Trick-or-Treaters and grimaced. Oh, joy. Kids. Leave it to him to pick a holiday where they ran absolutely wild. If any of the demon-spawn damaged his laptop, there would be hell to pay. He hoped Old Lady Pringle handed out raisins to the little Damien's instead of candy.

He paused to admire her animated zombie display on the front porch and the skull and bones wind chimes jingling in the breeze. He caught a glimpse of the solid black cat lazing on the side windowsill, basking in the sun. He took a deep breath before he rang the bell.

The zombie came to life, growling, and letting out gremlin-sounding noises when she answered the door wearing the traditional black witch's hat, a la Margaret Hamilton from the Wizard of Oz.

"Happy Halloween!" Grace beamed as she held out a deep cauldron-like bowl of king-sized Reese's' Peanut Butter Cups.

Looking at the dark-haired guy, her eyes widened. He was tall and lanky, with somber grey eyes. Additionally, he had attractive, etched cheekbones and a rugged jawline. His mouth held a stubborn, grumpy expression as if life was an overflowing sewer of shit he had to wade through. Perfect, she thought. "Oh, excuse me," she laughed.

"Hi, Grace Pringle?" He could barely get the words out as lust stabbed him right in the gut, and he hoped he wasn't just standing there with his mouth open. This wasn't the retired old widow he had been expecting.

"I'm Joshua Fisk, we spoke on the phone." Lord, she was a looker. Tall and willowy with huge blue eyes and blonde hair that looked like the honey in the glass container. Her lips were impish and tinted with a glossy peach. She was waif-thin, but he liked them that way. He was willing to bet she tasted just like honey. He was elated to have been wrong.

"Oh yes, Mr. Fisk, the writer! I thought you were one of the kids," she laughed at herself abashedly. "I've been expecting you. Please come on in. Welcome to my family home. The Pringle House has hosted several generations."

And her voice wasn't bad either, he mused.

At least her guest had discovered the bare minimum of manners, Grace thought, when she moved aside to let him in. When they spoke on the phone earlier, she found him brisk, sullen, and surly. But, besides her body-switching mission, she liked to flirt with handsome men. He dragged in his laptop and belongings, wrinkling his nose at the greenery hanging in the doorway in little bundles. "What's that smell?

"That would be sage," she replied. "It gets rid of negativity."

"If you say so." He dropped the subject as he looked around.

"This is nice." It seemed like a benign thing to say. The house was bright, open, and sweetly tidy. It hardly fit in with his idea of a haunted house with secret passageways, trap doors, and secrets lurking around every corner. "I like your wind chimes outside."

"Thank you. They caught my eye."

"They look so authentic."

She couldn't help but laugh.

"Are there any other guests here?"

"Some. We have been full up for the annual Scarecrow Festival, and there had been a family who checked out yesterday after our Haunted Cemetery Tour, and two couples who we barely see." She watched his body give a huge sigh of relief. How interesting. Fisk seemed gregarious in his interviews, even cocky. He was complicated, Grace observed. And it was always the complicated ones who were best in bed. "Would you like to check in?"

After giving her his Gold Card, with her handing him enough papers to sign his life away, she gave him his receipt and room key. It was one of those ornate, Victorian, heavy iron ones. "Yours is one of our best rooms," Grace assured him. "We don't usually get bestselling authors here."

"Excuse me, Ms. Pringle?" They were interrupted by a stately tight-lipped woman dressed in inky black from head to foot. "If you don't need me anymore today, I want to head home. John and I are hosting our annual Halloween Party tonight." Her accent was pure London and reminded Fisk of Diana Rigg.

"Oh, absolutely! I just need you to sign these documents first." Grace handed them over, and the woman wrote with a flourish.

"Do you work here?" Josh fought for something to say. He reached into his jacket pocket for a pack of Marlboro's and lighter.

"Mrs. Renfield is our housekeeper."

"Please do not smoke in here," Mrs. Renfield chided him in a scalpel-sharp tone.

"Just one cleaning lady with a house this size?" He frowned. Instantly, he thought of shoddy, half-assed work.

"You'll never see more immaculate cleaning." Mrs. Renfield's chocolate-colored eyes seared into Josh's. "Just be sure to leave a large tip," her words were clipped as she sailed out the door with a "see you tomorrow, Ms. Pringle."

Strange woman, Josh thought. She sure had Mrs. Danvers from Rebecca down. He gave the key the once over and switched it from hand to hand, testing its weight. "Very heavy and very Victorian. I didn't think they made these kinds of keys anymore."

"Well, at Pringle House they do," Grace smiled. "It's all part of the gothic experience. I love them. There's so much to imagine with keys like this opening doors. Well, as a writer, you must agree."

He made a noise of assent. "I assume you have Wi-Fi."

"Doesn't everyone?"

At seeing a stranger, and the social goings on, the black cat jumped off the windowsill and went to investigate Josh. She gave him and his belongings a quick sniff, arched her back, and let out a long hiss. Distrust glowed out of her golden eyes.

"Pandora!" Grace chided.

"Well, at least you look the part of a Halloween cat," Josh muttered. He disliked animals. He always felt nervous around them with the way they stared right through him. Like they knew something humans didn't. It was ... spooky.

Still wearing the stupid hat, all Grace needed was a broom to make the image of a witch complete.

She giggled out loud. "Yes. Pandora's very traditional. She's about the only thing in my life that is. I bet you expected a retired little old lady--a true hag."

He let the laugh escape him because she could read his mind.

"But I'm positive we have what you are looking for. Pringle House never disappoints."

"A haunted house, and true Halloween inspiration, so I can write my next bestseller." A frown formed creases on his face. "And a little R&R."

When the doorbell rang again, Grace answered the door and repeated her earlier performance for the next batch of Trick-Or-Treaters.

No one was as surprised as Josh to hear the clopping of horses' hooves on the street. "And across the street from the pharmacy, there's Pringle House," the uniformed carriage driver announced in an English accent worthy of *Oliver*. "After Josiah Henry Pringle immigrated to the United States from England, he built his home here. Charmed by the medicinal and psychological properties of the sea, he made his living in pharmaceuticals..." The clomp of hooves and rattle of the carriage lessened in the distance as it ambled away.

"Well, I've lived in harmony with all of the ghosts that have always lived here," Grace told Josh, automatically picking up the threads of their last topic. "They seem to all congregate here, watching the living. And making themselves known."

Grace laughed softly. "Listen to me, telling you what you already know! You have your own ghosts attached to you. We all do. And don't worry, if your next book is half as good as *Belladonna's Curse*, it will be fabulous!"

He grunted out thanks, thought she was one of those hippy-dippy freaks, and rubbed his temples. His head felt ready to crack open like a soft-boiled egg. After his bloody and decaying divorce, he reconnected with Maggie, an old college girlfriend who loved to write. Mainly for the sheer pleasure it gave her. It was one of the things they had in common, only Josh wrote for the local rag that made up shit about celebrities for a living. He wrote his own stuff on the side and could paper his walls with rejection slips.

Through some miracle, *Belladonna's Curse* had bulleted to number 1 on the bestseller list, not only frightening readers but reaching them, resonating with them. His brief affair with Maggie ended worse than his divorce. And his editor, Jack, had been ragging on him to come up with something even better than *Belladonna's Curse* for his next release. The fans were reaching out, giving him their own ideas. But Josh's creativity, his energy, his drive had left him. Plus, that something extraordinary didn't exist anymore...

What he really wanted was to be fucking left alone and retire. The next best thing would be to pump out another bestseller, and then take a vacation. But that didn't mean he couldn't enjoy this siren, Grace Pringle, along the way. She was all but purring like that god-forsaken cat.

Grace's lips turned upward into a smile. "Would you like a tour?"

"You bet."

Ewww...she hated guys who used that expression, Grace thought. It was so Cousin Eddie from the Griswold movies. But she needed a personal object from this guy for her spell to work, not to mention, his blood. Accepting her offer of wine, she poured two glasses in her special occasion crimson glass goblets out of the matching decanter.

The Sapphire Grape wine was nearly black and addictingly sweet. She added some dried ice on impulse, so it smoked, setting off foggy clouds in the air. Then, she grabbed a platter of cheese and crackers and some succulent fruits.

"Here we are, Mr. Fisk." She handed him the smoky concoction. He gazed at the bounty. "Wow! What's all this?"

"Service with a smile."

"How festive. Call me Josh."

"Alright then, Josh."

"What shall we drink to?"

"How about to new friends, tricks, and treats?"

"Oh, I like that."

She raised a long, peach-colored fingernail that matched her lipstick to trace the rim of her goblet, encircling it. Josh felt his stomach tie in a knot.

"Cheers." They clinked glasses.

He took a hearty swallow. "Jesus!" he exclaimed. "What kind of wine is this?"

"I call it Witch Fingers. Otherwise known as Sapphire Grape Wine. Do you like it?"

"It's very unusual."

She laughed, "Why be usual when you can be unique?" Grace sipped her wine, fixing her large eyes on him. "So, Josh, how did you become interested in writing? And writing horror at that?" She filled up his glass with more wine.

He repeated the story he always told during interviews. How he was always attracted to other worlds and realms and had a sixth sense of knowing they were there.

But the way Grace was looking so endearingly at him, as if he were the most important person in the world, he decided to tell her a little of the truth. "I was always a sickly kid," he said. "When other kids played outside, I was usually suffering from mono or flu. I became kind of obsessed with ghosts. Death really."

Grace made a sound of sympathy. "That's awful."

"I guess you think that's morbid." He helped himself to some of the cheese and crackers and some grapes. "Anyway, I grew out of it, and showed those bastard kids."

"By lifting weights, of course." She gave him a look of pure appreciation. "I don't find your story morbid at all. It's just sad."

"What about you?" This was good stuff, Fisk reasoned. He could use a lot of her information--and passion--for his new book.

"I was always drawn to the lives that the ghosts lived," Grace was saying. "It's wonderful to absorb yourself in their passions, ambitions, the paths they took in life."

"So, you're a romantic, are you?"

"I'll show you. How about that tour now?" She put her wine down, and he had no choice but to follow. After showing him the basics of downstairs, she gave particular attention to the study and library, where her Great-Grandfather Pringle's ghost roamed. He liked to smoke his trusty cigar, have his after-dinner brandy, and read *Great Expectations* aloud, fascinating Grace ever since she was a little girl. "His passion was to be an actor," she told Josh as she led him up the winding staircase. The cherry wood banister gleamed underneath their hands.

On their way up, she pointed out the family portraits that hung on the side wall. He nodded as she pointed out her great grandparents, great aunts and uncles, her parents, and siblings, and portraits from generations back. Josh barely fixed on a polite smile. He really didn't give a shit. Maggie had been the one with all the passion for research. And about almost everything. *Belladonna's Curse* had been her baby, her heart, he bristled. Where the hell had *that* come from?

If he was going to feel this needy, he might as well hit the Bahamas for a vacation.

"There are spirits all over the house," Grace told him. "But it's on the widow's walk that you can feel them so intensely."

Leading him up flights and windy passageways, they climbed up to the widow's walk. Once the door was opened, Grace went to the edge overlooking the beach and sighed in deep contentment. "Ah, can you feel that? It's wonderful." The chill waltzed all around her. Waves were picking up with the tide. The sun that was so bright and warming before was now setting. Even though, technically, it was still afternoon.

The full moon would be tonight, and she felt the anticipation bubble on her skin. She would have his body before she knew it.

"At night, you can see the glow of a candle, and hear the footsteps and sobs of ancestor Mary Pringle. Legend has it that she had a torrid affair with a sea captain, William Barrow, in 1904. Mary was only a young girl of seventeen--willful and beautiful-- when she met Barrow, at some party he had no business being at."

"Oh, a party crasher, huh?"

"Well, sort of. I believe that he supplied the shellfish for the area. But he would have rather been a pirate than a fisherman. Barrow was quite a bit older than Mary at 25 and a rakish one. He had a thirst for adventure and the hunt--of both the sea and of women. Mary had a taste for the unusual--including her taste in men. Barrow was in her every thought. After their affair, he had promised after this one sea voyage to find the treasure he knew was out there; he'd come back and marry her."

Grace paused and looked pointedly at Joshua. "Well, you can imagine what happened. He never did. Poor Mary came out here every night, sobbing and waiting for him. Heartbreaking, how she neither slept nor ate. Just waited, and sobbed, imagining if he was dead or had some horrible accident. She passed away when her heart gave out. She was still waiting..."

She sighed at the thought of Mary Pringle's broken heart.

"Yeah, well, she wasn't the first gal to fall for a bastard," Fisk announced, although inwardly, he couldn't really blame the guy. Mary Pringle must have been rather stupid to give it up so easily.

He wisely kept this opinion to himself. Being a misogynistic asshole wasn't part of his seduction skills. He had learned the hard way that the girls hated that. Besides, his mother had taught him *some* manners. Something flashed in Grace's eyes that he couldn't read. Something brutal and mysterious. Then they graced him as she approached. His heart hammered in his chest when she came close. Her perfume was intoxicating.

"Ah, but I think Mary was a woman of her time. In 1904, having an affair of any kind was unseemly for a woman. They didn't have the freedoms like women do today. Mary Pringle was a young girl, really. She could have easily become carried away when she felt that passion for Captain Barrow." Grace's elfin lips curled seductively as Joshua could only watch her mouth. "Maybe that's why Mary's ghost is still unsettled here. She wants to feel that freedom again, that heat." She ran her fingers down Josh's forearm. "Haven't you ever gotten carried away?" she asked.

His eyes locked on hers. Unable to stand it any longer, Josh's lips met Grace's and kissed her. Enthusiastically, she embraced him, met the kiss, and chomped down hard on his lips with her teeth. "Oops, sorry." Josh only laughed and flinched backward. After seeing the blood pour out, he grabbed a handkerchief and pressed it to his lips.

Jackpot, she thought.

"No apologies!" Josh made a sound of pleasure and kissed her again. Screw the pain, he thought. This time, Grace grabbed his hair and deepened the kiss. Grappling with clothes, they sank down in the Widow's Walk, unable and unwilling to wait. Soon, they were rutting and grunting like animals. When they finally made it to the bed in his room, it was almost time. Grace shivered in delicious anticipation for casting the rest of the spell.

"Now, that's what I call great turndown service! My compliments to the owner!" Josh grinned as he lay beside Grace. His eyes gleamed, and he barely felt the cut on his lip or the red marks where her fingernails had raked his back. "Care to go for another round?" he winked.

Did he actually think he was charming? Grace inwardly rolled her eyes at him but purred as she rose. "No time but thank you. I needed that." She leapt from the bed in all her nudeness and ran into the hallway, a second later she returned with a Polaroid camera and snapped it in Josh's face; she waited for the picture to appear.

"What are you doing?" he asked.

"Just a souvenir for me to remember you by." She leaned over to kiss him. He licked his lips in anticipation of hers, but she pecked his nose instead. She mentioned something about wanting her wine when she left the room.

That was new. Josh was dumbfounded when the door shut, and he heard her footsteps depart. Most women wanted to cuddle and talk endlessly about their feelings. Maggie had been the *worst* on that score. What are we going to do tomorrow? Next week, next month…Blah, blah, blah. He shrugged, got up, and put on a pair of jeans and an old sweatshirt.

Setting up his laptop on the desk, he unenthusiastically banged out the story Grace had told him about Mary Pringle and Captain Barrow. Verbatim. He didn't even have the desire to add any creative touches. Or fictional accounts. As unimpressed as he was with Mary Pringle and her lover, he had to write something to make Jack and the others happy. He wanted money to coast for a while, just to shut everyone up.

And hell, Grace probably would be *ecstatic* that someone immortalized her family, Josh reasoned. Not like Maggie. He was lucky to still have his balls intact with her. He still recalled how Maggie's face had gone white with horror, then scarlet with rage when he walked into the bedroom from the shower and discovered her reading over his computer.

"What the fuck?" she demanded, stalking over to him, and punching him in the gut. "How dare you! *Belladonna's Curse* was *my* book. And you fucking stole it, word for word!" Her face went dark.

"I know what it looks like, but--"

He didn't even have the decency to look abashed or even guilty. Maggie's eyes narrowed. "But nothing! It looks like you are putting your name on the book I wrote. That's stealing!" Every feature in her face contorted in outrage as she read aloud the e-mail he had sent to his editor. Along with the standard cover letter, there was another informal, cozy one. *"Dear Jack, this novel will knock you out! Take a look!"* She clenched her jaw, and in another moment, Josh thought she might just growl like an animal.

"What? You just wanted to fuck me to steal my book?"

Josh only gave a small reflexive smile at her spew of curses. "Hon, one doesn't necessarily exclude the other."

He earned a slap across the face for that. She ranted about suing him but never got the chance. When Maggie committed suicide, Josh felt numb and then relieved. People had gathered around him, so sorry for his loss, and told him how much of a waste her death was...she'd been so talented. So passionate about writing. None of them knew how much, Josh mused. Maggie had the talent, but he knew how to play the game.

Grace shut her eyes and took a fortifying deep breath as the room spun. She gathered all her essential elements together and nearly dragged herself to her Wicca Room. Being with Josh took more effort than she allotted. Drinking half her wine in a couple of large sips, Grace felt a little better as she sat crossed legged in her sacred circle again. She focused all her efforts on concentrating on the spell, even though she wished she could just shut her eyes, curl up and go to sleep.

If she did that, she'd never wake up.

At seeing her, Pandora woke up from a curl on the sofa, and ran to rub herself all over Grace. She received a pet in turn.

"Hecate, Chief Goddess, presiding over magic and spells for good and evil and grey, hear me. To you, I pray. Hear me, your loyal servant…" The caldron that she had prepared earlier boiled madly. Soon, Grace dropped Josh's bloody hanky in the pot, adding some yellow and red jasper stones for strength and good health to her circle.

"Give me the power. Let change come. Transform my flesh, my health into another." Instantly, she threw both nightshade and sage and dandelion in to appease both sides of magic for the goddess. "Hear me, Janus, and Eos, God, and Goddess of Transformation. Grant me what I seek." Grace poured essential oils on her skin and rubbed them in her hands. Then, she grabbed the photograph of Fisk and held it over the taper candle, so it caught fire.

"Accept thy sacrifice of Joshua Fisk." Watching it shrivel in the flame, Grace threw it in the bubbling cauldron. "So, mote it be."

A hearty bang filled the room when the concoction exploded. Instantly, the power went out, and darkness enveloped Pringle House.

When the thunder-like sound filled his ears, Josh bristled. Then he groaned, annoyed, as darkness surrounded him. *What the fuck?* Rummaging around in the desk for a flashlight, he only found a box of matches. Well, he did want the ambiance of a gothic haunted house. Pringle House delivered on that score, Josh mused. Soon, the room glowed in candlelight.

But then, after several heartbeats, Josh felt downright weird. Sickly. As unenthused as he was writing this thing, now he felt a punch of malaise. Worse than any flu out there. He hurt all over, and his stomach gushed with nausea. He brought a hand to rake through his hair and heard the little laugh in the air.

Maggie? It sounded just like her, he realized, looking at all the shadows in the room. Or someone else? What had Grace said? "You have your own ghosts attached to you. We all do."

Great. If that were true. Whatever bitch was hunting him, he didn't have time for it. *Go bother some other sucker*, he sneered. When he lowered his hand from his hair, he was astonished to see clumps of the honey-colored stuff in it. His eyes crinkled. Was it the lack of lighting, or did it look like his hand was considerably smaller?

"What the--?"

The voice that came out of his mouth was odd. The pitch was higher and downright feminine! *What the fuck?* Getting up out of his chair was hell on his back for some reason. And it took all his energy to get across the room to the dresser and mirror. Jeez, he really had to quit smoking, he thought.

Once there, he saw the image of Grace reflecting back at him. What was this? A nightmare? Had he fallen asleep working?

Wake up! He shouted at himself inwardly, and vigorously rubbed his eyes. That should do it. But the image in the mirror was the same: A freaked-out Grace Pringle.

"What the--?"

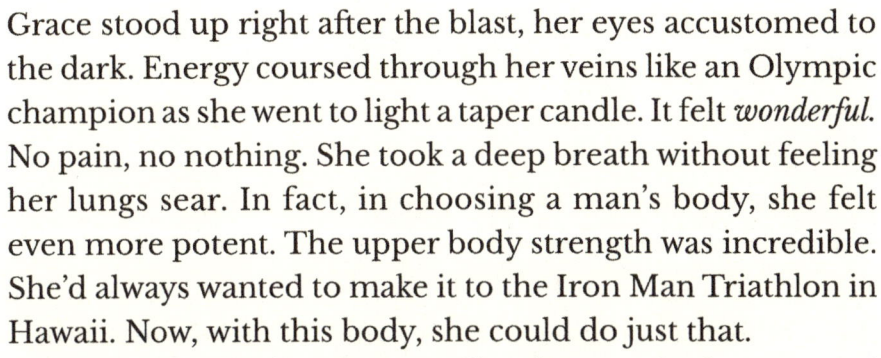

Grace stood up right after the blast, her eyes accustomed to the dark. Energy coursed through her veins like an Olympic champion as she went to light a taper candle. It felt *wonderful*. No pain, no nothing. She took a deep breath without feeling her lungs sear. In fact, in choosing a man's body, she felt even more potent. The upper body strength was incredible. She'd always wanted to make it to the Iron Man Triathlon in Hawaii. Now, with this body, she could do just that.

Pandora looked at her warily, then rushed over, and rubbed up against the new body lovingly.

"Oh, hello, baby."

They both jolted as they heard the scream. Pandora, with her feline instincts, wisely deserted the bedlam and went downstairs for some more kitty kibble and to keep her nine lives intact.

"Smart, aren't you?" Grace smiled to herself, lit a taper, and carried it to the bedroom. "Well, walking's--interesting," she murmured to herself. Having never been a man, it was something she'd definitely have to get used to.

Approaching the bedroom, she took a breath before she knocked and opened the door. "Is something wrong?" She asked when she popped her head in the doorway.

"What? What is this?" Josh's face turned various shades of purple, ending with a deep magenta. His jaw nearly hit the floor when he saw...himself... come into the bedroom. His own face illuminated by candlelight.

"Nothing."

"Nothing?" The echo was more of a growl. "Listen, lady. I don't know what your scam is here."

Watching the man struggle for words, Grace blinked and wondered how she could have kept standing for so long with that body. "Whoa, there. Take it easy. Too much excitement is not good for your health."

This body did feel downright frail. "Screw you! What the hell was in that wine?" His stomach surged, then dropped. "Witch Fingers, my ass. You...drugged me, and then what? Did plastic surgery on me?"

"Oh, come on now. Do you really believe that?"

"I could have been out for days!" He insisted. But it didn't explain how she had his body. His heart scampered in his chest, bafflement racing towards panic. "You did something." Eyes blazed with accusation. "I don't know how, just fix it. Now! Otherwise, you won't like what I'm going to do to you, and this business you've got here."

Swallowing a chuckle, Grace fixed her eyes on the apparition of a woman with dark hair, staring at Josh's computer. Her eyes were sad as she approached Josh, resting her hand on his shoulder. "That's not possible, even if I wanted to."

He shuddered at all the new information coming at him, but he felt compelled to see this through. He felt his lips form into a straight line. "Now, you listen, you screwy bitch--"

The hand on his shoulder gave him a spidery sensation that made him shiver. Maybe it was the fact that Grace Pringle was gazing at him with his own grey eyes. "You came here for R&R, and that's exactly what I've given you," Grace asserted. "You're filled with regrets and recriminations. Joshua Fisk, you have an amazing opportunity to rest your demons before your death."

"What demons?" He went white.

"For starters: Maggie, stealing her book--her life's blood, your so-called family, your wife..."

"Oh, I see. They all put you up to this crap. Well, it won't work! By the time I'm through, you'll spend a lifetime behind bars, and I'll spend it retired, whooping it up in the islands!"

"That long, hmm?" Grace commented dryly. Without another word, she left the room and let the door slam shut behind her.

He let out a primal scream and spewed a bunch of creative curses at the sound of the door finalizing the conversation. Peals of feminine laughter only made him glare around the room and grind his teeth. When he heard the distinctive crack and felt the object in his mouth, he spit it out along with a trail of blood. Oh God, he hadn't lost teeth since the Tooth Fairy put money under his Incredible Hulk pillowcases when he was little. The panic and anger restored him enough to get to the bedside phone before another bout of dizziness overtook him. Jeez, now none of his limbs could move, and he had to sit on the bed before dialing 911. The pain made him breathe in sharply before he could get the words out.

The next day, Mrs. Renfield found Joshua Fisk dead on the floor. Not long after, he was buried wearing Grace's face and her body.

Mobs of people attended her funeral, and they all wondered who the good-looking man had been to Grace Pringle as he sat along with Mrs. Renfield to mourn her.

Chapter Twelve

Devlin's Manse

BY DAEMON MANX

Profound sorrow is all-encompassing; it has a way of permeating and taking on a life of its own. It thrives, like a mold, in the darkest corners of the heart. Tragedy has a memory that cannot be purged by time. Although it can be displaced for a moment, it is never entirely forgotten. There is always a residue that lingers, like a bloodstain on the carpet, or the scar left from a wound. This is not only true with people, but for houses as well. The din of sadness can never be completely hushed in dwellings that have witnessed such atrocities. Although the presence of children can pacify the pain, for a moment ... there is always a residue.

Devlin's Manse remained vacant for a lifetime. It's dark walnut floorboards, ornate twelve-foot ceilings, and elaborate cherry wood mouldings spoke of a pride in architecture long since forgotten. The three-story Victorian design, popular during the 19th century, stood sentinel over 1500 acres of real estate. Rice and tobacco were the till of the land around the time, James "Old Buck" Buchannan was taking office. It had been decades since voices graced the halls of Devlin's Manse. Longer still since the resonating echo of children's laughter had danced upon its walls. But now ... something was stirring.

"Try to find me, James," the voice of a young girl drifted from behind a second-floor closet door. She pressed her face against the cracked opening to scan the room. The dresser, the chest of drawers, and the large four-poster bed remained undisturbed. Mary listened as the sound of approaching foot falls drew near, she retreated to the back of her hide-a-way, nestled between the old coats.

"Mary, where are you?" The boy rushed into the room, dropped to the floor, and pushed the duvet aside to search beneath the bed. An army of dust bunnies was all he found. Listening, he rose to his feet and noticed the door to the closet. He prepared to make his way toward it and was alerted by the muted sound of stifled laughter. It crept from the confines of the closet and greeted him where he stood. Quietly, he tiptoed across the floor and placed his hand on the knob. He held his breath and yanked the door open in one fluid motion.

"I've got you!" he shouted.

Mary screamed, but the look on her face was pure delight. "Oh James, you cheated!"

"No," he said. "I heard you laughing all the way downstairs."

Mary darted from the closet and took a running leap onto the bed; the thick comforter and array of goose-down pillows nearly swallowed the girl's small frame. "Don't you just love our new house?"

James followed her lead and dove headfirst after her. Rising to his feet he proceeded to jump in place. The tired old springs launched him higher with each pounce, but never came close to propelling the boy to his target of the ceiling. "What do you think?" he replied with a grin.

Mary crinkled her brow. "I think you shouldn't have your dirty shoes on the bed. That's what I think."

James took one final leap at the ceiling then fell onto his back. "Yes, Mom!" He let out a dramatic exhale.

Smiling, Mary leaned over and pecked him on the cheek. "You're it!" she cried, then leapt from the bed and darted out of the room.

"Ewww!" James wiped the kiss from his cheek. "Disgusting." He rolled from his position and took off in pursuit after her.

The room, silent once again, held onto the image like a photograph. The imprint on the bedspread remained for a moment ... if only for a moment. Then the open closet door let out a tired creak, and slowly swung shut.

The lush front lawn of Devlin's Manse sprawled for acres and reflected the care and time the new residents had invested in taking back the property from the grips of neglect. Magnolia trees adorned the grounds with a wooden swing suspended from the lower branch of one of the specimens. James pushed Mary while dappled sunlight played across her face as she arced back and forth.

"Higher," she called to the boy, who was more than happy to oblige and answered with another hearty push.

The scent of sweet magnolia blossoms filled the air. Although the trees were in full bloom, many discarded flowers littered the lawn, no doubt recent victims of the strong coastal southern breeze. Before taking flight on the swing, Mary had chosen the perfect bloom and tucked it delicately behind her right ear. The white pink of its petals danced like a flickering ember against the trailing flame of her long red hair.

"Higher, James. Higher," she called again.

"Aren't you tired yet?" he asked.

"No, but it's your turn. We can switch."

James allowed the swing's momentum to slow and then come to a halt. He grabbed the rope and helped Mary off.

"Hop on," she offered.

"That's all right," he replied, then took a seat in the shade with his back against the large tree. Mary sat next to him and lifted another blossom from the ground.

"Isn't it just perfect?" she asked, looking up at the house.

The once forgotten Manse stood before them in all its glory, revealing not even a glimmer of the years of disregard. The peeling paint, the rotting wood, all given a reprieve. Once broken windowpanes now refracted the noonday sun and suggested that the estate was healthy once again ... or perhaps, only in remission.

Mary twirled the flower within her fingertips and allowed her gaze to follow the large pillars that supported the second-floor balcony, and then up the front of the dwelling to the smaller third story windows. It happened in a flurry, one of the curtains was momentarily pushed aside and then returned to its position.

"Did you see that?" She jumped to her feet, dropping the blossom.

"See what?'" James looked up puzzled.

"At the window upstairs!" she shouted. "There's someone up there. I saw it!"

"What are you talking about?" he asked. "There's no one up there."

"No, James. I saw it." Her voice rose to a shrill. "The curtain moved. I saw it!"

"Well," he said, rising to his feet. "Let's go see then. But I'm telling you. There's nobody up there." James made his way across the lawn toward the house and Mary reluctantly followed.

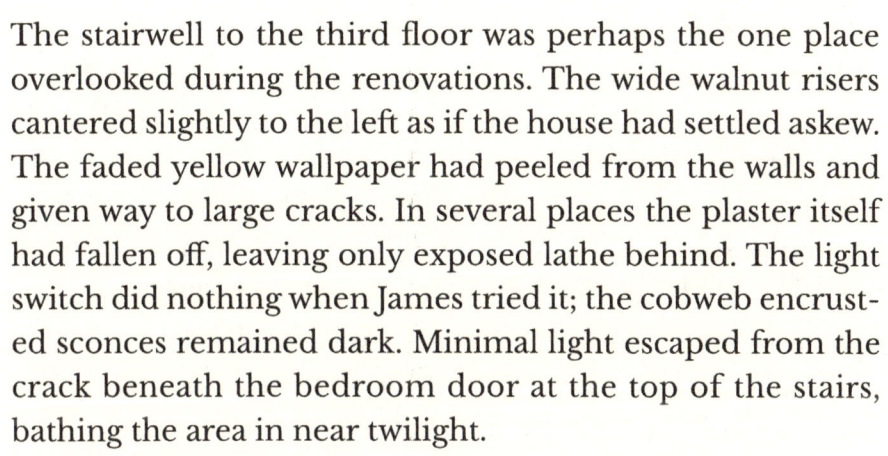

The stairwell to the third floor was perhaps the one place overlooked during the renovations. The wide walnut risers cantered slightly to the left as if the house had settled askew. The faded yellow wallpaper had peeled from the walls and given way to large cracks. In several places the plaster itself had fallen off, leaving only exposed lathe behind. The light switch did nothing when James tried it; the cobweb encrusted sconces remained dark. Minimal light escaped from the crack beneath the bedroom door at the top of the stairs, bathing the area in near twilight.

"I'm scared," Mary said as she crouched behind James.

"Don't be afraid. It's nothing," he reassured her. "You trust me, don't you?"

"You know I do. But I'm telling you, I saw something."

The stairs creaked and groaned as if they had not borne weight in far too long. Step by step, they made their way to the top, stealthily inching their way to the threshold. When he was within reach, James extended his hand to grasp the knob and then hesitated.

For a moment, the idea that Mary had seen something struck him as possible, and then he was sure of it. Something was lying in wait for them on the other side of the door, something that meant them grave harm.

He laughed at his foolishness, then grabbed the knob.

An icy cold shock seized his hand and froze it from the fingertips to elbow. He released his grasp at once and tucked his hand in the crook of his arm.

"What's wrong?" Mary gasped.

"It's ... it's cold." Confusion washed across his face.

He removed his hand from under his arm and examined it for a moment, it was fine. He reached for the knob again, but Mary pulled him back, nearly sending them both tumbling down the stairs.

"It's okay," he said. "It just surprised me, that's all."

His voice wavered as if he wasn't convinced, but Mary allowed him to continue and James touched the knob with his fingertips, then took it in his grip.

"Mary, the knob is freezing ... like ice." He tried to turn it to the right and then left but it would not so much as jiggle in the jamb. He let go and turned to her. "You feel it."

"I don't want to. Let's go, James. I'm scared."

"It's all right. It's just c—" But Mary had already descended the stairs and entered the hallway.

He tried the knob again, but it wouldn't budge. He pressed his shoulder against the door to find it just as cold as the knob. After a moment of futility, he gave up the attempt, and descended the stairs after her.

Evening floated in as if on gossamer wings. The sweet fragrance of Jasmine and Magnolia filled the air as the last streaks of violet gave way to even deeper shades of indigo. Fireflies rehearsed their ritualistic dance of light, as a chorus of crickets provided the soundtrack. They sat on the front porch of Devlin's Manse, soaking in the scents and sounds of summer.

"Are you mad at me?" she asked, her long nightgown hanging to her bare feet.

"Don't be silly. Why would I be mad at you?"

"I got scared and left you," she said, still shaken by the afternoon's events. "What if you..." Her voice wavered on the verge of tears.

"Hey, nothing happened, silly. I told you it would be okay." He reassured her. Although he wasn't convinced it had been entirely 'nothing,' he attempted to sound brave.

"I saw something," she repeated

"There's probably a draft up there that blew the curtains. That's why it's cold."

"James," her voice nearly drowned by a cacophony of crickets. "It's August."

After an uncomfortable pause, he leaned against her shoulder to shoulder. "Hey, I don't know, but I'm sure there's a good reason," he waited a moment, then added, "but I'm going to find out."

"Let's just leave it alone, I don't want to get in trouble."

His dark eyes looked into her green as the first stars arrived in the August sky.

"We're gonna be fine," he replied.

"Do you promise?"

"I promise."

"Okay, but I don't want to go up there again."

"You won't have to." He reached to grasp at a firefly that was too quick, and it easily slipped through his fingers.

Morning sunlight, filtered through linen window treatments, cast the sitting room in a dusty mellow glow. Dapples of amber diamonds reflected off the large chandelier suspended in the center of the ceiling while Mary sat at a small table set for a tea party of three: herself, an oversized teddy bear, and her baby doll, who lay tucked within her arms. She was hardly aware of the far-off voices of the grownups as she focused her attention on her baby, doting on his every need.

"That's my boy," she said. "I love you, Christopher."

Mary pretended to feed the little one his morning bottle while teddy sat watch with a dainty cup of faux tea set on the table in front of him. The distant sound of hammers and saws lofted in from somewhere in the house but were unnoticed as Mary allowed herself to be as lost as only a child could be, forever frozen in playtime. Thoughts of yesterday's fright had been set aside as if they had never happened. Mary raised the doll to her shoulder and pretended to burp him.

"Momma loves you so much," she beamed, a smile of pure joy spread across her face.

While Mary was submerged in teatime, James focused on a mission of his own. The basement of Devlin's Manse was dank and musty; a combination of scents filled the air: pickled fruit and dried meat mixed with mold, decay, and the dust of a thousand years. In the furthest corner from the stairs where James stood, sat a stack of old tables and chairs, covered in filth. A clutch of wooden boxes occupied the opposite corner and appeared to wear an equal amount of time and grime. Neither of which were the focus of his mission; what James was after lay under the stairs. He lit the candle he had taken from the kitchen cupboard and navigated his way through the dark.

Tiny creatures scurried back into their holes, and large black spiders curiously watched their new visitor. James was oblivious to his audience and to the sounds of construction from above. He made his way to the alcove beneath the stairs and halted when his foot struck something big and heavy. He directed the candlelight onto the object he had stumble upon and discovered a large chest. An ancient padlock adorned the front, holding the lid and the contents in place. He fumbled with it for a moment. It was a thick key-lock, caked in rust. On the very top of the chest set into the wood sat a rectangular piece of metal with an engraving on it. He wiped the dust away with his palm and revealed one word, the name 'JED' spelled out on the plaque. James tugged at the lock and wondered who Jed might be. He imagined one of the previous occupants who had left the chest behind. And despite his best effort he was unable to pry the lock open, which was fine, he had come to the basement in search of one key; now he would need to find two.

He raised the candle to the wall above the chest and slowly moved it to the right until the light revealed a masonry nail that had been driven into the wall. No key hung from the first nail, and he continued to search the darkness. There was no key to be found on the second nail he came across, or the third, and James's heart fluttered quick within his chest. He had been sure he would find what he was looking for. *They were down here.* He thought.

Creeping shadows suffocated the candle's reach like a wet blanket, sweat glistened on his brow despite the basement's sudden chill, and gooseflesh broke out on his arms and the nape of his neck. James found it increasingly difficult to swallow and anxiety quickly escalated into panic. A thought flashed in his head, *please don't let me find it.* He was overcome by the agonizing feeling that locating the key would be a very bad thing. He held the candle closer to the wall and revealed the fourth nail as a foggy plume of breath escaped into the icy air.

He was relieved for a fleeting moment, then a soft rustle and the sensation of movement jarred him back. James had no idea if the noise had come from across the room or right behind him. His frozen heart entered his throat and stagnated. Unable to move a muscle, he listened, then he heard it ... *thump!* It was followed by another, and then another.

James nearly screamed, then realized it was the thrum of his own pulse. Still, he waited, anticipating the repeat of the rustle, and half expecting something to seize him in the darkness. When neither happened, he wrestled the last vestige of his courage and extended the candle further into the dim. The umbra reluctantly retreated as the light fell across the stone, revealing the fifth and final nail. A single brass key reflected the flame like a lighthouse beacon. *Death lies upon these rocks.* Every nerve in the boy's body screamed for him to leave, to forget the key and abandon his search. *Whatever you do, don't touch it.* James stared at it, hypnotized by the dancing image of the candle on its shiny surface.

Last chance, boy; leave now while you still can. A voice that sounded exactly like his own, beckoned from somewhere in the dark. James let out a strangled cry, spun about on his heels and ran like a banshee up the old wooden staircase. Slamming the door behind him, he checked the lock and then made his way to the kitchen; he returned the candle to the cupboard and set off to find Mary. He made his way to the sitting room where he knew he would find her and tried his best to push all thoughts of the cold dark basement to the side. At least, that's what he should have done. Unfortunately, it was too late for that, and James remained where he was, reached out his hand, and took hold of the key.

A sharpened spike of pain penetrated his head like an ice pick; a concentrated pressure behind his eyes caused them to water and blur. The internal sound of muted jackhammers filled his ears and made him sick. *It must be the mold*, he thought, then shoved the key in his front pocket and made his way to the stairs. The fresh air from the first floor greeted him and helped clear his head slightly. James closed the door behind him and forced the experience to the back of his mind; forgotten was the fear, the sensation, and the voice. Not only this, but also forgotten, was any thought about the chest.

"Rock a bye baby, on the treetop," Mary sang to her doll. With just a hint of a tear in her eye, she pretended it was Christopher's nap time as she rocked him to sleep.

"When the wind blows, the cradle will rock." Her mind wandered to a vision of a time when she might rock her own child to sleep.

"When the bough breaks..." She held Christopher tighter, as James closed the basement door.

"The cradle will fall." Mary snuggled the doll and inhaled deeply, reminded of a smell that could only be baby, the scent of the skin, the warmth of the body.

"And down will come baby..." The tears welled up in the corners of her eyes.

"Cradle and all." The crystals in the chandelier began to chime as they lightly started to sway and strike against one another. The China cups and saucers shimmied across the table and teddy was thrown from his chair. His lifeless eyes gazed up accusingly at Mary. She drew the doll closer and shot to her feet, tipping her own chair in the process. Then the house started to shake on its foundation; the thunderous crash of heaving timbers sounded as if the place were being ripped apart. Suddenly, the China was thrown from the table and smashed against the wall. Tiny shards rained down on Mary and caught in her hair.

She screamed and pulled the baby in with a life-or-death grip. A moment later James exploded into the room, rushed to her side, and took her in his arms. The tremors continued for a moment longer, then subsided. The chandelier and its many crystals continued to pendulum, emitting a sickly-sweet calliope reverberance.

"Shh, it's alright," he tried to comfort her. "It's over now."

The room slowly settled, and the uproar was replaced by silence. Fine plaster particles, drifted in the air and gave the sunlight a faded feel. Mary continued to sob, James remained holding her, and Teddy closed his reproachful eyes.

The seismic anomaly that interrupted Mary's lullaby had been isolated to Devlin's Manse. The stairwell leading to the third floor had taken the brunt of the damage. The already cantered stairs now listed hard to port. Large fractures were evident in all the walls, and chunks of plaster littered the landings. The ceiling bowed and threatened to give way at any moment. The door to the bedroom was buckled in its frame; frigid air escaped from beneath the threshold and through the keyhole. But, this too, was forgotten.

―――◆○◆―――

Childhood solely has the unique and uncanny ability to distort time. The clock holds no dominion over this phase of life. It is childhood that is the master, and in command of either passing the summer in the blink of an eye or allowing a cold rainy morning to last an eternity. It freezes or it burns, it stands still, or it flies by, there is no in-between for children ... In the end, however it is perceived, it is only missed when it is gone-like childhood itself.

―――◆○◆―――

The morning sun gave way to afternoon showers. Low lying storm clouds rolled in off the Atlantic coast and blanketed the state. Periods of thunder and lightning sporadically occupied most of the day. It blocked out much of the ambient noise within the house and the constant drumming of the overflowing gutters was both disturbing and hypnotic.

Devlin's Manse had grown dark and cold. A chill had invaded like a predator and now had a strong foothold on the estate. Mary lay in bed with a thick blanket wrapped around both her and the doll.

The pain in James's head had returned with a vengeance, the ache in his temples and behind his eyes had intensified to a throbbing roar; he found it impossible to think. The constant throng of the rain made him nauseous. He had just closed his eyes and started to drift off from his position in the large armchair, when he smelled it.

At first, the faint aroma of burning wood; the distant smokey taste of hickory touched his senses, but he barely registered it. Then, it slowly increased and intensified; it crept up and overwhelmed him.

James coughed from somewhere in the fog of dreamland as his lungs filled with choking black smoke. He finally opened his eyes and was blinded. The room was a dark grey cloud. The house was on fire. Raking in a deep lungful of toxic smoke, he violently retched and fell to the floor. He struggled and clawed his way to the bed where Mary lay.

"Mary," he croaked, his voice barely registered a whisper.

Sirens assaulted his ears as hammers sounded at his temples. Outside, the rain beat relentlessly against the windows. From somewhere came the high-pitched sound of crying.

Mary's crying. He thought for a moment. But that wasn't exactly right. The crying wasn't coming from in the room, it was coming from inside his head. It wasn't Mary's voice either, it was the tormented wail of an infant.

I'm dying. He thought, as darkness overtook him. His final reflection, *I have to save the baby.*

The world was eclipsed; it floated on a shroud of shadows, deafeningly silent, glaringly dark, and sweetly bitter. It lumbered along on a dead slack tide, then was violently wrenched back by the suffocating rip. All the while, the rain continued, and Devlin's Manse retreated like a sleeping viper.

First, there was a push, then a tug, and then a shake.

"James, wake up."

James woke to find himself face down on the floor with Mary standing over him. "Wake up, wake up!" she yelled and shook him even harder.

"James, WAKE UP!"

Soupy disorientation impeded his perception. He struggled to hold onto the memory, aware for a moment of sound, and then movement; he recalled the smell of smoke, and then remembered the...

"...fire..." the words were barely audible.

He stirred, opened his eyes, then rolled onto his side and coughed uncontrollably.

"James." Mary tapped him on the back.

After a long while the fit passed, and the fog in his head dissipated. Alarmed and confused, he looked around and attempted to pinpoint the source of the blaze, only to find the room clear and cold. The marching band between his ears continued its assault, assisted by the oppressive sound of the rain, and the taste of burnt wood filled his mouth and sinuses.

"Fire," he gasped.

"James, what happened? Are you alright?" Mary asked, helping him to sit up.

He scanned the room again and found no sign of smoke, although he could smell it on his clothes and taste it on his lips. "The house was on fire," he said. "The room was filled with smoke."

"You must have been dreaming. I was right here, there wasn't any fire. Did you fall or something? You don't look good at all."

"I don't feel so well," he said, rubbing his head. "It was so real. The Baby!"

They both turned their heads to the doll in Mary's arms.

"You better lay down. I'll make you some tea." She helped him to his feet and walked him over to the bed.

"Mary, there was smoke everywhere. I can still taste it and I heard a baby," he said as she touched her hand to his forehead.

"James, you're ice cold." She helped him onto his back and looked at the doll. "Let's go make some tea, Christopher," she cooed, then exited the room. Behind her, the cohesion of reality sloughed away, and the silent house began to stir, once again.

James moaned faintly as Mary entered the hallway. The lucidity of the vision was overpowering, and he succumbed to it completely. He dreamt of darkened tunnels and torches, catacombs and chains, ancient secrets, and pain. There was a baby; there was none. He dreamt of hidden doors, unthinkable acts of cruelty, of a world where all was red and bitter. He dreamt of secret rooms, bookshelves, stairways, old wooden chests, and keys ... above all else, he dreamt of keys.

For a moment he was struck by the gnawing sensation that something grave had been overlooked, then in a flash, it was gone. He stirred as the thick grey smoke sifted through the cracks in the floor, seeped out of the lower portion of the walls, and covered the floor in a blanket like a London fog. It surrounded the bed as if he were lying on a cloud. In his dreams, James pushed the large object to the side and ascended the staircase. Somewhere close, was the key.

Mary opened the door and made her way to the back of the large area in search of the tea. The aroma of various spices filled the stocked pantry. Sacks of rice, flour, sorghum, and pecans lined the floor. Jars of pickled beets, beans, peaches, squash, and rhubarb filled many of the shelves; others were lined with honey, preserves, tea, coffee, and spices. Mary reached for the tea then jumped back when something small scampered across her foot. She looked down to see the field mouse as it disappeared behind one of the sacks. She laughed and regained herself.

At first, she felt more than heard, the low distant rumble of a faraway train in her belly and on her skin. Then the jars on the shelf began to shake. Suddenly, the pantry door slammed shut, and Mary was plunged into an abyss of darkness. She pulled Christopher close, and the room came to life. Glass jars exploded onto the floor as they lost their purchase upon the shelves. Grain bags erupted their contents into the air. Mary was showered by the debris and pelted by shards of broken glass.

"No!" she screamed and shielded the baby.

The world was thrown sideways then turned upside down. The combination of darkness and din dissolved the last of her resolve.

"Stop it!" Tears ran down her cheeks and fell to the floor.

Every deafening crash ripped through Mary like a seizure.

Then, the pantry door swung outward, and it was over. She slowly opened her eyes to find no debris and no sign of disaster. The pantry was empty, the shelves were covered in a thick layer of dust. Spiders stared silently back at her, and the skeletal remains of several rodents littered the floor. Mary shook uncontrollably; the room was as cold as an icebox, and she could see her breath. Outside, the rain was ceaseless ... inside, the memories came flooding back.

Mary stepped out of the pantry into the kitchen to find the cabinets gone. The table and chairs had vanished; the pots, the pans, China, and flatware, as if they never were. The room looked as if it had aged a hundred years. The flooring was missing in spots, pieces of the walls had fallen and much of the ceiling had given way.

Her cries hitched in her chest and Mary began to hyperventilate. Every breath shuddered in her lungs as insanity took control. Her tears fell like the rain.

"C ... Ch ... Christoph ... er ... r." She looked down to find his porcelain face had been replaced by bone, a small infant's skull wrapped in a tattered moth-eaten blanket. Empty sockets stared blindly into nothingness, a skeletal grin frozen in time.

Mary screamed and the perimeter of her vision shifted from grey to black; she fell to the floor in the middle of the old, abandoned kitchen.

As if transported from another world, a table phased into existence. It was followed by a set of chairs that faded into view. The ceiling re-materialized, along with the walls, and then the floorboards. Cabinets suddenly hung in place; pots appeared on a wood-burning stove. Everything looked as it had once been. But somewhere in time ... a baby is crying.

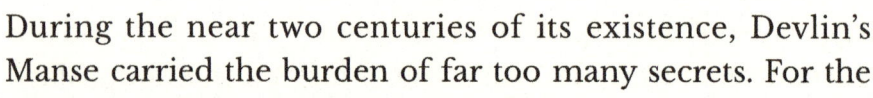

During the near two centuries of its existence, Devlin's Manse carried the burden of far too many secrets. For the greater part, it remained silent; however, some secrets were just too hard to stifle.

In 1827, Montgomery Devlin commissioned a team of architects to design an estate that would sit upon the family's 2000 plus, Charleston acreage. After two years of scrutiny and careful revisions, construction began in the spring of '29. Tradesmen and laborers were hired for no longer than two months, at which point they were terminated and replaced by an entirely new crew. It was Devlin's intention that no single worker would know all the secrets his estate would hold.

An elaborate tunnel system was constructed around the preexisting subterranean caverns. Dark passages, blasted out of the clay and bedrock, led from the main house throughout the property. Torches and lanterns illuminated the dark halls beneath the Manse.

The house itself was a 19th Century wonder of design. Walls that pivoted on fulcrum levers revealed hidden stairwells and secret rooms, virtually invisible to the naked eye. Faux floorboards gave way to trap doors, bookshelves could be moved to expose passageways, if one knew the exact pressure point.

Montgomery wasn't exactly a southern gentleman. He was a dark brooding, covetous man, with a flair for the macabre; however, he did have the capacity for love. He loved his nephew Edward, and he loved his privacy. And although there was never any evidence to support the accusations, it was suspected by many that Montgomery's passions were dark beyond comprehension. During his time as owner of the Manse, the city of Charleston suffered a plague like no other.

Shortly after the final nail was driven into the estate, the children of the area began to disappear in scores. Boys and girls, snatched from their beds in the middle of the night, were never to be heard from again. On more than one occasion, toys and pieces of clothing had been found near the plantation, but the constable was unable to lay the blame on old Montgomery Devlin, the man was as slippery as a snake.

But the lack of evidence didn't stop everyone, the servants who worked for Devlin had seen all they needed to reach their own verdict. The walls inside the Manse were not as thick as the bedrock tunnels that lay below. And as the first shots of the civil war were being fired at Ft. Sumter, Montgomery Devlin was dying his own agonizing death. He had been poisoned, presumably by one, if not all the servants. He convulsed on his bed for two days and in the end, turned blue, and was no more.

He was mourned only by his nephew Edward, who was eleven in 1861, and Montgomery's sole heir. Edward Devlin inherited the estate, all its responsibilities, as well as a mountain of debt. Fortunately, he didn't inherit his uncle's macabre propensity. Edward was a kind-hearted young boy, an even kinder young man, and proved to be a far savvier businessman than Montgomery ever was.

The war hit the south hard, and many of the plantations were unable to survive; however, great responsibility at an early age bred great adaptability in young Edward Devlin. As reconstruction began, he saw the potential that sharecroppers held, and he capitalized. He sold off parcels of the land piece by piece and converted the rice fields into a far more profitable crop, by planting pecan trees. He was able to overcome Montgomery's vast debt and take the family name out of the red. Unfortunately, the stain of his uncle's sins would never leave the Manse. A murky puissance would forever reside on the tainted grounds of the estate.

Devlin's Manse proved to have no love for children. Edward married Charlotte in 1870, and they were soon expecting their first child. It was a difficult pregnancy, and the baby did not survive the full term. One year later, they were expecting again. Charlotte gave birth to Allison in November '73. In February, she was found dead in her crib. Edward and Charlotte were devastated, and convinced it was their fault. In a way it was, had Edward never been born a Devlin his daughter may have survived.

Reeling from Allison's death, Charlotte withdrew, and Edward immersed himself in his duties on the plantation. By 1875, most of Montgomery's secrets had been obscured and forgotten. The labyrinth was long abandoned, most of the passageways and rooms had not been used in over a decade. Charlotte did favor one hide-a-way though, the third-floor bedroom, whose staircase was secretly hidden behind a row of bookcases on the second-floor hallway. It was accessible by depressing an exact piece of moulding at the baseboard, pulling the right side outward, and revealing the stairs to the third floor. Without knowledge of the staircase and the pressure point, the passage was undetectable. Charlotte spent most of her time in the hidden room, mourning Allison in quiet reflection.

Time slowly pacified the worst of the pain, and once again Charlotte was with child. She remained in bed on the third floor during the entire pregnancy, determined not to exert any undue stress on the baby; Edward doted on her every need. In 1879, Charlotte died in childbirth; a year later Edward died of a broken heart. Their newborn son would inherit the estate; the Manse, the land, the anguish, and the secrets ... it all belonged to Jed.

Lucidity slips, there is a bright blinding light, her vision momentarily seared out of focus. White-hot fades to dull yellow and she is looking at a summer sky with the sun shining on her face. There are people gathered nearby. She feels the presence of her family but cannot make them out until he lifts the veil.

It's her wedding day. The front lawn of the estate has been set for the occasion. The guests are seated in white chairs and her parents occupy the very first row. She stands beneath a trellis decorated with roses and magnolia blossoms and thinks, *I was happy*, then leans in to be kissed, perception slips again.

She senses the feeling of being carried weightless, blissfully in motion. Images vanish, a bookcase, the stairs, a bedroom, the chimney.

For a moment she thinks, *we have to wake up*. Then, she is back on the front lawn, she is being kissed.

"I love you, Mary," he says.

She looks into his eyes, "I love you, Jed."

The roar inside her head was deafening; hammers, pickaxes, and myriad implements of torture wicked away at her equilibrium, as the odor of decay filled her sinuses. Slowly, the shroud of unconsciousness receded and gave way to the relentless pounding of the rain.

Mary opened her eyes and attempted to focus on her surroundings. The desiccated corpse of a spider lay inches from her face, long dead, and sprawled turtle-like on its back. Then she remembered falling, she had been in the kitchen. She lifted her head and gasped; the room looked ancient and forgotten, long since abandoned and bathed in a hazy miasma as if not entirely there; almost as if she were looking through a—

"My veil," she said, and lifted a hand to her face only to find nothing, then slowly her vision cleared. Mary reached for her doll and pulled it close.

"It's okay, baby. Momma's here," she said, looking him over. "Fit as a fiddle."

Mary rose to her feet and the floor shifted beneath her. Then the room brightened, a polychromatic aura flashed against every surface. Suddenly, cabinets appeared on the walls; the pots, the pans, and the wood-burning stove materialized, and the room returned to the way it had been. Prismatic light diamonded on every surface; rubies, sapphires, and opals cotillioned before her eyes. Mary buried her face against the doll to shield them both from the horrible vision.

Creeaaakk!!!

The thunderous concussion jolted her back into the moment. Mary jumped as her vision of the kitchen shifted once again; she stared in disbelief at the throng of people standing before her: workmen attacked one of the walls with steel bars and sledgehammers, a woman wearing men's clothing held a roll of papers in one hand and a ball of light in the other. Mary tried to move as two men pushed a cart toward her, but was unable, then the cart and the men passed through her as if she wasn't there.

Her stomach somersaulted and the world turned grey; Mary pulled Christopher tighter and screamed, "This isn't real!"

A blinding flash of blue-white-blue, assaulted her perception, followed by a heavy clap of thunder, and the kitchen returned to normal. The men were gone, the woman was gone, the strange light had even vanished, and for a moment, everything appeared to be calm. All except for the rain, which was relentless, but it dulled in comparison to the din of insanity.

"James!" she screamed. "We have to get out!"

Panic set Mary in motion. As she ran from the kitchen the strange light returned behind her, but she didn't dare look back. Shallow breaths raked through her lungs but provided little oxygen and one clear thought hammered into her head with certainty, *if we don't wake up, we are going to die. Oh James, please wake up.*

She sent him a mental bullet.

"WAKE UP!"

James was catapulted out of sleep and nearly thrown from the bed. He woke to find the room frigid with a thick ground fog enveloping the floor. He shivered; thick plumes of condensation escaped from his lips. "Mary. Where are you?" he screamed, scanning the room.

"Mary, we have to get out of here!" James took to his feet and ran.

He tore through the hallway, rounded the corner, and nearly passed out as his vision blurred and shifted. The walls, doorways, and bookshelves disappeared, leaving only bare studs and old insulation where they had been. He stopped and stared at a section of ancient pipe, running through an ancient chase way, fastened by ancient fittings. A man appeared at the end of the hallway who looked to be operating a drilling machine of some sort. James ran to him, but the man vanished moments before he reached him.

The house lurched and started to shake once again. The floor jumped and the walls began to crumble, plaster fell from the ceiling in large sections, and the timbers buckled then splintered all around him.

"Mary!" he screamed, just as she rounded the corner at the end of the hall.

"There's something wrong with the house, it's trying to kill us!" She grabbed his arm and turned to run. "We have to leave!"

James pulled her back to him and suddenly ... he remembered what he had forgotten. He reached into his front pocket and pulled out the key. "We need to get to the third floor. I'm not sure how I know, but I do. If we can make it to the bedroom, we will be safe."

Mary looked at him and remembered as well. "Let's go," she agreed.

A large beam moaned in distress above their heads, then crashed to the floor inches from where they stood. James took off down the hallway pulling Mary with him. Sections of plaster and splinters of wood were thrown at them like shards of shrapnel as they made their way through the gauntlet of debris. Mary shielded Christopher from the brunt of the onslaught as dust and detritus rained down on them from every angle.

Finally, they arrived where the staircase had been, only to find it replaced by a wall-sized bookcase. James fitted the tip of his shoe into a small notch in the baseboard and pressed firmly. There was a loud clunk, then he placed his hands on the right side of the case and pulled outward. The bookcase slid away easily, revealing the concealed stairwell.

"How did you...?" She looked at him

James stared back at her with eyes that had glazed over, his face was as white as death and his lips had turned a cold dark blue. "I'm not sure," he said, a foggy plume of breath escaped into the air.

The stairs tilted before them and revealed the numerous missing risers since last they saw it. The walls and the ceiling began to buckle and fold inward. Ice and frost spread out in crystal tendrils before them. Mary pulled Christopher closer, and his tiny fingers grabbed onto her dress.

Cautiously, they navigated the staircase, while Devil's Manse did its best to stop them. An earth-moving tremor ripped through the narrow passage, raining larger sections of plaster over them. Then the floorboards under their feet began to give way as they made their ascent.

James wrapped his arm around Mary and lifted the key to the lock just as the bottom stairs splintered and were replaced by nothingness.

"Hurry, James," she cried through lips that had turned dark blue.

More stairs were pulverized behind them.

"The house doesn't want us here," he said as he slid the key into the lock.

"James," she said. "I love you. I always will."

Christopher coughed and James turned the key.

"I love you too ... both of you."

For a moment, the door was there, and then it vanished. The world exploded in a blinding blue pulse and the last of the stairs shattered beneath their feet. The past, the present, and the future, fused together into one existence ... and it was summer once again. She stood beneath a trellis of rose and magnolia blossoms on the front lawn. The sun shone down on her face through a veil of white lace. Jed lifted the veil and kissed her.

Charleston Gazette

August 7, 2023

The Historical Society of Charleston has been hard at work on the restoration of Devlin's Manse, which has lain vacant since the disappearance of the Devlin family in 1902. The plantation and the estate were declared historical landmarks, and construction began in the spring. Early Friday morning, after removing a large second-floor bookcase, workmen discovered a hidden stairwell, which led to a secret third-floor bedroom. The room was virtually obscured from the view of the exterior. When Jake Jefferies pried open the door to the room, he discovered a portal to the past and the answer to a century-old mystery. The skeletal remains of the Devlin family were found in their bed.

James Edward "Jed" Devlin, his wife Mary, and their infant son Christopher vanished in 1902. Foul-Play had been suspected, but no bodies were ever discovered. It is now believed that the family perished in their sleep. "It looks like the chimney flue was partially blocked and it's possible the family asphyxiated in their sleep," said Jefferies. The family is assumed to have died after being overcome by smoke inhalation. Medical Examiners from the Charleston Coroner's Office have positively identified the remains as that of the Devlin family.

Also, a large wooden chest belonging to James Edward Devlin, bearing the insignia J.E.D. was recovered from the basement. Along with family photos and a China tea set, workmen recovered a teddy bear and Mary Devlin's wedding dress in pristine condition. All items will be put on display at the Charleston Historical Museum. Mysterious reports of unexplained voices and the sound of a crying baby have baffled workers since renovations began. Perhaps closure to this century-old tragedy will finally allow the souls of James, Mary, and Christopher, some solace ... Rest in Peace.

Afterword

Profound sorrow is ageless and can never be completely forgotten for long. Not even the innocence of childhood can prevent the flood. To ease the pain, some houses hold onto their secrets as long as they can. But in the end ... there is always a residue.

"Try to find me, James," the voice of a young girl drifted from behind a second-floor closet door.

Chapter Thirteen

Flesh and Chocolate

BY JAMES G. CARLSON

Halloween night, 1992

Felix Donovan aimed the prongs of his fork at his dinner plate and impaled the first of six chicken nuggets. He was prepared to scarf all of them down in record time. Not because he was famished but because his mother wouldn't let him leave the table until he finished. So, making quick work of the breaded chunks of meat, he dug into the mac and cheese, impatiently shoveling each bite into his mouth, and swallowing without really tasting anything. He was far too excited about trick-or-treating to care about something as mundane as a family meal. Besides, he'd soon be up to his eyeballs in all sorts of candy. The only food he was genuinely interested in this evening.

"Can I go now, Mom?" he asked, his words delivered with youthful energy and eagerness.

"I said you had to eat *all* your food," his mother replied, looking at his plate.

"I did."

"Not the broccoli." She pointed to the small pile of neglected vegetables there.

"Aw, Mom."

"Don't '*Aw, Mom*' me. That was literally the only healthy part of this meal."

"But broccoli is sooo gross."

"A small price to pay to get out there and enjoy the holiday with your brother and your friends. So, less whining, more eating."

"He's not coming with me," stated Parker, Felix's older brother.

"Yes, he is," said his mother firmly.

"No way is that brat hanging out with Tig and me."

"Let me put it this way"—she fixed him with a stern look to match her tone of voice. "You either take your brother out trick-or-treating or you don't go anywhere tonight."

"That's bull—"

"Careful," warned his mother. "You're not going anywhere if you finish that sentence."

"Fine," groaned Parker, poking angrily at the mushy lump of cheese-coated noodles on his plate.

"All done," declared Felix around a mouthful of half-chewed broccoli.

"Okay." His mother gave an amused grin. "Go get ready."

Still chewing, Felix darted from the table, down the hallway, and thundered up the stairs to his bedroom. He threw open the closet and retrieved his Halloween box. Contained within was a new latex monster mask he had recently come across at the mall. He knew then and there that he had to have it. The price tag had pulled his mother's face into a momentary expression of doubt, but her desire to please him had won the day. He held the glorious thing in his hands now, studying the artistry of its wonderfully hideous design, admiring its black mohawk and scarred features and wide mouth of pointy teeth. It was perfect.

He emptied the rest of the items from the box: a pair of latex monster gloves to match his mask, a black robe of lightweight fabric, and a plastic jack-o'-lantern bucket for collecting candy. He had tried on this ensemble several times in the two weeks leading up to the holiday, each time gazing at his reflection in his mother's full-length mirror. Now, at last, it was time to wear it out in public. And on the most magical night of the year. He could hardly wait.

Wasting no time, he hastily donned the black robe over his sweatshirt and jeans. Carefully lowering the mask over his head, he lined up his vision with the eyeholes, all the while savoring the oddly satisfying rubber smell that came with wearing the thing. Then he fed his fingers into the gloves, bending and straightening the long gnarly fingers with his own.

"Nice costume, dork."

Felix turned in the direction of the voice to see his brother leaning against the frame of his doorway. "Shut up, Parker."

"Ready to go?"

"Yeah." Felix looked at his brother's ripped jeans, then at the grungy gray cardigan he wore over a Pixies t-shirt. "But where's your costume?"

"You're lookin' at it, pal."

"But that's just a normal outfit you'd wear any ol' day of the week."

"I'm fifteen now, Felix, almost sixteen. I can't go around in that kiddie shit anymore."

"It's not kiddie sh..." He paused for a moment, not sure he wanted to repeat his brother's foul language. "It's not kiddie stuff. It's scary and awesome."

"Whatever you say, dude." Parker ran his hand through his longish brown hair.

Seeing there was no changing his brother's mind, Felix grabbed his orange candy bucket and made for the door. But when he got there, Parker blocked his exit and snatched the bucket from his hand.

"Hey, what gives?" asked Felix, trying to reclaim his property.

"If you're comin' with Tig and me tonight"—Parker handed his brother an empty pillowcase—"— "you're collecting candy like the big boys do."

Felix nodded to his brother, happy to be accepted into the big boys' club.

"Alright, let's hit the bricks, little man."

"Stop treating me like a baby. You're only four years older than me."

"Those four years make a big difference. Believe me, you'll understand when you get to be my age."

Parker proceeded to wrap his arm around his brother's shoulders in a half-hug, half-chokehold, roughly pulling him into the hallway. But that was just Felix's older brother, always full of contradictions and mixed messages. One minute he was kind and affectionate, the next, he bullied and insulted him. An odd cycle of love and torment that proved quite confusing.

Felix and Parker headed out after saying goodbye to their mother, promising to return at a reasonable hour. Their neighborhood was your typical suburban labyrinth of safe streets populated by respectable abodes that were neither too boastful nor overly modest. The boys' mother had only managed to keep the house because of their deceased father's life insurance payout. They knew their time there was coming to an end, evidenced by the For Sale sign in the front yard, but they were determined to make the best of it until then.

When they reached the streetlight at the end of the block, they found Tig waiting for them. The streetlight had just switched on and threw its yellow vaporous illumination several feet in every direction. Tig leaned against the pole, a candy cigarette protruding from the corner of his mouth. He wore a shirt whose graphic depicted a cyborg cop serving up justice on the mean city streets. Around his head, just above his ears, was a red and white headband Felix recognized from a popular teen movie about karate. And on his feet, red and white sneakers that a character had sported in a quirky movie about time travel. Tig called himself a "film buff" and regularly rented VHS tapes from a store in the new strip mall. He and Felix's brother had their differences, with Parker's tastes leaning more toward music and girls than movies, yet the two got along surprisingly well. In fact, they'd been best friends since the third grade.

Felix didn't have a best friend. The other kids thought he was weird. But he didn't mind. That gave him more time to draw his homemade comics, read scary books, and write his own stories. That also gave him time to play in the woods, where his vivid imagination could plunge him into any number of wild, fantastical scenarios. In some of those scenarios, he even imagined that his father was still alive, and they were sharing the adventures.

"'S'up, fellas?" said Tig, still pretending to smoke the candy cigarette.

"Hey, Tig," Parker replied.

Tig looked at Felix. "Didn't know you were comin', little dude."

"My mom made me bring him." Parker shook his head, sighing.

"It's cool," he told his friend. "I don't mind." Then his eyes returned to Felix. "Badass costume."

"I don't know who's more of a dork," said Parker to Tig, "you or my weirdo brother."

"You know you love me." Tig leaned forward and made kissing sounds with his lips.

Parker pushed him away, laughing. "Fuck off, man."

Felix couldn't believe his brother used the f-word. But he was in the big boys' club now. He couldn't tell his mother. Being part of this sacred circle of three meant no snitching to parents, no matter what. Besides, he'd experimented with swearing, quietly, in the privacy of his room. But each time, he had thought of his mother and instantly felt guilty.

"Where are we gonna start?" Felix asked his brother.

"Oh, we're not trick-or-treating here," answered Parker. "We're going over to River's Fork where the rich people live. They hand out big candy bars and other cool shit."

"Yeah," Tig chimed in, "none of that bite-sized crap that just teases the tastebuds. I actually heard one of the houses over there passed out fifty-dollar bills instead of candy last year."

"That's the stupidest thing I've ever heard," said Parker. "Who the hell would pass out that kind of money to a bunch of kids?"

"Chill out, man. It's just what I heard. Damn."

Felix looked at his brother with worry. "That's pretty far from here."

"It's less than two miles if we take the train tracks and then cut over and walk the fishing trail beside the river."

"You wanna go in the woods? At night? In the dark?"

"Sure." Parker shrugged. "Why not?"

Felix nodded as if his brother had offered a perfectly reasonable argument as to why they should embark on this perilous journey. After all, he was an official member of the big boys' club. Had to act grown-up, respect the code, even if he didn't fully understand it. That's how Felix suspected most people matured, anyway—they pretended to be grown up until they became real adults. But, in truth, he didn't feel grown up at all, which was fine. He enjoyed being a kid. Loved it, really. But he also wanted to be included in events involving cool teenagers like Parker and Tig. As far as Felix was concerned, those two were about as cool as you could get.

Strolling out of the neighborhood, they lost daylight fast as the sun's fiery crown ducked below the horizon. It was a crisp, cool evening, and the soft breeze carried just a hint of straw bales and cinnamon. Ideal for Halloween. Felix examined the delightfully macabre decorations in people's yards. Spiderwebs made from cotton stretched from branch to branch throughout the trees and bushes. Big screaming skulls. Zombie arms reaching out of the ground. Skeletons dangling from trees. Tombstones. Coffins. Some houses even went so far as to use fog machines and spooky sound effects.

For Felix, there was no better night of the year.

"How are we gonna see on the tracks and in the woods?" Tig asked. "It's getting kinda dark."

"Got it covered." Parker handed the other boys glowsticks.

Bending the plastic casing and shaking the liquid inside, Tig's stick began emitting a sickly green glow. "Cool."

Felix and Parker did the same.

Holding their glowsticks, the boys ran through the damp grass by the cemetery, scrambled up a slippery embankment to the train tracks, and started toward River's Fork. While Felix and Parker stepped carefully over the shifting ballast stones and cross ties between the rails, Tig ran ahead and began skipping from tie to tie while singing a song Felix didn't know.

"Thanks for bringing me with you guys," Felix said to his brother in earnest.

"You bet, buddy," Parker responded. "Honestly, having you along doesn't suck as bad as I thought it would."

"It's weird not having Dad around this Halloween. I mean, he always came out with us, and we had so much fun together. I think he liked this holiday as much I do."

"Yeah, Dad was all about Halloween."

"I miss him, Parker."

"I miss him too."

"I hate that he's gone." Felix suddenly found himself struggling to hold back tears.

"It totally sucks." Parker reached out and tenderly squeezed his little brother's shoulder.

"What are you two buttheads doin' back there?" shouted Tig from up ahead. "Come on! Moonlight's a-wastin'!" Then, directing his gaze to the waning crescent moon above, he unleashed a loud wolf-like howl into the night air.

The brothers laughed and quickened their pace to catch up to their friend.

Fifteen minutes later, the three boys left the tracks without encountering a single train chugging along its rails. A good thing too, as getting out of the way wasn't always an easy feat. Sometimes you ended up with your back against a tree as you watched tons of linked machinery go by from several feet away. You could feel the ground shake and the mighty whoosh of air created by its motion. Other times, you were forced to step off the tracks only to find yourself ankle-deep in a swampy area. And if you were in the tunnel and a train came, you'd better haul ass in the opposite direction.

The boys trudged through some thick vegetation, getting snagged on leafless branches and tangles of old vines. Parker and Tig cursed nature. Felix, however, pulled his mask up so he could see better and then stepped through with feline grace. This delivered them to the fishing trail, a narrow dirt affair that ran parallel to the river for miles.

While Felix found these woods beautiful in the daytime, they were downright eerie at night. Something about them at that very moment sent a serious shiver through him.

"You sure this is a good idea?" he asked his brother.

"Don't be a pussy," was Parker's only reply.

Felix instantly regretted asking his question. He didn't want to be perceived as a baby, yet that was surely what he'd just accomplished.

They walked beside the dark, babbling water of the river for several minutes. Until they saw the distant glow of streetlights and heard the excited chatter of kids.

River's Fork, the wealthy section of town, was just up ahead.

Compared to the boys' neighborhood, the houses of River's Fork were mansions. Fancy vehicles occupied driveways or peeked out from three-car garages. The holiday decorations there proved grander and more interactive than those Felix had observed back in their decidedly humbler area. Animatronic monsters growled and lunged. Gnarled hands pushed coffin lids open a couple of inches to make you wonder what fearsome thing lurked inside. Dressed like a grotesque scarecrow, one overzealous homeowner stayed very still on his cross until kids approached, then jumped down and chased them through his yard. Screams and laughter filled the night. Fog machines, light spectacles, and sound effects drew the senses from all directions. A true Halloween paradise.

Felix, Parker, and Tig went right to it, going door to door and collecting treats. A few adults nearly withheld candy from the older boys on account they weren't in costume. Parker explained that he'd been tasked with overseeing Felix's trick-or-treating fun and hoped to get some candy out of the gig. And Tig argued that his ensemble was a collection of costumes, each item referencing a modern cinematic masterpiece. At this, the adults shook their heads and grudgingly dropped sugary goodies into their bags.

Before long, the pillowcase of each boy was over half full. The weight of it in Felix's hand made him feel accomplished and excited. He couldn't wait to get home and gorge himself on junk. Between the festive atmosphere and substantial candy haul, he was glad his brother had convinced him to come to this neighborhood.

That was, until two sneaky older boys came up behind him and snatched his sack of candy right out of his hand. Then the offenders sprinted down the street, laughing and hollering.

"Hey, you fuckers!" shouted Parker as he took off after the thieves. "Give back my brother's candy!"

Too stunned to give chase, Felix stood frozen for a moment. But once the shock wore off, the tears began. He removed his mask and gloves and threw them in the grass under the nearest streetlight. Then he seated himself on the curb. He didn't make a sound as twin salty rivers flowed freely down his cheeks.

Tig sat beside him and placed a hand on his back. "Don't worry, man. I'm sure your brother will get your candy. Don't tell him I said this, but he's actually kinda tough. Definitely tougher than me. Again, don't tell him I said that. I told him I know karate, which is a huge friggin' lie."

This elicited a reluctant chuckle from Felix. He smiled at Tig through the tears and snot, grateful for his kindness and understanding.

"You know," Tig continued, "Parker likes being your big brother more than he lets on. He's just too angsty to tell you himself."

Felix had no idea what *angsty* meant. Judging from context, he assumed the word was simply a synonym for teenager. "Really?"

"Cross my heart." Tig drew an X on his chest with his finger.

That's when Parker returned, breathing heavily, face red from exertion. "Lost 'em," he panted. "They took off down the fishing trail. Recognized 'em, though. Jay and Mikey Mancini."

Felix knew the Mancini brothers. They were two of the most notorious bullies in town. He'd had a few run-ins with them, and none had ended well. On one occasion, when he had taken a shortcut through an alley in town after school, he encountered them. They had pushed him against the brick wall hard enough to make his teeth ache. Then, they had taken his comic book and waved it in his face, telling him only pussies read such garbage. Finally, they had thrown the comic on the ground and urinated on it. Leaving the ruined book there, Felix had run all the way home, the occasional tear escaping the corner of his eye. He promised himself that he'd be big and strong one day. He promised himself he'd fight back.

"Let's go find 'em," Tig said to his best friend. Then to Felix: "You game, dude?"

"Fuck yeah."

"Damn!" exclaimed Tig, slapping Parker's arm. "Little man just dropped an f-bomb! He means business!"

Rising from the curb, Felix picked up his mask and put it back on. It was no longer enough to wear the monster; he needed to become the monster. Of course, he knew he wouldn't win a fight with either of the Mancini brothers, forget facing both at the same time. He was too small, too weak. But if they caught up with the dastardly candy-snatchers, he'd certainly watch Parker and Tig rough them up. And if he was lucky, he'd get to give them a good kick in the ribs once they were down.

All three boys took off down the street, the soles of their sneakers slapping the asphalt. They crossed the border separating the neighborhood from the woods and quickly located the fishing trail. That's when they circled up for Parker's instructions.

"Tig, you head back toward our area. Since the Mancini brothers live over there, they might've gone that way." He looked at Felix. "You walk the edge of the cornfield and keep a sharp eye on the woods. If you see 'em, holler for Tig and me. Don't confront them on your own." He placed a hand on his chest. "I'm gonna go farther down the trail in the other direction. Maybe they thought it'd be clever to go that way. Got it?"

Felix and Tig nodded.

Parker produced three glowsticks, the ones meant for their journey home and therefore the last on his person. "Let's all meet back here in twenty minutes at the most."

With that, the boys split up.

Using the glowing chemical reaction in his stick to see the treacherous ground, Felix moved through the woods toward the edge of the cornfield. The stalks had been severed in the recent harvest, leaving the ground between the rows strewn with big dead leaves and browning tufts of silk. He walked as quietly as possible, with measured breaths, trying not to advertise his position any more than necessary. Again, he pulled up his mask, folding the latex face over his head to better see his surroundings.

At the end of the field, he entered a dense, old-growth part of the woods where he'd never ventured before. Beneath the towering trees, portions of large roots lay across the detritus-littered ground. Hairy vines hung from the branches overhead, twisting around one another. Tall, brown weeds leaned dejectedly in the mild autumn temperatures, preparing to surrender to the chill of winter. As he went deeper into the woods and further from civilization, he came upon something unexpected—an old, crumbling stone wall about two feet high. He followed it until he arrived at something equally unexpected—a small stone hut with a thatched roof. Maybe the Mancini brothers hid inside, biding their time until the coast was clear, snacking on their ill-gotten treats. Felix knew he had to check.

There was no door, so he poked his head into the hut to have a peek around. Because the interior was too dark to see anything, he extended the hand in which he held the glowstick. Its weak, queasy illumination touched on a dirt floor sprinkled with straw, a weathered wooden bench, and a rickety-looking table with lumps of melted candle wax. And in the corner, a considerable pile of bones belonging to various birds and small animals. No sign of the Mancini brothers.

Sighing, he turned to head back the way he came. But before he could make his departure, a voice sounded from inside the hut. A dry, raspy voice that said, "Oh, a young visitor. How splendid."

With the initial jolt, Felix went rigid as much from fear as surprise. Slowly, he rotated to see who had uttered those words. Peering into the hut once more, his eyes fell on a haggard old woman sitting on the ground, her back against the stone wall. Thin strands of straight white hair hung from her scalp to brush the straw and dirt upon which she sat. Her clothes were tattered and filthy, her skin withered and gray. And she stared back at him with eyes whose pitch-black pupils were circled with irises of candy-apple red.

"Well, do come in," she continued. "Only scoundrels and the dimwitted linger too long in doorways, and you, good sir, strike me as neither."

Though afraid and uncertain, Felix didn't want to appear rude. He stepped into the hut, stopping just beyond the threshold. There he could see the woman even better, and this did nothing to put him at ease. She was quite possibly the oldest person he'd ever seen. In some ways, she looked like she should be long dead. Even more disconcerting, rusty chains ran from secure wall mounts to heavy manacles clasped around her wrists and ankles. Felix couldn't imagine who would do such a thing to an elderly person. Suddenly his fear was joined by both sympathy and confusion.

"And what might your name be, young man?" she asked, her words like brittle leaves tumbling and scraping across the quiet streets at midnight.

"Felix Donovan," he answered in a slightly tremulous voice.

"Pleasure to meet you, Felix Donovan. I'm Mary Proctor."

"Nice to meet you too, ma'am."

"And how old are you, Felix?"

"Eleven. Almost twelve."

"Oh, what a glorious age. Old enough to start acquiring the wisdom that accompanies maturity, yet young enough to still appreciate the magic in the world."

"Miss Proctor?"

"Yes?"

"Why are you chained to the wall?"

"Why, I was imprisoned here by some very bad men. A long, long time ago."

"Why did they imprison you?"

"It was a more ignorant era. Superstition and fear ran rampant through the colonies. Neither the townsfolk nor holy men understood people like me. Thus, my kind was chased down and persecuted, subjected to torturous trials. And when they were unable to execute us, they bound us not only with iron but with words from their sacred little books."

"I'm sorry that happened to you."

"Aren't you sweet?"

"Well, I should be going. My brother and his friend are probably waiting for me."

"Do stay a while longer. I've been alone for so very long."

"Okay," Felix agreed after a moment of consideration. "I guess I could stay a few more minutes."

"Have a seat." Mary gestured to the wooden bench. "Tell me about yourself."

"Not much to tell." Felix lowered himself onto the bench. "I'm just a kid."

"Very well. How about you tell me why you're in the woods at this hour?"

"I was trick-or-treating with my brother and his friend when two older boys, the stupid Mancini brothers, stole my candy and ran off. So, I went looking for 'em."

"I see. You're not only smart and polite but also brave."

"After searching the woods for a while," Felix continued, "I found this place."

"And a good thing you did, as this place is only visible to others once a year on this very night. This is a special night, after all."

"I think so, too."

"Of course, it used to be something quite different than what it is today. Something meaningful and beautiful, something magical. We gave thanks to nature. We rejoiced at life and remembered the dead. It was our sacred tradition...until the Church got their greedy, power-hungry hands on it."

"I like the way it is now."

"That's because you can feel the ancient spirit of the holiday. I can tell that it moves you."

"Yeah, I guess."

"And where are your parents, Felix?"

"My mom is at home. My dad passed away eight months ago."

"Oh, dear. Losing a loved one is never an easy thing to bear. My condolences, Felix."

"Thank you, ma'am."

"What if I were to tell you that I could bring your father back?"

Felix regarded the old woman with unveiled skepticism.

"It's the truth," she insisted. "I can bring him back for one night only. Tonight. But you must do something for me in return."

"What would I have to do?" asked Felix with a trace of doubt.

"Oh, it's nothing of any real consequence. To be free from these infernal binds"—she held up her manacled hands—"they must meet with the blood of an innocent willingly given. Only a few drops. A small price to pay when you think about it."

"You mean my blood?"

"Yes, of course. You are an innocent, aren't you?"

"I think so."

"Well then, what do you say?"

"I guess I could do that."

"Wonderful."

"What do I have to do?"

"Go to that pile of bones over there and pick out the sharpest one you can find."

Standing, Felix went to the pile of bones and rifled through them. The overwhelming smell of decay surrounding the remains made him want to retch. Soon his hand met with a short length of yellowed rib that had been snapped off in such a way as to create a pointed tip. He held it for the old woman to examine. "Will this do?"

"That's perfect," said Mary. "Now press it to the palm of your hand. Hard enough to draw blood. Then drag it across the skin to increase the size of the wound a bit."

Felix did as she instructed. Wincing, he pressed the tip of the bone into his flesh, drawing blood. It hurt as he drew it across the tender skin there. But the thought of seeing his father again made it all worth it, made it bearable. "Okay, now what?"

"Now," she said, holding out her arms, "touch the blood to my chains."

Bravely, with no small amount of purpose, Felix approached the old woman. He began reaching for her chains. But something gave him pause, like a bubble of contemplation that had floated to the surface of his mind and popped. "One more condition before I do this."

"What might that be?" She smiled, exposing a mouth of jagged, blackened teeth.

"You get my candy back from the Mancini brothers."

This caused Mary to cackle. "You drive a hard bargain, young man. But you have yourself a deal. I shall temporarily raise your father from the grave. And I shall retrieve your precious candy for you."

Satisfied with this arrangement, Felix touched his bloody hand to the rusty chains. The links seemed to absorb the crimson offering as if thirsty for it. At first, anyway. But then, after a long moment, they began to dissolve as though undone by the stuff. The boy watched in amazement as tiny particles of iron and rust fell to the ground in little piles of fine powder.

Her bones creaking painfully, Mary stood with some effort. She stretched her arms, her skin like leather left out in the rain too many times and then dried in the hot sun. Angling her face up to the ceiling of sticks and straw, she closed her eyes and entered a state of concentration. The next thing Felix knew, the hut began dismantling itself. Each stone separated from the one upon which it sat, hovering in the air several inches apart. The roof lifted off until suspended a few feet above the rest of the impossible structure. Mary then arched her back and jerked her arms. In response to her movements, the primitive building materials went flying away from them in all directions, disintegrating into rubble and dust as they went.

"Wow!" said Felix, wholly impressed with the spectacle. "That was so rad!"

Mary looked at him with her red eyes. "If you liked that, young man, you will undoubtedly appreciate this too."

Directing her gaze to the white sliver of moon in the night sky, she mumbled words in a language Felix didn't understand. But he didn't need to understand them to know they were imbued with magic. Right before his eyes, the old woman started to transform. First, her hair. The scattered strands of white dangling limply from her scalp turned into voluminous tresses of shining silver. Then her skin smoothed and healed, defying the ravages of time. Finally, her face underwent a series of changes. Her features became less bony and emaciated. Her teeth turned a healthy shade of white. And her eyes, although still candy-apple red, now possessed a mild glow that Felix found enchanting.

"What are you?" asked Felix, his voice marked by wonder.

"I was called many things in my time. Witch. Demon. Necromancer. Resurrectionist. Conjurer. Enchantress. Frankly, I don't think any of them do me justice."

"Well, I think you're pretty neat."

"How nice of you to say."

"Well, I better go now."

"I owe you a great debt, Felix," she said, "and it shall be paid. But you must know this before I bring your father back—he will not be the same man you remember. He will be but a dim light of that man, and that light will fade throughout the night. He will also be forced to feed on things you might consider unpalatable, even grisly. Alas, souls can only be pulled back and housed within a corpse for so long before being called back to the afterlife. Do you understand?"

"I think so."

"Knowing this, do you still want me to perform this favor for you?"

Felix nodded.

"Very well."

"And my candy?"

"Not to worry," she said with a laugh, "I haven't forgotten the terms of our bargain."

"Now what?"

"Now, go home, Felix Donovan, and await the arrival of your father. And your candy, of course."

"It was nice meeting you, Miss Proctor."

Smiling at Felix, she burst into a murder of crows and flew off into the night.

Felix stared at the sky through the branches overhead, watching the dark shape of the birds fly out of sight. He could hardly believe what he'd just experienced. What was more, he couldn't believe he might get to see his father again. With that thought in mind, he ran back the way he came, jumping over exposed roots and fallen trees, darting around soggy patches of earth. And he kept going until he arrived at the boys' meeting place.

When Felix came running up to the other boys, Parker instantly demanded to know where he'd been.

"I was—" Felix took a beat to rethink what he was about to say. Surely, he couldn't tell them the truth—that he'd just had an encounter with a magical person chained to a stone wall in a primitive hut. Parker and Tig would think he'd fallen and hit his head or something. "I was lookin' for the Mancini brothers and got a little turned around in the woods. That's all."

"We were worried as fuck, dude. I said to meet back here in twenty minutes, and you were gone for over an hour."

"Sorry."

"Come on. Let's get home before Mom puts together a search party to find us."

"I really am sorry, guys."

"It's okay," said Tig. "I won't get in trouble. My dad's probably half-drunk on the couch by now, watching old reruns on the tube until he passes out. He won't even notice I'm not there."

"Yeah, well, our mom is gonna kill us," said Parker.

"If you survive your mom's wrath, do you guys wanna hang out tomorrow?" asked Tig.

"You mean, me too?" asked Felix.

"Of course, man. It was kinda fun having you with us tonight."

"Tig's right," agreed Parker, "you're not so bad. For a little dork, that is."

Felix didn't answer. He simply pulled his monster mask down over his face and started walking toward the train tracks. Parker and Tig followed. None of them spoke on the way.

After a rather long lecture on the importance of not giving their mother a stroke from extreme fear and worry, the key parts expressed in a raised voice designed for impact, the boys went their separate ways. Parker stomped off to his room to sulk, as his mother made it very clear that they were grounded until further notice. Felix, on the other hand, went to sit on the front porch. He told his mother he wanted to keep the jack-o'-lantern company while its candle burned out.

On the porch, Felix mentally replayed the exceedingly strange events of the day. He stared up at the moon, wondering where Mary Proctor had gone. What's more, he wondered if she would keep her promise to him. For a moment, he wondered if she could even do what she claimed. But he'd witnessed enough to know that she was capable of extraordinary things. No, there was very little doubt in his mind that she'd deliver.

He looked at the jack-o'-lantern he and his mother had carved together. Parker had refused to participate, claiming that pumpkin carving was a lame activity for stupid little kids. Still, the angry eyes and toothy mouth with upturned corners gave it a sinister quality, and he was proud of the work they'd done. He watched the flame of the candle flicker inside.

But then something in his periphery caught his attention, prompting him to turn his head.

A dark figure shambled up the walkway.

As the person drew nearer, Felix's heart started beating wildly in his chest. His breath caught in his lungs. He recognized that face. Time and rot had altered it somewhat, but it was unmistakably his father.

She had done it! Mary Proctor had returned his father to him!

Felix stood and gave his father a closer inspection. Once covered in thick brown hair, his head now showed bald spots where locks had fallen out. The flesh of his right cheek had torn and now hung from his jaw, exposing molars and a section of jaw bone. A putrid ooze drained from his nostrils, dripping over his lips and down his chin. The color had faded from his eyes, leaving them pale and cloudy. His burial suit was covered in dirt from having clawed his way out of the grave. The buttons of his shirt had snapped off, leaving it to hang open. Where the skin didn't cling tightly to his torso, it had come away altogether. Felix not only saw some of his ribs but also the maggots and worms squirming behind them. Clutched in one of his hands was Felix's pillowcase full of Halloween candy. In the other, a sack Felix didn't recognize, its bottom wet and red.

"Hi, Dad," said Felix, descending the three steps to the walkway.

His father produced a groan in place of words. Felix assumed that was all he was capable of now. Not ideal communication, but he'd take what he could get.

Stepping forward, he wrapped his arms around his father and squeezed him tight. Still holding both the pillowcase and sack, his father returned the hug the best he could. He smelled of rot, like bloated roadkill decomposing in the summer heat, only worse. But Felix didn't care. He was too thrilled to see his father again to be revolted.

After a long embrace, Felix peered up at his father's face. "Wanna sit with me?"

His father replied with yet another groan.

Felix took his seat on the top step of the porch. His father clumsily followed and then plopped down beside him.

"Don't you just love Halloween, Dad?"

His father didn't groan this time. Instead, he extended his arm, presenting Felix with his retrieved pillowcase of candy.

"Thanks," said Felix, gladly taking his hard-earned treats.

Reaching into the pillowcase, Felix withdrew a full-size chocolate bar and peeled the wrapper open.

After watching Felix do this, the dead man reached into his bloody sack and withdrew something of his own. What he held in his hand was something that should have shocked and appalled Felix to his core. But all he'd seen and experienced that day had unburdened him of such reactions. For now, at least.

Gripping it by the hair, his father set the head of Jay Mancini on the porch beside him. Then he reached into the sack again. When he pulled his arm out, he held the head of

Mikey Mancini. Turning it upside down, he leaned forward and began gnawing hungrily on the shredded stump of his neck. He tore off strips of skin and chunks of meat, one after another, working his way up to the face.

With a shrug, Felix raised his chocolate bar to his mouth and took a big bite. As he chewed the rich, sweet, melty goodness, he looked lovingly at the man beside him. He didn't see a flesh-eating monster freshly risen from the grave; he saw his dad, the man who had affectionately raised both he and his brother, who had loved his mother and treated her well. He saw the man whose passing had left a gaping chasm in his life, and whose presence now seemed to fill that sad, empty space.

"I missed you, Dad," he said, still savoring his chocolatey treat.

Felix's father scooted closer to him and put a rotting arm around his shoulders. The dead man then turned his blood-smeared face, his cloudy eyes falling on his boy. He groaned through a mouthful of human flesh as if to return the sentiment: *I missed you too, son.*

Taking another bite of his chocolate bar, Felix contentedly sat with his father on one side and the glowing jack-o'-lantern on the other. The crescent moon hung in the sky, pale and sharp, like a celestial broach pinned to an endless sheet of dark fabric. And a black cat trotted across the street and disappeared behind a neighbor's house.

Halloween truly was the best night of the year.

Chapter Fourteen

Riding the Ghost Train

BY JACK WELLS

What is it about slipping into middle age that suddenly instills in a man the predilection for self-reflection? Why must we wait until our bodies begin to complain before we take stock of both ourselves and our deeds? How are we so ignorant of the harm we perpetrate upon those we love? That men survive the impetuousness of youth, not to mention the folly, is both astounding and incomprehensible.

These are the thoughts that accompany me as I step into the horse-drawn carriage that awaits outside of my home. The shame I carry is burden enough that my shoulders seem to ache, and I furtively glance from side to side, hoping that none of my peers are watching.

I do not wish for them to see me in this wretched state.

That I am the subject of gossip within the community is not unknown to me. No stranger to the bottom of a bottle, I have mistaken my neighbors' front door for my own on several occasions and am known to be argumentative when deep in my cups. There are many kinds of drunkards, from happy to morose; I am of the unfriendly variety.

But the haze of alcohol also served as a suit of armor, and I endured the stigma with inebriated indifference, like a stone statue unfazed by decades of inclement weather. The stares and whispers never penetrated.

Sticks and stones, as they say.

And yet, just this previous night, I crossed a threshold that had been hitherto unimaginable. In a pique of rage, I became the vilest of suburban habitants. There is a new stigma attached to me now; a new title that I will bear until the end of my days.

Abuser of women.

Was it merely the alcohol? Or has my incessant drinking unlocked some part of me that has always existed, coiled tight and waiting to strike? I would like to blame my actions solely upon the liquor-induced stupor; but that is not where the culpability lies. That I only lashed out once makes no difference. Drunk or not, I struck my wife in front of our children, and in doing so, I have created a new and fractured reality that we must all learn to live in.

She said she forgave me. As I poured the contents of each and every bottle down the drain, self-loathing pounding me like heavy waves, she swore that we could move past it. I promised that it would not, under any circumstances, happen again. That I could change. That I *wanted* to change. I made a vow to never touch another drop. And though she has every reason to distrust my words, I could tell that she believed me.

But nothing is ever as straightforward as we anticipate. Forgiveness does not equate to *tabula rasa*, and one does not harm an angel without repercussions.

And, so, I am taking a sabbatical, from work, from home. From the murmurs of the rumor mill. And from the discoloration that mars my wife's cheek. I must let the poison run its course and remove myself from any means of acquiring more. I must abscond somewhere remote.

As fate would have it, there exists such a place.

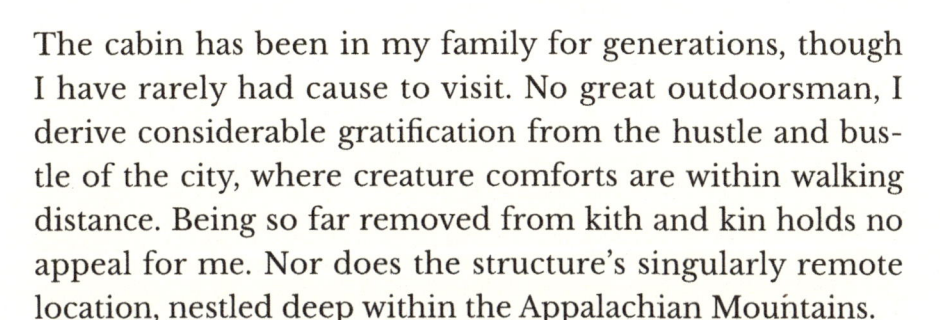

The cabin has been in my family for generations, though I have rarely had cause to visit. No great outdoorsman, I derive considerable gratification from the hustle and bustle of the city, where creature comforts are within walking distance. Being so far removed from kith and kin holds no appeal for me. Nor does the structure's singularly remote location, nestled deep within the Appalachian Mountains.

And yet, my promise lingers like a phantom, always on the periphery of my waking mind. If I am to face my devils, if I am to wrest my life from their clutches, then I must do so alone. My family has suffered enough. I cannot ask them to walk through this particular hell with me.

I will not.

My journey up the mountainside is uneventful; the carriage's spring-and-leaf suspension bouncing me as if I were a babe on my mother's knee; the clopping of hooves like some organic metronome, lulling me into a fitful doze with their measured meter. The din of the city fades. Even my regrets fade, if only temporarily. In that null hour between lucidity and dream-state, all of my failures cease to exist. I am no longer *that* man. He is below me now, sinking like the city is sinking, dispersing into the depths while I rise above, looking down upon my submerged self as if beholding a stranger.

My mistakes seem so small from this height. So inconsequential.

I awaken some hours later, the driver's knock against the carriage roof startling me back into mindfulness. Never have I slept so soundly when not occupying my own bed. I peer out the window, though night has fallen, and details are scarce. But the outline of the cabin is perceptible against a backlight of stars, the silhouette eerie and ominous to my cosmopolitan inclinations.

Exiting the buggy on stiff legs, I knuckle the small of my back, coaxing feeling back into my extremities. The driver has already offloaded my luggage, such as it is. Just two meagre trunks contain everything I expect to need for a week in the backwoods. Before me, my erstwhile abode beckons.

It is a single-story affair, clad in clapboard and fading paint. The front of the structure had always resembled a face in my youthful imagination. That appearance has somehow perpetuated into adulthood, and now, with the porch sagging and the windows half-shuttered, the resulting visage is both forlorn and frightening. As though the place is unhappy to see me. A single Tulip tree towers over one corner of the roof, a stalwart sentinel ever watchful through the seasons. Its pointy limbs drape the edifice in a jagged embrace, while yellow leaves cling desperately, swaying in the evening breeze with a susurrus of sound.

The cabin. I haven't been here since I was a young man, and the memories are far from pleasant. Fragments return unbidden; my father arguing with his brother, nearly coming to blows; my mother's pleading voice; the children, myself included, waiting on the porch, neglected in the wake of perplexing adult matters. I never did learn what the row was about. I just know that it must have been a matter of some significance, creating a rift in our family that has yet to be mended.

But such remembrances are best left undisturbed. I push the thoughts from my mind and fish the wrought-iron key from my pocket. The carriage and horses have long since departed, and I feel strangely exposed on the stoop, a lone man hemmed in by endless acres of foreboding back country. The hairs on my neck tingle, as if a thousand eyes watch me from the darkness.

Suddenly spooked, goose pimples appearing on my arms, I unlock the door with haste, escaping into the safe confines of my manmade dwelling.

No longer abetted by clear starlight, it takes some time for my eyes to adjust to the cabin's murky interior.

For holding such a spot of intense repugnance in my memory, my temporary lodgings are, in reality, quite discouraging. The place is smaller than I remember; a ceiling low enough to touch; cluttered furniture encroaching upon narrow walkways; the wood burning stove that has appropriated an entire corner as its domain. Everything, from the furnishings to the assorted bric-a-brac, are flanked by walls that feel closer than they should.

Lighting the cabin's lanterns is a test of both my ability and my patience. Electricity is still relatively new in Pittsfield, yet I have already grown accustomed to its convenience. Cold fingers fumble through the unfamiliar motions of filling oil reservoirs and saturating wicks. I eventually manage, though not without uttering a few blasphemies. Flickering flames cast serrated shadows hither and thither, untethered darkness that capers across the walls and ceiling like grotesque goblins.

A storm is blustering in from the east, the wind whistling through the cracks and gaps in the framing. My nostrils are filled with a chilly tang, the promise of snowfall made manifest. In my haste, I had failed to consider potential changes in climate. A quick accounting of the cabin's stores sets my mind at ease; one of my estranged relatives has left the place well-stocked with firewood and canned goods.

My visit may be less cozy than expected, but I am in no discernible danger.

I go about the business of settling in, fluffing pillows and dusting surfaces. For such a large monstrosity, the cast-iron stove is ponderous in its heating, although I have filled its belly with plenty of fuel.

The busywork keeps my mind from revisiting that which brought me here. I am grateful for the mental respite. And yet, not everything is going in my favor. I sense a chill across my flesh as I work, one that has nothing to do with the temperature. Again, I perceive that I am being observed.

The source of my unease is obvious upon further inspection; the flat eyes of dead animals seem to follow my every move. A wolf resides near one wall, killed mid-snarl, its hateful expression still affixed even in death. Above it, on a dusty bookshelf, roosts a northern barred owl. Like most members of the strix genus, this bird's eyes are beady and devious. But it is the animal closest to the door which produces within me the most dreadful unease.

Mounted on a plaque the size of my wife's vanity mirror, the elk's neck and head are stupendous, topped by antlers that are fearsome in their abundance. The creature must have weighed more than a thousand pounds when it was felled. Though it lacks a body, the elk still gives the impression of powerful vivacity, as if the rest of it will come crashing through the wall at any moment.

Whichever taxidermist was utilized certainly knew his craft.

I tear my gaze away from the stuffed trophies, returning to the task of making the cabin habitable. While I toil, the first pangs of hunger gnaw from within, and I give the small dining table my undivided attention. A thought occurs to me then, bringing with it no small amount of shock: tonight's supper shall be the first one not accompanied by a drink in more than a decade.

It is a notion that is both exhilarating and terrifying.

My sleep is fitful; filled with both dreams and cravings, both which haunt me through the night.

I am shivering when I awaken, my breath visible in the air. The source of the cold is immediately apparent; somehow, the front door came open during the night, though I am certain I had latched it prior to climbing into bed. Through the doorway, a white wonderland is visible. As expected, the evening storm brought several feet of snow, a large quantity of which is spilling across the threshold.

And yet, it is not the nippy air that chills the blood in my veins, but instead the tracks that lead into the cabin from outside. The continuing snowfall has mostly obscured their finer details, and whatever scant knowledge I possess of fauna escapes me; I cannot tell what sort of animal created them.

Or whether it was an animal at all.

Despite my overactive imagination, however, the odds of the tracks belonging to a human are slim. For a start, they do not appear large enough. In addition, the carriage driver is not set to return for six more days, and there are no other lodges within walking distance.

The cabin is not large, and I rummage through it in a panic, searching for whatever interloper has invaded my solitude.

Nothing seems to have been disturbed. The only creatures to be found are the dead ones already in residence, and I discover no other oddities, save for the wet spots on the floor, leading from the doorway to the side of the bed.

I shiver anew, terror causing my entire body to shake; whatever it was, it had stood over me while I slept.

With the door re-latched and the fire stoked, I hurriedly poke through every nook and cranny. My search bears fruit; a double-barrel shotgun is hidden in one of the linen chests, well-oiled and sturdy. The only shells I am able to find are birdshot, but they are better than nothing.

Perpetually on guard, my muscles ache from unreleased tension. I stalk the cabin like a night watchman, stomping to and fro, unable to quell my nervous fidgeting.

I try to eat, but the dry rations taste like ash in my mouth, and my stomach roils in protest. Water is the only palatable option. Yet no matter how much I drink, that revolting flavor clings to my teeth. The toothbrush I brought feels strange in my hand, but I am desperate to be free of the pasty residue. It is only when a sharp pain lances across my gums that I realize I am, against all reason, gripping my safety razor instead. Shock and agony wage war across my senses. Hours pass before I am able to stem the flow of blood; in this, at least, the copious snow proves useful.

Though it has been lingering in the back of my mind nearly this entire time, the desire for a drink is suddenly overpowering, a compulsion that assails my self-control with the force of battering rams striking a portcullis. The dull glow of alcohol would steady more than just my nerves. However, the cabin is bereft of spirits; not even a bottle of laudanum or paregoric can be found.

Cursing my weakness, I settle in by the stove, cradling the shotgun in my hands. The promise I made weighs heavy upon my heart, shame eating at my belly like a feral rat. Only one day in and I'm desperate for hooch. I truly am a wretch of a man.

How did I fool myself into thinking this would be easy?

The dreams of the previous night still linger, refusing to dwindle into the unlit depths of reminiscence. Their tendrils run deep, infecting every long hour, pervading my every thought. They were violent and hateful; I may not remember them with perfect clarity, but that much remains.

I curse my crumbling fortitude and the stubbornness which has led me here. My conceit is nearly a physical thing—an active fault line that compromises the mantle of my wishes and intentions, undermining my every action.

If I am to prevail against my base urges, I must be stronger than this. And I shall be. But, alas, not tonight. I am too out of sorts to enact any alterations to my temperament. Mayhap tomorrow will be kinder.

Despising my very existence, I stumble to bed, bleary-eyed and desolate.

My second morning starts out much the same; door ajar, wet prints on the floor, the air deathly cold.

These new tracks appear different, more pronounced in both size and depth. I still cannot fathom their origin, but whatever made them must be colossal in stature. How I managed to sleep through such heavy footfalls is truly a mystery.

The prints, in and of themselves, are most disquieting, but they are not the sole inconsistency within the cabin. Both the wolf and the owl have been moved from their original positions. The owl now roosts on my nightstand, far too close for comfort. The wolf, for all intents and purposes, appears to be guarding the door, incursive snowdrifts pooled around its paws. It faces the bed, rictus snarl seemingly more pronounced than before.

Even more ominously, the elk is no longer simply a head and a neck; its broad chest and long forelegs now adorn the placard as though they had always been there. The sheer size of the shaggy brute makes my knees buckle. Am I misremembering the trivial particulars within my refuge? Are my anxieties eroding my sanity?

I once again search high and low, finding nothing. What has done this? What *could* do this? Perhaps this place is cursed, insomuch as any physical exemplar can exceed the maledictions which we inflict unto our own hearts and minds.

A profound terror grips me, and I yearn to plunge through the doorway and escape the strange tableau, just as swift as my legs can carry me. A fool's errand, to be sure. I have not the appropriate attire for traipsing through a blizzard. Mother Nature also opposes me; the snow is now higher than the doorframe, as if the very elements conspire against me. Digging out would be no easy feat.

There is but one recourse available to me, and that is to hunker down and ride out the storm.

Not content to trust in the latch, I have stacked two linen chests against the door. Their combined weight should prove an immovable obstruction. The windows I have blocked with wooden shelving. No fortress, to be sure, yet it shall have to suffice.

But though I can barricade every ingress and arm myself against physical threats, I am defenseless against the machinations of my own mind. In the dark disquiet of solitary thought, each facet of my existence is magnified to gargantuan proportions, with my mistakes looming largest of all.

I keep the shotgun close, both barrels loaded, cold hands gripping it like a lifeline. My arms shake like unsecured railway tracks. The sweat dripping from my brow, in spite of the frigid air, is indicative of a fever.

Some rational part of my brain recognizes the symptoms, providing a name for my ailments. Riding the ghost train. Barrel-fever. Both exist as saloon vernacular for *delirium tremens*, itself merely a fancy appellation for one's detoxification from liquor dependency. That I am suffering the effects so soon is disconcerting. I had hoped to hold out longer.

A face takes root in my mind, that of my wife. The bruise is purpling, standing in stark relief against alabaster skin, her expression one of astonishment and hatred. Darkened skin around her eye calls to mind the black orbs of the owl. Was this how she looked at me, in that snatch of time after my fist connected? I am unable to recall. But if she did, one could hardly blame her. Attempting further recollections yields no clarity; my dishonor has colored each memory, painting them in a patina of negativity, replacing certitude with nagging doubts. I knew there would be repercussions for my malicious deed; perhaps I am living through them now.

Through the miasma of withdrawal, I sense an awakening of other senses. As if I alone can somehow unravel the mysterious threads of the unknown and unknowable.

All the while, the dead animals regard me with eyes that seem animated. Perhaps they've been watching me from the start.

In my burgeoning delirium, I begin to ascribe characteristics to each of the creatures. The owl, forever a symbol of wisdom and veracity, undoubtedly represents my pride. My temper is handily embodied by the snarling wolf. And the elk, that majestic and terrifying beast which dwarfs the others, is the physical incarnation of my regret. Such thoughts are truly the ravings of a madman, but rarely is the truth an easy pill to swallow. Deep down, in my heart of hearts, I know that I have touched upon something factual.

How many hours have passed since the morning? With the snowpack higher than the cabin, a gloomy darkness prevails, interfering with my circadian rhythm. Time stretches like glue, distended and delicate.

Lamp oil cans seem to mutate into whiskey bottles before my eyes, but after several instances of coughing up the vile substance, I no longer fall prey to that illusion. Fool me once...

Who, who? Whether the enquiry comes from the owl or my own imaginings is trivial compared to what is being asked. Who indeed?

I'm afraid the answer is quite simple; there is only myself to blame.

My belly rumbles, aching to be filled. But these are hunger pangs like I've never known. The truth is more than evident; it is not food my body is craving, but an altogether different form of sustenance. I realize, in this very moment, that I would sell my very soul for even the cheapest of bathtub gins.

And yet my exhaustion is greater than my appetite; my eyes growing heavier with each exhalation. I do not wish to sleep, to be so undeniably exposed, but my body and resolve are powerless to prevent it. The shotgun barrel thumps against the floor and my eyelids make good their betrayal.

Slumber overtakes me.

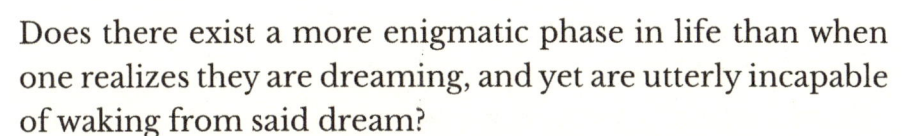

Does there exist a more enigmatic phase in life than when one realizes they are dreaming, and yet are utterly incapable of waking from said dream?

In my nocturnal reverie, I have been transported home, to some undefined time in the future. My children are older, taller, no longer clinging to their mother's skirts. I welcome the change. Being able to speak to my progeny without simplifying the topic is, in a word, liberating.

But that sword is sharp on both ends; they are old enough now to see through pretenses. There is judgement within their eyes, and maybe hatred as well.

My wife, too, has changed. Gone are her carefree disposition, gentle smile, and kind expression. The lines in her face have deepened, carving into angular planes which once were rounded. Hair that was formerly as golden as summer wheat has turned pale. In my dream, she is nearly a stranger.

No great deductive reasoning is required to understand this future; the bottle clasped in my hand lays bare the origin of their altered behavior. My choices have led to this, as inexorably as the setting of the sun. The fault lies with me, as it frequently does. *Mea culpa.*

And yet I do not relinquish the liquor.

The dream shifts, morphing into another scene entirely. My wife stands firm in front of our children, blood trickling from her nostrils, while I rave and rant about, spittle flying from cracked lips. What I am angry about is unclear. But in my stupor, it matters not. Anger begets anger, and the letter opener held in my wife's hand like a weapon ignites within me an incandescent fury. How dare she threaten me, as if

I am some lunatic who has unexpectedly barged into her home?

I now comprehend that the dream is, instead, a nightmare, one from which I am desperate to awaken. I know what transpires next and have no desire to experience it. But my dream persists; there is no stopping.

In an instant, my hands are wrapped around her throat. The blade is lost in the commotion, and our children beat at my arms and face in desperation, their fists ineffective in the face of my wrath. I will *not* be deterred. My wife glares at me in defiance. Gasps escape her lips, and the thrum of her heartbeat pulses against my palms. I squeeze tighter, and then tighter still. The spark of life fades from her eyes, her limp body crumpling to the floor.

And still my rage has not been quenched. I turn to my children next. Their footfalls as they flee sound louder than cannons, the noise strangely out of sync with their motions.

The cacophony jolts me from my torpor, igniting my every nerve; it is not coming from my dream.

It is originating from within the cabin itself.

I jump to my feet in a flash. My weary arms can barely manage to lift the shotgun. A lingering horror clings to my conscience; the atrocities committed in my dream went beyond the pale, and they have hounded me into wakefulness. Such a twisted future cannot be allowed to take place.

Nevertheless, in this moment, I have more pressing concerns.

In the faint glow of the stove's smoldering embers, I witness a sight that nearly stops my heart. The elk has almost broken free of its confinement, most of its body now emerging through the wall. The front hooves beat a deafening staccato against the wood, and an ear-shattering bugling escapes its mouth, interspersed with raspy grunts as it attempts to extricate itself.

Meanwhile, the wolf is returned to life as well, and has withdrawn into the shadows, growling and snarling with unmistakable menace. The owl screeches by overheard, close enough that I feel the beating of its wings. Sharp talons brush my hair; I duck down in just the nick of time.

Despite clasping the shotgun, I do not feel that I can prevail. These creatures hold every advantage in the low light. My only recourse is to flee, to dig myself out somehow, blizzard be damned. Furniture blocks my way as I scrabble towards the door, only to find that it is gone; stacked chests guarding nothing. The windows have vanished as well, unbroken surfaces where they once were situated. Whatever fell magic has brought the animals to life has also stolen away all manner of egress.

I am trapped with my demons.

As if my very thought has summoned it, the wolf snares my pant leg betwixt its teeth, yanking me from my feet. I land bodily upon my weapon. Within moments, the wolf's jaw has latched onto my ankle, biting deep. I scream in torment, trying to bring the shotgun to bear while it savages my flesh: ripping, wrenching, tearing. The pain is like nothing I've ever felt, hot and acrid like lava.

The creature relinquishes its hold, drawing back for a lunge, and I finally manage to bring my weapon to bear. I pull both triggers just as the wolf pounces, the deafening roar is like music to my ears. A veritable torrent of birdshot strikes the animal full in the chest, mere inches from the barrels, sending it careering backwards, its lifeless husk thumping to the ground in a most satisfying manner.

From the darkness, the owl screeches in remonstration, and the elk seems to double its efforts; the pounding of hooves is ceaseless, as if it possesses dozens of feet, each drubbing against the wall in a frenzy. The room seems lighter now, as if lit by braziers that are just out of view. My mangled leg makes standing difficult, yet I manage it all the same. In the corner, that which embodied my temper lies dead, fur still smoking from the point-blank impact.

Optimism wells within for the first time since my arrival; a lone vessel of hope atop a dark sea of despair. If I can kill my ire, then I can vanquish my other sinister aspects as well. The latch on the breach slides easily; I load two more shells into the gun while searching for the strix.

But the devil bird is faster than I. It swoops in from behind, sharp talons grazing painfully across my scalp as it soars past. I turn, tracking its flight with the gun. However, it is far too fast, my lameness slowing my motions considerably. The blood trickling into my eyes is also proving a hindrance. Several seconds pass, the beating of my heart competing with the elk's hooves, each thumping impossibly loud. The beast is almost free; hindquarters pulling through, forelegs stamping on the floor. I will need to contend with him shortly.

First, however, the owl. My pride.

I sweep the weapon from side to side, not knowing where to aim. I can sense my foe, however, somewhere in the clutter, beady eyes surveilling, stalking me as surely as a predator in tall grass. It will strike while my attention is diverted, as conceit is wont to do. Of this, I am certain.

The elk steals my attention for a trice, and some preternatural impulse warns me of the bird at my back. My ploy has proven successful. I kneel down as the owl sails overhead, directly into my line of fire. Thunder once again fills the air. My opponent, vitiated by a salvo of small steel, bursts into a flurry of bloody feathers that drift to the ground in silent defeat.

I have overcome both my anger and my pride; my shoulders already feel less burdened. The room is brighter as well, as though the sun itself has been contained within the cabin's walls, burning away shadow and distress with fiery intensity. For the briefest of moments, I see my wife's face, filled with the vibrant vitality of which I am familiar. She smiles at me, the warmth of her expression heating my skin, scintillating radiance igniting my each and every nerve.

Such a vision can mean only one thing; that terrible future glimpsed in my dream need not come to pass. My downfall can be avoided. So long as I remain steadfast, I can…

Before my mind can finish the thought, a sharp agony flares across my back, white-hot and debilitating. I need not even glance down; the antlers piercing through my chest extend for several feet in front of me, dripping with ichor.

My wife's aspect dissipates, drifting apart as if a dandelion on a breeze. The light tapers as well. I am back in the cabin, door and windows obstructed, gloominess ubiquitous and stifling. My wound steams in the cold air; that my tomb is glacial seems fitting. The beast steps back, extracting its horns from my rent flesh. What little strength I have fails, unresponsive limbs spilling the shotgun to the floor with an impotent clatter. My body follows shortly thereafter. I cannot inhale no matter how I struggle.

We stare at each other for several minutes, my remorse and I, while my very lifeblood stains the floor beneath me. Compunction seeps out with it. What a buffoon I was, believing that I could subdue my regret by running away. By facing it alone in some godforsaken wilderness. I should have known such an act would lead only to folly.

But it is now, and shall forever remain, far too late.

Chapter Fifteen

A Dream of Dead Leaves

BY JEREMY MEGARGEE

Long I've searched the desolate spaces
Pumpkin patches gone to rot and graveyards with broken gates
For just a glimpse of her in her natural state
Alive and full of jack-o-lantern flames...

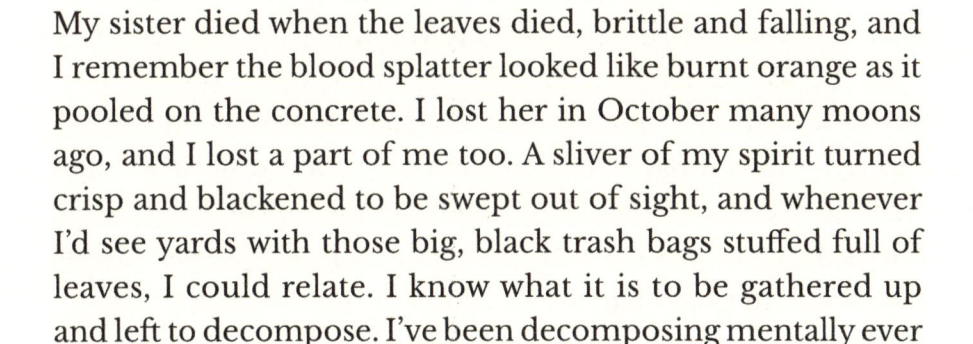

My sister died when the leaves died, brittle and falling, and I remember the blood splatter looked like burnt orange as it pooled on the concrete. I lost her in October many moons ago, and I lost a part of me too. A sliver of my spirit turned crisp and blackened to be swept out of sight, and whenever I'd see yards with those big, black trash bags stuffed full of leaves, I could relate. I know what it is to be gathered up and left to decompose. I've been decomposing mentally ever since Fiona committed suicide.

She was a child of the harvest time, and spooky season was in her blood. She'd dance at masquerades under cold, yellow moonlight. She'd take pride in her costumes and her home décor. There was always a dark glint inside of her, but it was warm and welcoming, and when her pallid hand with the chipped purple polish fell across mine, I'd feel whole.

She was young and I was old, so I always had that desire in me to protect her from this world. She loved her monsters, those misfits of fang and fur, but I knew about other kinds of monsters. The ones that prowl among us in human skin, the beasts that hide inside of people, and I never wanted her to have to encounter those. Much like revealing that Santa is a myth, I did my best to keep Halloween safe for Fiona. Pure, pleasantly macabre, and born of outsiders that for one special night want to feel that they belong.

I take some degree of solace in knowing that she chose her favorite time of year to seek an end. I don't know why she tore off the plywood and snuck into that eyesore of an abandoned house on a dead-end street. I've turned it over and over in my head, trying to figure out why she climbed those sagging stairs and found her way to that shattered attic window. I often wonder what she was thinking before she took the plunge. For one strange and blissful moment, did she want to be like the bats that she loved so much? Did she want to fly like them and listen to the music of the night?

All the softest parts of her cracked open when she landed, and when I had to identify her in that basement morgue, I thought I was looking at a broken porcelain doll. My sister was still there under all the crisscrossed wounds and twisted bones, but she was forever changed, emptied of something that made her who she used to be. I almost expected one of those ruined hands to reach up, a weak butterfly seeking my cheek, and I hoped she'd say my name one more time.

Olive.

I think that I do hear her calling to me some nights, but it's just the wind, and sometimes the wind can mimic cruelly.

I'm almost nocturnal now, because I have this sense that there's nothing left in the sun for me. The joy has been stripped clean, and what is left is raw to the touch, not fit for other people to see or endure. I keep to myself, I live in solitude, and I think about my sister. I imagine what she'd be like now if she hadn't died back then. My heart is in the past, the present has no flavor, and the future seems like something that will be no different than what came before.

I walk to the house sometimes around two o'clock in the morning. I never liked to go in. I'd just stand out front and stare up at it, damning it for taking her, silently cursing it for getting to spend a few final moments with Fiona when I was afforded no such gift. But lately, I've felt brave, and I've been going inside and wandering halls with discolored walls. It stinks of mildew, and it is an altar to the forgotten.

I don't know how long the graffiti has been there, perhaps before her death, or maybe the artist came after. I can't stop looking at it. I can't stop reading it. The words drip in sloppy orange spray paint, and there's some attachment that I can't shake. It feels like her, or some association to her, and I can even smell the paint on the walls, like pumpkin pie that is close to going bad, but a single bite is still possible, and I just know it'll be sickly sweet to taste...

Long I've searched the desolate spaces, pumpkin patches gone to rot and graveyards with broken gates, for just a glimpse of her in her natural state, alive and full of jack-o-lantern flames.

I feel her still in desolate spaces. I think of veils between worlds and rotting vines where the pumpkins roll overripe down unknowable hills. Gates that keep the living from the dead, but all gates can break, can't they? Maybe a glimpse is still possible. There's something in that snippet of poem that haunts me. Where did she *go*, what did she become, did she wither and fade with the leaves, or is there a chance for a reunion?

I'm not sleeping these days. I only dream.

I dream of unfamiliar vistas. Cornfields dried to mazes of husk, and hunched shapes in the rows; big, gleaming, curious eyes that blink erratically if I look at them too long. The moon lords over, fuller than I've ever seen it, and there's the desire to stand on my tippy toes to graze fingertips across the craters. My nostrils flare, and everything is scent here. Wet earth, browning vegetation, and squash vines that creep like serpents in the undergrowth.

There's a parade of scarecrows crossing the field, their movements lethargic and jerky, limbs just stuffed husk, scraps of clothing clinging to insubstantial frames, and battered hats with wide brims, no faces in the shadows beneath, or perhaps the shadows are the faces. A woman flits in and out of their ranks, a shy creature adorned in a gown of autumn colors, sewn leaves of red, brown, and orange. There's jack-o-lantern fire in her irises, and when she opens her mouth to laugh, a sputtering flame dances on her tongue. I never see her clearly. She is just a shifting promise peeking out from behind ragged scarecrows coats and crouching between twitching twig limbs, but I don't need a closer look to know my own sister.

I know that it's her even if she's fundamentally changed. The gown, the internal flame, and the tempting ballerina movements are new, but that face is the same face that I grew up with. I feel in my bones that wherever I am is not of the world I know. It is a haven for the harvest. A place where the moon marks the day instead of the sun. Through the dream, I've found a door, but it is only temporary. I can't stay. I can't follow my sister. Fiona cavorts in a different plane of existence, and the glimpses are meant to bait me.

I awaken drowning in my own sweat, the taste of pumpkin in the far back of my throat, and that other place lingers before it fades into fragments. I hear the cawing of crows and I get my hopes up that I'm still there, but it's just a few morning birds on the telephone wires beyond my open window. I'm never able to hold onto the dreams. They slip like sand through the fingers as I autopilot my way through morning routines, and by the time afternoon comes, almost nothing of those images remains. I wish I could bottle the dreams and drink them when I'm sad. I don't think of them as nightmares, but somber fantasies that enthrall as much as they confound.

The world I return to is often devoid of anything that makes it worthwhile to roll out of bed. There are expectations here, and I'm too tired and indifferent to adhere to them. I want that eerie violin song that rides the wind in the other place. I crave to know what it's like to house a flame inside of yourself.

Fiona knows, and I think she wants to show me.

I carve the triangular eyes into the soft pumpkin flesh, and I disembowel slowly, tossing guts and seeds behind my shoulder. I've been told that there are sacrifices necessary to cross the threshold. Rites to honor and customs to be observed. Fiona comes to me even in the waking moments now, and I see her in all reflective surfaces.

She speaks the backward tongue of the mirror, and she wears a thousand different masks, for in that realm that she inhabits, she can be anything or nothing according to her whims. Always the eternal flame guttering in her eyes, and her mouth, and her heart, and she can communicate through the unloved critters of this plane of existence. I hear her from the mandibles of a spider that lives in the sink. She whispers to me from a rat in the bedroom wall when I rest. She sings me lullabies through the wings of roosting bats in the springhouse.

She said that she jumped because she became disillusioned. The color drained out of her life, and she sought to find it again in a new place. That old forlorn house wasn't chosen at random. It is a window into a different world. It sits in gloom and dust and collects the dead leaves when the October breeze makes them swirl. Its porch is a tongue, its door is a slanted eye, and the innards are that of a great gutted pumpkin, and when a person comes and chooses to transition, a human seed finds growth before sprouting into something else entirely.

But I can't become like her yet. I can't see the truth of the house unless I arrive with seasoned eyes. She tells me through centipedes where I must go. She shows me maps born of mole burrows in the dirt. It's a far place, and a thin place, and Fiona claims that it'll test me. If I'm worthy, it'll know.

She sends me walking, and I go.

I'm expected at the graveyard with the broken gate.

The hill is devoid of civilization, a pocket of isolation far beyond the limits of the city. It's all green and choked in weeds with cracked stones reaching up from the wild growth like pitted fingertips. If the graveyard ever had a name, it's been lost, much like the honor of the place. The gate is broken, and in pushing it open, it breaks even more, sending cloudy rust flakes billowing around me.

The dead are quiet here, long undisturbed, but it's clear the wildlife inherited the land. Fat groundhogs watch me malevolently from their holes, and foxes slink red and deceptive through tall grasses. Birds have their quarrels up above, and the mosquitoes find me and start to suck, resentful that I'd dare to pass without a blood toll.

The centerpiece of the place is on the top of the hill, and it's a trudge to get there. It's a mausoleum, emerald-green in the sun with black stains on the exterior from lack of cleanliness. I climb the steps to enter and admire the stained-glass windows that still hold a degree of majesty. The door yields, hinges creaking, and then I'm in the gloom of the interior. Marbled walls with names and dates and wide slots, some of them shattered, allowing a glimpse at the caskets within.

It's the graffiti on the far wall that draws me. I approach slowly, almost with reverence, and I let fingertips gaze across those dripping orange words.

> *She whispered to me once in a long-gone dream*
> *Of a city of monsters and unfixable things*
> *Past the arctic wastelands, through the obsidian rings*
> *Where the leaves are brown and crisp forever*
> *Always cool and somber, timeless October*
> *If only you'll go there*

Did Fiona write this? Is she the author of the words? I get the sense that she isn't. I think she saw the words like I'm seeing them, and what happened after was pure compulsion.

It became her ambition in life to find access to that timeless October.

There's a shifting noise in the dark, and I notice a marble table that I overlooked. There's a naked cadaver seated there, legs crossed, flesh desiccated and gray, all shriveled limbs and a sunken face that looks at me with mild curiosity. There's been butchery done to the face, and I get the sense that it was self-inflicted long ago. Eyes gone, just dark chasms carved into triangular jack-o-lantern holes, and the mouth torn at with a knife; a Glasgow smile paired with the jovial grin of a pumpkin freshly bladed.

I think the proper reaction is to scream when faced with such an unnatural perversion, but the moving corpse has no such effect on me. I knew in my heart I'd find some sort of messenger here. An envoy of that other place where Fiona dances immortal in fields of harvest.

He gestures calmly with one hand to the seat opposite him at the table, and the movement causes a dried fingernail to clatter down to the tabletop. The corpse lets it sit there, paying the loss no mind at all.

"Are you the poet?"

I nod up to the spray-painted words on the wall as I sink down into the chair.

"No. But if you're found fit to cross over, you'll meet the poet."

His voice is strangely soothing, a melodic rattle from deep in that lifeless throat. It reminds me of a black tomcat fighting sleep next to a fireplace.

"I don't ask for much. No lies, just vulnerability. I might not have eyes, but I have the flame, and it sees the truth of you."

He taps dead fingertips on the marble, and he studies me with the wounds where his eyes should be.

"What do you fear, Olive? What unsettles you in the marrow of your bones?"

"Life itself. The performance that is life. I go through it comparing myself to others, fighting envy, pushing down insecurity, and hoping that others never find me out."

"What would happen if they saw you, all necessary masks dropped to the earth?"

"I think they'd cast me out. I think they'd realize that I'm not like them. A fraud, or a poor mimic."

The carved smile on his face widens, and I can hear the mummified skin making taut sounds as it stretches.

"Well, if you're not meant for here, those mortal pastures out there, perhaps you've always been meant for somewhere else. What do you think?"

"I think you're right. I think my sister is somewhere else. That *particular* somewhere else. Can you tell me for certain?"

The cadaver with the wounds for eyes makes no response to this. It seems to almost shut down for a moment, just a rigid inanimate body again, nothing keeping it upright, but then the head upturns, and in those triangular chasms, two flames sputter into life. The burn is beautiful, and it smells of hay bales to be seated upon during a wagon ride through the woods.

"One last question, Olive. This one matters the most, so be open and true. What does Halloween mean to you?"

I heave a sigh and I let my eyes drift across the walls and the ceiling. I feel the emotion surging in me even before the thoughts gather together in my head.

"Halloween is that one night when I can be anything other than myself. It's pure catharsis. Monsters are welcomed, and demons are invited in. No judgment or withering gazes. You can be strange on Halloween. You can be different on Halloween. You don't have to hide what you are."

I lift my eyes up to meet his candle flame gaze, and I feel the tears spilling down my cheeks. I make no effort to wipe them away. There is no corpse with wounds for eyes. I'm alone in the mausoleum, and either he got the answer he needed and drifted from this realm, or he was never there at all. It doesn't matter. It felt good to speak that truth aloud for the first time.

I think that I know what comes next. What waits after the graveyard with the broken gate. Fiona feels closer than ever, almost like she's pressing against a veil, and I'm desperate to press back. I must go where she went, walk where she walked, and do as she did...

It's a supermoon tomorrow night, and the trick-r-treaters will bask beneath its glow. The sweets I'm hunting last longer, and I'll have to give new meaning to the tradition.

I'm off to meet the poet, and to add to the poem.

The abandoned house on the dead-end street stops being a house the moment the door closes behind me. There's a subtle shift, and discolored wallpaper peels upward and drifts into nothingness like bits of ash. Beyond termite-eaten boards there's a pulsing substance underneath, moldy gray in color, and it takes me a moment to recognize it as the interior flesh of a rotting pumpkin.

I smell it too, the aroma hiding beneath the mildew and old wood. Decaying vegetable matter hits the nostrils, and I accept my predicament. I relate to Jonah at the moment he was swallowed by the whale, but it's not a whale that has me in its insides, but a dead otherworldly pumpkin that masquerades as something else. I reach out to touch the walls as they gently retract, and the soft rotting pumpkin flesh is warm under the fingertips.

I'm seeing the truth of the place, and I understand on a deep level that the game has changed for me. I'm closer to Fiona than ever before. I'm experiencing what she experienced moments before the fall.

Music plays softly from somewhere in the deep innards of the house, an orchestral piece reserved for moonlit glades, and it soothes the anxious thoughts that have started to develop in my head. I focus on the piano melodies, and I begin to traverse the pumpkin rooms, careful of my footing lest a shoe push through the more decomposed sections of floor.

A man I once loved appears before me in the sitting room. He hurt me a great deal in the past. I was a meek mouse back then, and self-esteem was a foreign concept. This version of him is barely corporeal, his skin the same mottled gray of the rotten pumpkin walls.

"You're lucky that I loved you. It was out of pity. I lowered my standards. I made sacrifices that you didn't appreciate. There's nothing worthwhile in you."

A wry smile crosses my lips, and I reach out, caressing his cheek with the back of my knuckles.

"I believed that once. It scared me so much to lose you. But I found so much after. The self-worth you had hoped I'd never find."

The former lover frowns, and then his entire body topples down into mush, the rot eating him up. I move on because it would be a waste to spare his remains another look.

I wander into the bathroom, and there in the bath is the mentally ill mother that Fiona and I grew up with. She looks withered, her white hair drifting in stagnant water like a sad halo.

"You'll stay with me, won't you? You and Fiona. I need you both. I can't get along on my own. Everyone else is out to get me."

I sit for a moment on the edge of the tub, and I brush a lock of that stringy hair behind her ear.

"You tried with us. If your brain had been kinder to you, I know that you would have tried harder. I don't blame you for the chaos, but we have to go. We have to grow up."

I'm already up and walking away before she can guilt me to stay by her side, and when I do glance back, it's just the fleshy mush of formless pumpkin rot floating in the dirty bathwater.

The glamour doesn't last after that, and no visitations from my life before return to greet me. I don't begrudge the house such illusions. It is seeing if I've cast off old hurts. It wants to know that I'm strong enough to exist in that other place. To dance among demons in timeless October, one must first conquer the demons that dance in the head and the heart.

I take my time ascending the winding staircase, fingertips reaching out to graze the soft innards of the gatehouse. I hear the rattle of a spray paint can, and I follow it to the highest point in the house, tucking my head and shoulders down as I enter into the attic. The poet is there in a far corner, just a black silhouette of static that fizzles in and out of existence. There's no discernable gender or identity to the figure, as insubstantial as will-o'-the-wisp, but I approach and speak to it all the same.

"What does the poem mean?"

The figure responds in whispers, voice crackling like a flame.

"Different for everyone. I'm more of a conduit. When people think of Halloween, their heads swim with hopes, dreams, and fantasies. I make verse of those fantasies, poetry from those that hunt and crave for an October that never has to end."

The paint sprays outward, and the smell of the burnt orange fumes makes me swoon.

"There are so many dim and desolate places in the world, and *our* people visit them. I leave pieces of the poem in all of these places. The poem is a promise, and we are its keepers."

I walk closer, and I feel the sudden compulsion to extend my hand.

"May I?"

The poet flickers and fades, verse unfinished, and it deposits the can of spray paint into my hand before becoming one with the shadows around it. It seems that for what comes next, I must be alone.

I stare up at those bare walls, and I think of what's in my soul. Yearning, curiosity, and the desire to leave so much of this behind.

I'm still here, somewhere stuck in the between
Hollow and heartsick, lost girlhood, lost steam
Sometimes still in sweet October I imagine holding her
That pallid kindred Queen
Sister waits undying in permanent Halloween

The can is empty, so I let it slide from my grip and clatter down against the floorboards. I hope that others see what I've written, and I hope that when they're ready, they follow in my footsteps. I walk slowly to that gaping attic window, mindful of the shards of glass that remain, and I stretch outward while holding tight to the flimsy wood of the window frame.

The glow of the supermoon paints my face, and the night breeze cools the sweat that has collected at my temples. I'm afforded a grand view of the neighborhood, tiny, costumed forms exploring the streets with sacks in hand, and I can't think of a better sight to see.

They'll eat their treats and go to bed, and then the next day all will be normal, but not for me. I don't want Halloween to end. I want to see Fiona again. I want this to be my forever.

I inhale sharply through my nostrils, breathing in all that is autumn, and I let my eyelids flutter closed.

I leap.

I fall for what feels like centuries.

When I finally open my eyes again, jack-o-lantern flames burn in the irises.

Meet the Authors

Heather Miller
   Bio: Heather Miller is a writer of old-fashioned horror. She dreams of long candlelit passages and things that go bump in the night. Her writing is influenced by the old Gothics that she grew up reading, and the terrifying tales she heard at her grandmother's knee. She released her first novella, Knock Knock, in 2021, and her short stories have been featured in Twisted Pulp magazine and the upcoming anthology Into the Forest from Black Spot Books. Heather lives with her husband, five kids, and a small menagerie of animals in a century-old house (likely haunted) in a tiny town in Oklahoma.

   Story Inspiration: The Far Field
   I grew up reading the old Gothic ghost stories, so when the call went out for stories for this anthology, I knew that this project was perfect for me. I sat down to think, to brainstorm a story, and the first thing I thought of was old, haunted houses. I knew there would likely be lots of those in the collection, though, and I wanted to do something different. I began mentally tossing around other places that could be

haunted: hospitals, schools, churches. Then I asked myself the question: why does it have to be a building at all?

There are haunted forests, haunted caves... and then in my mind's eye there spread this quiet, secluded autumn field, all brown grasses and nodding flower heads, with a gray sky overhead. Into the field walked the shadowy vision of a young woman, and something in my brain said YES! I want to know her story. So, I wrote for her a tale of longing and betrayal, and finally, of vengeance.

Jo Kaplan

Bio: Jo Kaplan is the author of It Will Just Be Us and When the Night Bells Ring. Her short stories have appeared in Fireside Quarterly, Black Static, Nightmare Magazine, Vastarien, Haunted Nights edited by Ellen Datlow and Lisa Morton, Miscreations edited by Doug Murano and Michael Bailey, and elsewhere (sometimes as Joanna Parypinski). Currently, she is the co-chair of the HWA LA chapter and teaches English and creative writing at Glendale Community College. You can learn more at JoKaplan.com.

Story inspiration: Hallow House

So many of my stories deal with unconventional hauntings... that is, places that are "haunted" in some way, but not by traditional ghosts, and "Hallow House" is no exception. Part of my inspiration for this story actually came from reading Piranesi by Susanna Clarke and thinking about labyrinthine spaces. I've also been thinking about consciousness and the fractal networks of the brain, in part for a novel I'm writing at the moment, and I wondered what if Hallow House was not just a place, but an entity?

This led me to the question that my character Jordan poses in the story: "If animals are conscious, why not other things? Why not plants? Why not fungi? Why not computers, or trains, or houses?" This felt like such a strange, delicious question to me, and I let that strangeness guide me through the deeper and deeper recesses of my unconventional house to see where it would go.

Michael J. Moore

Bio: Michael J Moore is a bestselling author, and globally recognized freelance journalist. His books include *Highway Twenty*, which appeared on the preliminary ballot for the 2019 Bram Stoker Award, *After the Change*, which is used a curriculum at the University of Washington, *Secret Harbor*, *Nightmares in Aston: Wicker Village*, and *Cinema 7*.

His work has appeared in dozens of anthologies, magazines, journals, and newspaper, is used in classrooms around the world, has been adapted for theater, and has appeared on television. Follow him on Twitter, @ MichaelJMoore20 or on Facebook.

Story Inspiration: Nory's

When I was growing up, there was a locally owned Pizza-restaurant a couple towns over that had a reputation for having the best pizza in Skagit County. It operated in a building that was much older than the business and utilized big brick ovens that seemed to have been built into the structure.

Rumor around town was that those ovens hadn't always been used for pizzas, that the place had once served as the local crematorium, and if they really had been there since before it was a pizza joint... well, who knows? Years later, I got to thinking about that mom-and-pop spot (it's since become a major chain in the Pacific Northwest), and the next day a first draft of "Nory's," was ready for revisions.

Jae Mazer

Bio: Jae Mazer was born in Victoria, British Columbia, and grew up in the prairies of Northern Alberta, where she completed her Bachelor of Arts, human services major. While reading feverishly, and writing the odd short story or journal article, Jae got her Master's in Clinical Psychology, and worked in the field of mental health for ten years. After spending the majority of her life battling sasquatches in the Great White North, she migrated south to Texas to have a go at the armadillos.

Jae always had an obsession with reading and inherited a love of all things dark and horror from her dad. One day, she decided that she had devoured enough words that she could spin a decent yarn of her own. Now she is an award-winning author with a dozen novels under her belt, short stories in various publications, and is an affiliate member of the Horror Writers Association.

Story Inspiration: Behold, Death Arrives, A Duet of Ash and Fang

It's no secret I like folk horror. And when Daemon contacted me, inviting me to write for a gothic collection, I immediately thought forest. Historical fiction. Ghosts. Curses. And being strongly connected to my Canadian roots, it didn't take me long to weave a tale set in the time of the witch trials, featuring a classic Canadian folk creature in a Canadian setting. Sprinkle in some specters, a creepy abandoned church in the woods, and violent religion, and BOOM. Gothic Canadian Lore!

Diana Olney

Bio: Diana Olney is a Seattle based fiction author, and words are her world. Her stories have appeared in several independent publications, and her novella, She Devil, was released this year in a collaborative book with fellow author Daemon Manx. She also won first place in Crystal Lake Publishing's flash fiction contest for her short story, "Shadow Dust." Currently, she is in the midst of creating many new monsters. Visit her at dianaolney.com for updates on her latest nightmares.

Story Inspiration: Hell Hath No Fury- Where the Mundane meets the Macabre

When I hear the words of a good story, they are spoken in whispers. The kind you hear when you're alone in a dark room, warning you to take a second look at your surroundings. "Hell Hath No Fury" begins with one of those warnings.

Our protagonist, Claire, is haunted by her past, so much so that she has started to carry her ghosts with her. Exorcizing these spirits, however, is easier said than done. Modern monsters take many forms, and they feed on what we give them.

This sort of haunting happens all the time. These days, we don't have to look down to see Hell, because it's already right in front of us. So, the next time you're alone late at night, searching the shadows for answers, the question you must ask yourself is this:

"How did I get here?"

Christy Aldridge

Bio: Christy Aldridge comes from the backwoods of Alabama. She spends most of her time writing or procrastinating from writing with her four cats and Pitbull, Stitch. She's published seven books and been featured in several anthologies.

Story Inspiration: A Halloween Ghost Story

I was inspired to write this story while doing my "52 in 52" challenge. It was a challenge consisting of me writing a short story every week for a year based on a Ray Bradbury quote about it being impossible to write 52 bad short stories in a row. This one came around Halloween time and I think even Bradbury would find it charming.

Matt Scott

Bio: Matt Scott is the author of over fifty short horror stories as well as a stand-alone collection. He lives and writes in Southern Colorado. He and his wife, Heather love to explore the most colorful state with their fur family.

Story Inspiration: Mine

The inspiration for 'Mine' came from Poe. He is a big influence on me. I pictured The Raven and then I pictured a harried man, a nervous and anxious man, perhaps Tell-Tale Heart snuck in there a bit, just a crack. But ultimately, I wanted to see a man to be at the end of his rope, and then wait around long to see what he would do.

Tony Evans

Bio: Tony Evans is a crafter of horror and dark fiction, a spooky storyteller, and a lover of all things creepy. He is the author of over two-dozen short stories that have appeared in various print and online horror magazines and anthologies, two short story collections, two novellas, and one novel.

Tony was born and raised in the Appalachian foothills of eastern Kentucky where stories of 'holler witches', haunted coal mines, and evil entities that lurk in the woods are still prevalent to this day, and these Appalachian folktales play a heavy influence in his writing and its style.

Tony currently resides in New Albany, Indiana, where he spends his time coming up with bad story ideas, great dad jokes, and trying to entertain his wife and two young daughters – his favorite little monsters.

For a look into his daily life and to stay updated on all his fiction, current and new releases, and horror related projects, follow Tony on Twitter/Instagram: @tonyevanshorror, or visit tonyevanshorror.com.

Story Inspiration: The Dare

My inspiration for this story comes an old tale my mom always talked about when I was a child. I can't remember the exact details, but the general premise was centered around someone's house being haunted because it was built with haunted wood. As odd as this sounds, it is a welcome breath of fresh air, to me at least, in a genre where the haunting always seems to be linked to someone dying in a house, being tortured in a house, or a house being built on some type of burial ground.

Guy Quintero

Bio: Guy Quintero is a former reconnaissance soldier with three deployments under his belt. Quintero combines his military background and a life-long fascination with the occult, bringing a mix of bone-chilling horror and heart-pumping action. His inspirations are Stephen King and Tom Clancy. He hopes to follow in their footsteps someday.

Story Inspiration: Cries of the Night

Quintero has been fascinated with the things that go bump in the night since he was a young boy. The inspiration for 'Cries of the Night' derives from a mixture of vampiric lore, combining them into greater levels of nightmarish terror for the antagonists of his story.

D. E. Grant

Bio: Growing up with five sisters left me with a lot of time on my hands and reading and exercising my imagination became my favorite pastimes. I would make up stories about houses and cars I passed by. I would think up stories while walking through the woods in rural South Carolina and tell them while I sat beside waterfronts. I would also read stories about the creatures that went bump in the night. I was entertained and inspired by reading Stephen King and Dean Koontz. My time spent alone nurtured and helped develop my storytelling skills.

It was further fueled when I took a creative writing course in high school. It was there I discovered my love for writing, as I wrote poetry as well as short stories from pictures. Life happened and I put those skills on hold but my dreams of being a writer were never too far away. After serving in the United States Navy, I settled into civilian life and built careers in hospitality and restaurant management and allied health.

Fast forward to the present time and having the time to resurrect my literary dreams, I drew from my enjoyment of dark creatures that lurked in the shadows and wrote and published my first book at age 55, Cursed Plantation. Since then, I have written a sequel, Cursed Legacy, and have almost completed Cursed Bloodline at this point in time. I also co-authored The Collector with five other amazing writers.

Currently, I am living my best life in central Florida with my wife, muse and best friend Daphne, and my "co-author" Cisco, my six-month old cat.

Story Inspiration: The Feeding
The thoughts and ideas of things that goes bump in the night and can reach out and chill one's soul inspired my opportunity to write The Feeding as vampires have always fascinated me as nocturnal creatures feasting on the lifeblood and essence of the living. From Dracula to Barnabas Collins from Dark Shadows to Spike and Angel from Buffy the Vampire Slayer, the undead has intrigued me, as they used the living to maintain their uncontrolled urge and living death.

Danielle Manx

Bio: Danielle Manx enjoys writing speculative fiction, and her tastes are broad and eclectic. She writes everything from romance stories to Hitchcockian thrillers and was elated to put her passion for Gothic Horror into this project. To Danielle, writing is all about creating a mood and transplanting her readers into it. Danielle works as a journalist in the Tri-State area, where her writings have appeared in various publications.

She lives in New Jersey with her brother, Author Dameon Manx, and her insatiable rescue cat, Sidney.

Danielle has begun to seek publication for her fictional voice, including Green Shoes Sanctuary, where her short stories Recall, and The Last Box Of Ribbon Candy were published in October and December as part of the winning writing prompts for those months. Additionally, her short story Riddles and the 5 C's will appear in the Last Waltz Publishing's anthology Monochrome Noir.

Story Inspiration: Belladonna's Curse

I was inspired to write Belladonna's Curse because I am enthralled with all things Victorian. The homes are so stately and elegant, and it's wonderful to imagine who lived there in the past. Even as a young kid, I liked to spin stories about them. When I began to write, I looked behind the beauty and wondered what secrets and horrors those houses held. I was always drawn to the Gothic-Horror element ever since I can remember. Whether it was Rebecca's Manderly or Turn of the Screw's Bly, or Dracula's Castle, there was also always a romantic element in there that spoke to me. Adding in characters that were multi-layered, how could I resist?

Daemon Manx

Bio: Daemon Manx is an American speculative-horror author. He is a member of the Horror Writers Association (HWA) and the Horror Authors Guild (HAG) and has been featured in magazines in both the U.S. and the U.K. He has recently been nominated for a Splatterpunk award for his debut, Abigail in the best short story category. In 2021 he received a HAG award for his story The Dead Girl.

In 1991, Daemon was involved in a motor vehicle accident with Ronald Reagan's motorcade, when he crashed into the former president's limousine on a New York City Street shortly after Ron and Nancy stepped out of the vehicle. No one was injured, except for maybe the pride of the secret service agent who was directing traffic.

After an on-going battle with addiction, Daemon spent eight years in the state prison system where he fought to turn his life around. He earned a college degree, discovered his passion for literature, and on October 31st will celebrate ten years clean and sober.

Daemon is the owner of Last Waltz Publishing, an indie horror label focused on elevating new authors. He lives with his sister, author Danielle Manx and their narcoleptic cat, Sydney where they patiently prepare for the apocalypse. There is a good chance they will runout of coffee far too soon.

Story Inspiration: Devlin's Manse

I wrote the opening line of Devlin's Manse over ten years ago. Some stories sit with you ... what can I say. At the heart of this story is emotion, the driving force being sadness. I have always believed that strong emotions like profound sadness and enduring love are energies that cannot be destroyed ... that they continue to live ... even after we are gone. I have had reoccurring dreams of an old, abandoned house. It is in disrepair, but somehow, I know every room as if I have lived there before. The house sits on a large piece of land, also forgotten.

It has been the setting for many happy occasions, but now there is only sadness and regret. The house of my dreams remembers what it has witnessed. Sometimes I can go years without reliving the dream, but ultimately it returns, along with the overwhelming despair. That's the most familiar part of my dream, it's the memory of the pain; in the end there is always a residue.

James G. Carlson

Bio: James G. Carlson is an award-winning author of horror, science fiction, and dark fantasy. His short stories have appeared in various anthologies from small presses. He has also released two collections of dark fiction, SEVEN EXHUMATIONS and THE EVER-DESCENDING STAIRCASE, as well as three novellas, THE LEGION MACHINE, RED FALLS, and the Splatterpunk-nominated MIDNIGHT IN THE CITY OF THE CARRION KID.

From the weird state of Pennsylvania, James drinks too much coffee and writes at a desk surrounded by animals and family in the mad zoo he calls home.

Story inspiration: Flesh and Chocolate

Inspired by events that transpired in our youth, Flesh and Chocolate is loosely based on my big brother and me. He and I went trick-or-treating—our first time without adult supervision (I'd even graduated from the plastic pumpkin to the pillowcase)—and my candy got stolen by some neighborhood bullies. This took place when I was eleven or twelve. We lived in the Philly area at the time, but it wouldn't be long before my parents moved us an hour north to Allentown.

There weren't any monsters in the real version of events...except the bullies, of course.

My brother became a hero that night. First, he attempted to reclaim my candy. Failing that, he informed our parents of the bullies' identities, as he'd recognized the scoundrels. My mother marched over to their house and brought back not only my candy but the bullies' candy too. Their mother apparently agreed with mother about how awful their actions were.

So, what began as a terrible Halloween, turned into a memorable holiday with so much candy. And it gave me some usable material for Flesh and Chocolate. Thanks for reading. I hope you enjoy it.

Jack Wells

Bio: Jack Wells is a burgeoning author located in Northern Utah. He has been writing on and off since grade school, though most of his early works consist of bad poetry and even worse song lyrics. He is best known for Monochrome Noir, an alternate history mystery/thriller series set in a grayscale 1986 Los Angeles. When not putting pen to paper, Jack can be found spending time with his sweet but quirky family, hiking, kayaking, and sipping whiskey by his fire pit. One can often catch Jack taking spontaneous late night road trips throughout northern Utah with the latest retro synth music providing a surreal soundtrack.

Story Inspiration: Riding the Ghost Train

Riding the Ghost Train is heavily inspired by the works of Poe and Dickens, particularly in how the main character is haunted by his recurring mistakes. While both authors were masters of supernatural horror, they also turned their gaze inward quite frequently, examining the many ways in which man is his own worst enemy. Despite the outdated prose (or perhaps because of it), their stories have a timeless quality that is unrivaled.

Jeremy Megargee

Bio: Jeremy Megargee has always loved dark fiction. He cut his teeth on R.L Stine's Goosebumps series as a child and a fascination with Stephen King, Jack London, Algernon Blackwood, and many others followed later in life. Jeremy weaves his tales of personal horror from Martinsburg, West Virginia with his cat Lazarus acting as his muse/familiar. He is an active member of the West Virginia chapter of the Horror Writer's Association, and you can often find him peddling his dark words in various mountain hollers deep within the Appalachians.

Story Inspiration: A Dream of Dead Leaves

A Dream of Dead Leaves is really my love letter to spooky season as a whole. It borrows a snippet from a poem I wrote many years ago (entitled Queen of Halloween) and I essentially built this story around the poem using it as framework. I wanted to capture the nostalgia of autumn and how sometimes we wish that it would last forever. For those of us that love Halloween, this one is for you. Never stop seeking timeless October...

Also By Last Waltz Publishing

Tales My Grandmother Told Me by Heather Miller

Down by the Riverwalk by Matt Scott

Monochrome Noir: A Gathering Storm: Book 1 by Jack Wells

Monochrome Noir: A Rising Tide: Book 2 by Jack Wells

Abigail by Daemon Manx

Piece by Piece by Daemon Manx

Drawn & Quartered by Daemon Manx and Diana Olney

Coming Soon:
Monochrome Noir: A Fatal Flood: Book 3 by Jack Wells
Monochrome Noir: A Drowning Man: Book 4 by Jack Wells

Available on Amazon or on the Last Waltz Publishing website.

Made in the USA
Monee, IL
15 October 2022